rebel

Montgomery Brothers ~ Book 3

laura pavlov

Rebel

Montgomery Brothers, Book 3

Copyright © 2020 by Laura Pavlov

All rights reserved.

❀ Created with Vellum

dedication

Dear Eric,

Since Rebel is releasing on your birthday month…HAPPY BIRTH-DAY, E$! I cannot begin to tell you how much your support means to me. From encouraging me to keep going, to listening when I'm having an off day, to recommending the best Netflix shows, to saving the day when it came down to the wire with the house stuff!! You are always there for me, and I am so grateful for YOU!!

Love you,
Laura xo

one

. . .

Jack

I STOPPED by the bakery on my way up to the office. No better way to start my day than with a few of Harley's donuts and a cup of coffee. My sister-in-law made pastries that could bring a man to his knees.

"Hey, there," Harley said from behind the display case.

"Sheesh, girl. That belly of yours gets bigger every time I see you. Should you still be working?" I asked when I stepped behind the counter and took her in.

"Thanks, Jack." She rolled her eyes. "I'm more than aware of my size. No need to point it out. And don't get your brother all riled up about me working. I'm putting in half-days as it is, and he's having a freaking fit. Just because I'm carrying two tiny humans in my stomach does not mean I can't do anything. I'm still capable." She placed both hands on her lower back and closed her eyes.

"You have nothing to prove, Harls. You have great employees and you've planned for this. I think you've frozen enough baked goods to cover a year's worth of maternity leave. There's nothing wrong with taking it easy these last few weeks." I laughed, grabbing a chocolate donut and pulling her in for a hug. The girl looked like she was about to pop, and she refused to slow down.

"But I don't want to. I feel great. The doctor said everything looks perfect. It's just Ford being a control freak," she huffed, pushing the dark hair that sprung free from her ponytail away from her face.

"That's because he loves you so damn much," I said, and her features softened.

"Yeah, yeah, yeah. Let me grab you a coffee."

The door dinged and Monroe Buckley stepped inside. She'd just started working for Montgomery Media this week, after we'd made her an offer that she couldn't refuse and stole her away from CBS where she'd interned. Ford thought we needed a fresh voice, and he felt strongly that Monroe was it. She'd just graduated with her master's from Stanford University and the girl's resume could hold its own against anyone in the field of journalism, even the most seasoned.

He didn't need to sell me on her. She also happened to be my best friend, Buck's, little sister and he'd been bragging about her since the first day of our freshman year in college.

"Are you ever *not here*?" Monroe rolled her eyes as she sauntered in.

"Nice to see you too," I said with a laugh.

"No one said anything about it being nice to see you." She raised a brow and smirked.

We weren't exactly the best of friends. She hated me for reasons I didn't understand. And now I was her boss. We'd gotten off to a rocky start and she didn't attempt to hide her disdain for me. And I wasn't okay with it. *People love me.* I'm the life of the party—a guaranteed good time. But Monroe Buckley couldn't stand the sight of me.

"You know, most people don't get away with speaking to their boss that way." I perused her from head to toe as she scanned the baked goods in the display case.

Her light brown hair ended just past her shoulders on her slight frame. She wore a cream blouse and dark jeans with a pair of heels. She glanced up at me, and her indigo blue eyes locked with mine—and there was no humor there.

She shrugged. "That's a matter of opinion. I'll take a blueberry muffin, please."

"FYI, I don't work here. Just helping Harls out."

"I wasn't judging. Just figured since you're behind the counter and all." She chuckled.

Snarky little thing.

"You need to give her a bag. We don't just put the pastry in their hands, for god's sakes," Harley chuckled as she came around the corner and handed me my coffee before reaching for a bag. "Hey, Monroe. I heard you're going to bring a hip perspective to the paper with your column. I can't wait to read it."

Monroe had been a shrewd negotiator, and she and Ford had gone back and forth for hours before they'd finally come to an agreement. Ford, my oldest brother, was the president of Montgomery Media, and I managed the newsroom, oversaw new hires, and handled all the PR responsibilities for both Montgomery Media and Montgomery Wines, our winery in Napa Valley. Our middle brother, Harrison, was the president of Montgomery Wines—so we all had our roles in the family business.

Monroe would write a bi-monthly column for us drawing in the younger crowd about trendier current events, as long as we'd agreed to let her have an anonymous political column as well. Apparently, that's what she was passionate about. It was a big undertaking, but this girl clearly didn't back down from challenges.

"Yeah, we'll see. I'm not going to lie—I think half the reason I agreed to come work at Montgomery Media is because DeLiciously Yours is downstairs." She reached for the muffin and winked at Harley. The girl was nice to everyone—with the exception of me.

"Not because you wanted to have a cool boss?" I teased.

"Definitely not," she hissed, and Harley covered her mouth with her hand when she laughed.

"Thanks for the muffin, Harley. I'll see you later." Monroe smiled at my sister-in-law before walking past me without so much as a side glance before heading out the door.

"Oh, my. She really does despise you," Harley said with a chuckle.

"I don't know what the hell her problem is. I'm a likable guy," I said, crossing my arms over my chest. "Go put your feet up, girl. You're working too hard. I'll be back later."

I made my way to the elevators and stopped the door just before it closed. Monroe had a mouthful of muffin and her cheeks flamed pink when I stepped inside.

"Hey, no shame in trying to wolf down some pastries in the elevator. Next time just make sure the door isn't about to close on someone."

She finished chewing and glared at me. "It's not the job of the person in the elevator to check to see if anyone's coming. You should have called out for me to hold the door."

"I disagree."

"I wasn't asking your opinion."

I narrowed my gaze. "How about you tell me why you're so hostile. We have to work together, so you need to drop the attitude."

"Oh, so anyone who doesn't agree with your *elevator etiquette* has an attitude?" She chuckled and stepped off.

"Noooooo. This has nothing to do with etiquette and everything to do with your attitude." I followed her into her office and shut the door.

She sat down behind her desk and I dropped in the chair across from her. "You know. You may have just helped me choose the first topic for my column."

"Let me guess... how to treat your boss with disrespect?"

She rolled her eyes. "Are you always such a narcissist?"

"Probably. I mean, look at me." I chuckled and raised a brow in challenge. "So, what's the topic?"

"Social etiquettes. From the workplace, to the elevator, to small talk, to the dating world. I mean, we face these challenges daily, right? What's politically correct these days? Do I hold the door for a guy I don't really care for, or let him wait for the next one?" She paused and smirked before continuing. "Or what if a guy asks you out and you aren't interested. You've got two choices, A, you ignore him, and you're labeled a tease, or B, you tell him you aren't interested, and you're labeled a bitch."

"What about C?"

"There is no C."

"Well, what if you like him?"

She shrugged. "Okay, there's a C. Say you actually like him. If you tell him you like him, you're a stalker. So, you keep it to yourself, and then he sleeps around because he didn't know you wanted to be exclusive, and then you hate him. Yes. There's a lot to run with here. I mean, there's also a ton going on in the political arena, which is slightly more riveting, but I agreed to do this, and you just helped me get there. So, thank you, Montgomery. *You've been a huge help.*"

"Why do I feel like that's a backhanded compliment?" I asked.

"Because it is." She chuckled. "You're a bit slicker than I expected."

"I'm full of surprises."

"I'm sure you are. But not everyone loves surprises, so…" Her gaze moved to the door.

Seriously? She was kicking me out of her office?

"I was just leaving," I said, pushing to my feet with irritation.

"Sure, you were."

I laughed. I liked how snarky she was.

"Send me over the idea for the column."

"Yes, sir," she said, her smile anything but genuine.

"Now was that so painful?" I asked as I paused at the door.

"Yes. Very much so."

I shook my head and made my way to my office, dialing Buck as I walked.

"Hey, Montgomery. My sister seems really happy there. How's it going?" he said, getting right to the point.

I dropped down behind my desk, turning my chair to take in the views of San Francisco. Montgomery Media was in the heart of the city, and I had a corner office on the top floor. Tall buildings lined the busy street, and my eyes flickered between the Bay Bridge and the Golden Gate Bridge from where I sat.

"She's doing well. But she hates my fucking guts."

He barked out a laugh. "Nah. That's just Monroe. She's still pissed that we hooked up with her teammates years ago when we visited. She's all bark and no bite. She'll come around."

"It's not like I hooked up with Monroe. It was her teammate."

"Dude. Do not joke about that shit. My baby sister is off-limits."

"There's nothing to worry about there. She's barely civil to me, and obviously I'd never cross that line." Buck had always been protective of Monroe for as long as I'd known him. The one thing you didn't mess with was his little sister—he adored her.

And he had nothing to worry about.

Because Monroe Buckley was the last person I was interested in.

two

. . .

Monroe

SENATOR REYNOLDS STOOD in front of the cameras with his prim and proper wife and two perfect children tucked neatly beside him. He was a complete fraud, and I rolled my eyes as he thanked his family for their undying support. Every media outlet had come out to hear him speak today, as he'd garnered a lot of attention since announcing his intent to run for president in the next election.

"Buffy here, she's been by my side all along. I wouldn't be here without her," he spouted, and the crowd cheered.

Yeah, he wouldn't be here without her, because he'd be at a strip club or a poker game. Everyone knew his reputation, which is why I was so surprised that he'd thrown his name in the hat. The man didn't have an honest bone in his body.

I was a journalist, and I looked at candidates with an open mind. My job was to report the facts—not my personal opinion. And Simon Reynolds represented my particular political party of choice—but that didn't mean I wouldn't call the man out. He was shady as hell and he'd opened the door to be exposed, and that's exactly what I planned to do. Thankfully, there were several other candidates running against him, but for whatever reason, Reynolds was the front runner in the early polls.

My phone vibrated and I glanced down to see a text from my pesky boss. Jack Montgomery could not seem to stay out of my business.

Jack ~ We have a meeting in 20 minutes. I expect you to be there.

I rolled my eyes. My job was to report the news. The guy wanted to meet about every little thing, and I didn't appreciate being micro-managed.

Me ~ I'm at the rally for Senator Reynolds. I'll be back in 30 minutes.

Jack ~ Montgomery Media has a professional relationship with Simon Reynolds if you want to schedule a one-on-one, just ask. Our meeting is in 20—I'll see you there.

I dropped my phone in my purse and shook my head. I didn't need a one-on-one to know who Simon Reynolds was. The man lied on the daily. Nope. I'd just investigate him until I found what I needed. I'd been exposed to people like Senator Reynolds my entire life, and I'd learned that the real story was not on the surface.

My father, Ryan Buckley, had been the quarterback for the San Francisco 49ers for more than a decade back in the day. He'd gone on to become one of the most recognized faces on ESPN as a sports broad-caster, as well as dabbling in acting, and landing a few big roles in large films. I'd grown up in an affluent family, been surrounded by famous people most of my life, and I'd always wondered what they were hiding. What the real story was. Who they were deep down. My father called it a curse—I called it a gift. I was curious. Determined. And I wouldn't quit until I found what I was looking for.

Fortunately, Mr. Perfect, with his white teeth and his supermodel family waved goodbye, so I could head back to the office to meet my overbearing boss.

"You think he's the real deal?" Brett Waters, the lead reporter for CBS, said so only I could hear.

I'd interned at CBS my last year of college, and considered taking the position they offered, but I wouldn't be covering politics for many years if I'd accepted. Brett was their guy, and he wasn't going anywhere anytime soon. Ford Montgomery had offered me a deal that I couldn't refuse. Yes, I had to jump through hoops and write a bi-monthly column for the younger generation about fashion, and relationships, and all the trendy shit people my age loved. But he'd agreed to let me write a political column which would be anonymous for the time being—and I'd jumped at the opportunity.

"I'm not sure yet," I lied. Brett was a snake, and he'd been a complete jerk to me during my internship. The man suffered from small penis complex if you asked me. He acted like he was God's gift to the world, but he was petty and spiteful, which told me he was insecure and threatened by anyone and everyone who came into his arena. My father taught me at a young age that wisdom is something to be shared. He always told my brother and me that if you strive to be the best you can be, then you have nothing to worry about. There's enough room at the top for everyone. Brett Waters wanted to be alone at the top, and that was a red flag for me.

"Really, Stanford?" he said, and I cringed at his annoying nickname. Not because I wasn't proud of my alma mater—I was. But I didn't like that he put labels on people. He did it with everyone. He called his personal assistant "Blowfish" because she'd had a little too much filler injected into her already oversized lips, and he dubbed the other intern, "Boomer" because he'd attended the University of Oklahoma. We all found it annoying, but Brett was the golden boy at CBS, so everyone tolerated him. "Little Miss Research doesn't have the deets on this guy? I find that hard to believe."

"Well, didn't you once tell me to keep my research close to my chest?" I asked as I turned to leave. It was the one and only tip the man had ever given me, and he followed it up by saying, "And lucky for you, you've got a nice set of tits," in the next breath. So, I wasn't sure how genuine the tip was.

"Ah, yes. But that doesn't include sharing your knowledge with your mentor." He smirked as his camera crew packed up beside him.

Mentor, my ass.

The man had never allowed me to shadow him, had shared very little about his career or himself with me, and he'd had me escorted out of several meetings because he didn't feel *"interns were of any value."* Yet he had no shame hitting on me every time we were alone in the breakroom and appeared surprised each time I turned him down.

I chuckled. "I'll be sure to remember that when I run into my mentor." I had no crew with me, I'd just snuck out of the office to attend the rally solo.

His head tipped back in a chuckle of his own before his icy gaze locked with mine and a chill ran down my spine. "Careful, Stanford. You'll need friends in high places."

I forced a fake smile. "I'll keep that in mind."

"I don't see a crew here with you. I noticed Dan Arbor from Montgomery Media up front with a whole slew of people. Why are you even here?"

I pulled the strap of my satchel over my head and shoulder and shrugged. "Call it curiosity. Just wanted to hear what he had to say."

"I figured. Long road for you to get there, I'm sure." He snickered.

I turned on my heels and headed for the office. I didn't say goodbye or bother looking back, but I could feel his eyes boring into my backside as I left. The weasel's creep factor was a solid ten. My skin crawled every time he was around.

I stepped off the elevator, and Sam, the assistant to both Ford and Jack, greeted me with a smile. "He's waiting for you in his office."

I was five minutes late, and I'm sure I'd hear about it.

"Thank you."

I knocked on his door and he called out for me to come in.

"Sorry I'm late." I dropped to sit in the chair across from his desk.

"Are you though?" he asked, running a hand through his thick dark hair. Jack Montgomery was a beautiful man—there was no denying it. And he knew it, which irritated me all the more.

"What do you mean? Of course, I am."

"Why did you go to the rally? Dan was already there with his team."

"I'm aware. But I write an anonymous political column as well, so I needed to be there to hear his speech," I said.

He scrubbed a hand over his face, and I wondered what it would feel like to graze my fingertips over the dark scruff peppering his jaw. Yes, he was basically my nemesis. But hey, I hadn't had sex in almost a year, and a girl could fantasize without acting on it, right? His eyes were an intoxicating whiskey brown with pops of gold and amber. His skin tan, lips full, and his body was a male masterpiece. It didn't matter that he annoyed me, and his ego was as large as his big fat head. I still found him attractive. Hell, every woman within eye view turned to stare at the man wherever he went. I was only human, after all.

"Monroe." He paused to study me.

"Jack," I said, mocking him. The guy was a joker, but he did appear to take his job seriously, which surprised me. I'd only been here a few weeks, but he checked in relentlessly, and everyone here respected him.

"This has to stop. I know you're Buck's sister, but you need to show me some respect at the office. If you're leaving, you need to tell me where you're going. That's how this works." He motioned between us. His striking gaze drilled into mine, and my chest squeezed with something. Guilt? I wasn't even sure. I'd been a jerk to him since I started, and he'd been nothing but nice to me. He was my brother's best friend, I could cut the guy some slack.

"Okay. I'm sorry."

He cocked his head to the side. "Just like that?"

"Yes. I'm not a complete asshole, Montgomery. I can admit when I'm wrong. It doesn't mean I have to like you, but I can be respectful."

His head fell back in laughter, and I couldn't help but smile. The man was ridiculously handsome. He looked like a young Ryan Reynolds with darker hair. His laugh was infectious the way it bounced off the walls.

"I am curious why you despise me so much. I mean, I came to see you race, and I hooked up with some chick who hit on me. Is that a crime?" He folded his hands on his desk and waited for my response.

"You hooked up with *Tiffany Crupp*." I crossed my arms over my chest.

"See, I don't even remember her name. What's the big deal? It was years ago."

"She hated me," I said, shaking my head.

"Because you won that race that we came to?" he asked, studying me like I was about to tell him some sinister secret.

"I guess so. She'd been number one on our team all four years, and I came in as a freshman during her senior year, and I think she resented me for beating her. I don't know. It's not like I've won every race in my life. People beat me sometimes, it just made me work harder. I didn't hate them for it. I blamed myself for losing, not others for beating me."

His lips turned up in the corners and he nodded. "Hell yeah. I get that. You know, sports are competitive, and some athletes can't handle losing."

Jack was a collegiate phenom at the University of Southern California and was predicted to be a first-round draft pick when he surprised everyone and decided not to go pro after college. He understood the meaning of winning and losing better than anyone.

"I guess so."

"So what? She hated you and in turn, you hated me for hooking up with her? That makes no sense."

I wouldn't tell him that I had a massive crush on him at the time, and told my teammate and friend, Gwen, and Tiffany overheard the conversation. She made it a point to hit on Jack and then rub it in my face. It didn't matter. I hardly knew him at the time, and I got over my crush immediately—and traded it for some good healthy hatred for the guy.

"Maybe I just disliked you, did that ever cross your mind?"

"No one dislikes me. What can I say, I'm a likable guy," he said, holding his arms out to the side.

"Why do you even care? We don't need to be friends, Montgomery."

"Well, you're Buck's little sister, we're working together, seems we can get along, right?"

"Fine. I'll make an effort to be more respectful."

He laughed again before narrowing his gaze at me. "You're an odd little bird, Monroe Buckley."

"I've been called worse."

"Okay, so, from now on you tell me when you're going to a rally or to something for your anonymous column. We're on the same team. I need to know what's going on."

"I don't like being micromanaged," I said, raising a brow in challenge.

"Then I guess you should work for yourself."

I laughed. "Touché."

"What did you find out about Senator Reynolds?"

"Aside from the fact that he's a complete douchebag... nothing new."

"Wow, tell me how you really feel," Jack said with a laugh as he leaned back in his desk chair.

"Sorry, I forgot—you have a professional relationship with him." I rolled my eyes.

"I've known him a long time, but that doesn't mean I like him. It's no secret that he's got a wandering eye, but between you and me, I don't think it's a secret from Buffy either. She tolerates it because she likes the lifestyle that she's living. Not sure why they're even together, but it seems to work for both of them." He shrugged.

"He's not the first guy to cheat on his wife and he won't be the last. But he threw his name in the hat to run for president, so he's opened himself up to be scrutinized. Not the wisest move seeing he has a lot of skeletons in his closet."

"More than what we already know?" he asked, and it surprised me that he appeared genuinely interested.

"Yeah, I believe so. I think he leads two lives—one for the public, and one for himself. And I'm fairly certain it's much darker than what we know. I'd like to do a bit more digging into it and see if my instincts are correct."

He smiled and leaned forward, forming a teepee with his fingers and resting them on his desk. "All right. But finish the article for this week first and keep me abreast on what you find."

His response surprised me. I was prepared to battle him, and he'd been more than fair.

"Thank you. Will do." I pushed to my feet and walked toward the door.

"Good work on the Reynolds stuff. Keep it up." He winked.

Jack Montgomery was sweet—I'd give him that. Add that to his undeniable good looks, and it's no surprise he had women dropping at his feet. But I was a big believer in the three-strike rule, and he had at least three strikes against him already.

Laura Pavlov

He was my brother's best friend.
He slept with my nemesis.
And he was my boss.
Three strikes and you're out.
Jack Montgomery was definitely out.

three

• • •

Jack

"I JUST RECEIVED a call from Simon Reynolds inviting us to his yearly fundraiser at his home. I think he's hoping to get our support," Ford said, leaning back in his desk chair.

I popped in the last bite of my pumpkin donut and spoke over a mouthful of cake. "Damn, your wife makes the best fucking donuts."

He shook his head and motioned for me to continue.

I took a sip of coffee to wash it down before speaking. "I think he's got a shit ton to hide, and he's opened himself up for a lot of scrutiny by throwing his name into the presidential race. Monroe went to the rally as well, and she's definitely working on something. Even though her piece is anonymous, it's in our paper, so we need to prepare for his wrath."

He nodded. "Well, let's hope Dan finds as much if not more than Monroe. We're paying him a lot of money and he has all the resources at his fingertips. Sounds like she's just a lot hungrier for the story."

"She's like a dog with a bone." I rolled my eyes.

"How's that going? I know she had a problem with you at the start. But the girl is definitely on a mission and there's no stopping her," my older brother said.

"We had a power struggle at first, but she's been easier to work with this week. We had a heart to heart, and she actually seems to get it now. At least she's checking in with me and keeping me updated on her whereabouts."

"How's the column coming? The one we're actually paying her to write."

"It's good. Ready to go to print. Hell, she spent so much time researching Reynolds I don't think she gave much effort to her column. She just writes that shit like it's nothing and it's fucking brilliant. She has her next three proposals to me already, and they all look solid. You know, the basics—dating life for twenty-somethings living in the city, fashion hot spots, and etiquette faux pas. I don't know where she comes up with it, but the girl is talented. And her work ethic is insane. She beats me here every day."

"Yeah, that's why we had to fight hard to get her. She's got a bright future ahead of her. And I think she's going to draw in the Millennials and Gen Y age group. She's exactly what we needed."

"Agreed."

"Everything else running smoothly in the newsroom?" he asked.

"Yeah. There's a lot happening in the political arena, so let's see what Dan Arbor and his team come up with. What do you want me to tell Simon Reynolds? Should we attend the party?"

"Hell yeah. And you're going to have to go. Harley needs to get off her feet, for fuck's sake. She's carrying two babies, and she wants to keep working. Frustrates the hell out of me." He ran a hand through his hair.

"Dude. She's an independent woman. Hell, that's part of what you love about her. She'll slow down when it's time. But let her do it on her own, don't force it. She's not going to do anything to put those little girls at risk, you know that. So just calm the fuck down and let her figure it out. And of course, I'll go to the party. No worries at all."

"Sounds good. Thanks for the advice. You do spend a shit ton of time in that bakery, so you'd tell me if you thought she was overdoing it?"

"Of course, I would. She's not, but I'll keep you posted." I knocked on his desk before leaving his office.

I spent the next two hours walking the newsroom and listening to a few pitches. I stopped at Monroe's office to find her engrossed in her work. I knocked on the open door before waltzing in and dropping down in the chair across from her desk. She'd made her office her own fairly fast. There were black and white prints on the walls with pops of pink. Her desk had a photograph of her and her father and Buck in a white shiny frame, and a fake floral arrangement sat beside it. She'd brought in her own white velvet desk chair, and her desk was tidy and neat.

"Well, just go ahead and make yourself at home then." She glanced up and met my gaze. Such an odd little bird. Her eyes the darkest indigo, similar in color to a blue jay.

"Thanks. Don't mind if I do. What are you working on?"

She pushed to her feet and moved to shut the door before returning to her desk. She leaned forward, eyes darting left and right as if she were about to tell me something sinister.

One could hope.

"I guess, seeing as you're my boss and all, I need to share what I'm working on. But I don't want anyone to know. You strike me as a bit of an *over-sharer*, with a gift for gab. I can't have that."

My head fell back in laughter. "It's called being social. Speaking to other humans. You should try it."

"I'm serious, Montgomery. I want to trust you. This can't go anywhere." She intertwined her fingers and settled her hands on her desk.

"Good Christ. I'm not going to tell anyone. Seeing as I own this paper, I actually want it to succeed." I shook my head and tried to cover my smile.

"Okay. But if this story leaks, I'll know it's you because I haven't told a soul. I mean, aside from my source." Her tongue darted out to wet her lips, and I couldn't help but notice how plump and pink they were. She was a pouty little thing, and her full lips turned down as the words left her mouth.

"I'm a vault when I want to be. Spill it, Buckley."

"Senator Reynolds is into real kinky sex, not that I'm judging, but the kicker is… it's not with his prim and proper perfect wife, Buffy. I'm talking back alley, dark, underground, S&M, career shattering, scandalous stuff." She leaned back in her chair and rested one palm on her cheek as if she just couldn't handle what she was telling me. Her blue eyes danced around the room, and her mannerisms were fast and sharp.

Was I surprised by this information? Sure. Not that he was cheating on his wife, because everyone knew that he was a piece of shit husband. But throwing his name in to run for president meant he'd be dissected to the nth degree. A guy with a dark sex habit including being unfaithful to his wife would be the first thing they'd expose. He was in his mid-forties playing family man with his wife and two kids for the public, all while leading a double life. He was digging his own grave.

I ran my hand over my day-old scruff as I contemplated the information. "I'm surprised he'd go to a public place that could be traced."

She gasped. "I tell you the guy is a complete douchebag and you're only surprised that he does it in a public place?"

"Listen. Simon's an asshole. It's no secret. But he's sly, and he covers his tracks. I wouldn't think he'd be stupid enough to engage in something that could be traced, that's all I'm saying. He's a pretty slick guy."

She leaned forward and whispered as her gaze darted to the door to make sure no one was entering. "That's the thing. This is an *exclusive club*, and it costs a small fortune to be a member. Only the richest of the rich can get in. They promise complete anonymity."

I chuckled. She was cute as hell when she was conspiring. "So, how'd you find out then? I'm guessing the press is about to pounce on this. I'm sure Dan is all over it."

"Trust me. He's not. This is not public knowledge. My best friend Gwen's, boyfriend's, sister's, roommate works at this club." She raised a brow.

"What? That's like saying your cousin's, uncle's, neighbor's, grandmother knows a guy. How reliable could the source be when it's that removed? You can't run with a story with unreliable sources, Monroe. That's not how it works."

Her head fell back, and she groaned. "No duh, genius. This isn't my first rodeo. But a tip is a tip." She reached for her phone and held it up for me to see a blurry photo that definitely resembled Simon Reynolds. "She snapped this picture for me last night. He goes every Tuesday evening. He's a regular. Apparently, he likes it rough. You know, the whole whips and chains and beating him senseless type of stuff. And he doesn't go with his wife. He has a lady he sees there."

"And how do you plan on exposing this?" I crossed my arms over my chest. For whatever reason, I felt protective over Monroe Buckley. Hell, she was my best friend's little sister, for starters. And maybe it was her lack of fear—her desire to run into a burning building at whatever cost to get her story, that concerned me.

"I made an appointment for next Tuesday. I have to bring a hefty deposit, but I don't mind putting the money up for this, because duty calls."

"The hell you will."

"Excuse me?" she huffed and pushed to her feet.

"You're not going to that underground dungeon alone. Absolutely not. And we have funds for work-related expenses." I raised a brow and dared her to challenge me. People often mistook my laid-back demeanor for passive. I was anything but. And when I wasn't okay with something, there was no changing my mind. And I was most definitely not okay with Monroe Buckley going to a secret S&M club to expose a presidential candidate by herself. No fucking way that was going down on my watch.

"You can't stop me." She crossed her arms over her chest and stood in front of me.

"The hell I can't. I'll tell Buck, I'll go public with the info and blow the story up, whatever I need to do to stop you from going."

She narrowed her gaze and a little wrinkle formed between her eyes. Fucking adorable. "You wouldn't."

"Try me," I said, pushing to my feet and towering over her for effect. She was a tiny little thing. She stood about a foot shorter than me, but I was almost six feet four inches, so I guess that didn't make her short per se. Her frame was thin and feminine, yet every inch of her was toned from her running days.

"But you promised to keep this between us," she huffed.

"That was before I knew you were going to put yourself in danger."

She stormed back to her desk and dropped into her chair. "Okay, note to self—don't tell my arrogant boss what I'm doing again."

I put my hands on her desk and leaned forward, crowding her space. "You will tell me what you're doing, and we'll figure it out together. But I'll be damned if I let you go into a dangerous situation on your own. I won't tell anyone, and I won't blow up your story. I run a newsroom, after all. I don't make a habit of blowing up stories. Nobody would work for me if I did."

She studied me as I dropped back down in the chair across from her. "What does that mean? What are you going to do?"

"I'm going with you. You know, to this club. We'll go together. Call and tell them we're a couple. Lots of couples are into that kinky shit."

A smile spread across her face and her cheeks pinked. "You're joking?"

"Normally, yes. I'm a bit of a joker. But this time, I'm dead serious. Buckle up, sweetheart. They might let me whip you a few times." I barked out a laugh.

"You're such a pig. You'll have to wear a disguise. We can't risk getting recognized and blowing the whole story."

"Don't you worry about me. I've got all kinds of disguises. What do you suggest? Assless chaps? Leather speedo? Or just go in the buff with a pair of sunglasses?"

"No. Just no." She waved her hands in front of her face. "Dress like you're going to a club, and wear a hat and glasses, or a wig."

"I'll figure it out. But what's your plan when we get inside?"

"I'm going to fake a stomachache, and just ask for time to lie down. Then I'll find the bastard and snap a few pictures and make a run for it," she said, tucking her light brown hair behind her ear.

"That's a terrible plan. Too much room for error. Let me think on this. I'm sort of the king of plans. Ask my brothers."

"We can't ask anyone. No one can know what we're doing, Montgomery. I'm serious. This is the kind of story that someone puts a hit out on you for. And I wouldn't put anything past Senator Reynolds."

I laughed. "He's a scumbag, but he's not a murderer. Take it down a notch, Nancy Drew. Why don't you go with me to the party he's throwing in a few weeks. We just got the invite."

She rubbed her hands together. "Yes, please. I'd love to see the dirtbag in his element. Acting like a perfect gentleman with Buffy on his arm. Unless we expose him before then."

"We need to have a lot of proof before we go public with the story. We don't need lawsuits. And we're going to have to bring Dan in at some point. He's our political guy. You don't want to step on toes."

"That's up for debate. If he was good at his job, he'd know about this, right?"

"Well, he doesn't have his uncle's, brother's, mechanic's, dental hygienist giving him tips," I said, and I couldn't hide my smile.

"Hey, it takes a village."

"Thanks for keeping me in the loop. Now get to work on your real job. The Millennials want to know what Kombucha drink to order or if they should give goat yoga a try." I pushed to my feet and made my way to the door.

"On it," she said, sticking her finger in her mouth and mockingly pretending to vomit.

"Don't bite the hand that feeds, *Blue Jay*."

"Sorry that I happen to care about what's actually happening in the world and not what the latest French braid style is." She smirked. "And why must you call me a bird?"

"It suits you. See you later."

"If you're lucky," she yelled as I walked out the door. A big grin spread across my face. Because I was going with Monroe Buckley to a sex club in less than a week.

Now that's something to smile about.

four

. . .

Monroe

TUESDAY COULD NOT COME SOON ENOUGH. I'd done enough research on the hottest tennis shoes out there, and the best dating apps for single twenty-somethings for a lifetime. I was ready to get to the gritty truth about Simon Reynolds, a.k.a. the current presidential front runner.

I stopped by Jack's office. He'd turned out to be a fairly cool boss. He gave me enough slack to do what I wanted at work, all while keeping me in check. It was a gift, I suppose. Because normally it would annoy me to have someone in my business like this—but he had a way of acting like he cared, which made it less offensive. I knocked on the open door as he sat behind his desk and popped a cookie in his mouth. The guy couldn't stay out of the bakery downstairs, yet his tall, lean physique clearly hadn't suffered. I know he still worked out all the time, as he and Miles followed a similar workout program. Not that I was looking.

I wasn't.

At least I tried not to.

But sometimes he happened to walk past my office and the door was open.

Or when he spoke at our staff meetings, I had no option but to watch the way his broad shoulders filled out his dress shirt, and the way his abs flexed against the cotton fabric when he laughed.

Did it just get hot in here?

"What's up, Little Bird?" he asked around a mouthful of pastry.

"Have you ever heard of not speaking when your mouth is full?" I asked, dropping in the chair across from him.

"Yep. Just don't give a shit. And it's sugary goodness, it's hardly offensive. Just makes me all the sweeter."

I rolled my eyes. "Anyway, Romeo. What's the plan for tonight? It's Tuesday. Operation *Dirty Reynolds* goes down at ten p.m. sharp. Do you want to meet in the alley behind the entrance?"

His head fell back in laughter. For whatever reason, Jack Montgomery appeared to find everything I said hilarious—even when I was dead serious. "Hell no. We aren't meeting in any dark alleys. Give me your address and I'll pick you up at nine forty-five. My driver can drop us off."

Now it was my turn to laugh. "We can't take a driver to an undercover operation. We'll stand out like sore thumbs."

"You said this is a club for the wealthy. You don't think Simon has a driver?"

I thought it over, chewing on my thumbnail as I did so. "Fine. He can drop us a block away and we'll walk it in. Don't forget your disguise. You're a public figure. We can't have you recognized."

"Stop worrying. We'll be fine."

"I'm not worrying, I'm thorough. I'll text you my address."

"Thanks. Your brother called. He said he's coming into town in a few weeks for your birthday?"

"Yeah. He always does. Not sure why, it's not that big of a deal."

"Your dad's having a dinner for you?" he asked.

I groaned. "Yeeeees, per the insistence of *Thirsty Thelma*. She's hosting the lame soirée. Lucky me."

Thelma was stepmother number four, and they just kept getting worse. I wasn't sure what my dad saw in these women, but I loved him, so I tolerated his slew of crazy wives. Ever since Mom died, he's dated… questionable women. Apparently, my mother was irreplaceable, so he stopped trying.

"You want the day off for your birthday?" He looked up to meet my gaze.

I chuckled. "No. I prefer to work. Plus, I'm new here. Why are you offering me random days off? Let me guess. You take your birthday off and treat it like it's a national holiday?" I asked.

"I do."

"God, you're so predictable, Montgomery. When's your birthday?"

"December twenty-fifth. It really is a national holiday." He laughed.

"Of course, you share a birthday with Jesus Christ. It's so—"

"So, what?"

"It's so *you*," I said, unable to hold back my laughter.

"What can I say? I'm a Christmas miracle."

"Okay, boy wonder. I need to get back to work. See you tonight."

"Hey, Blue Jay," he called out when I reached the door. My stomach dipped every time he called me by the ridiculous name.

"Yeah?"

"Wear something sexy." He winked.

I shook my head and made my way down the hall to the break-room where everyone ate lunch. I usually just grabbed my food from the kitchen and ate at my desk.

Two girls that I'd seen a few times since I started, stood off by the microwave gabbing. They smiled when I walked in and continued their conversation.

"I turned up my flirt game yesterday, but still nothing," Sabrina said. She was the assistant to Dan Arbor.

"Trust me, girl, he won't bite. He either has a girlfriend, or now that he runs the newsroom, he won't cross the line." Bailey pulled her microwave lunch out when the timer beeped. They were obviously talking about Jack because he oversaw the newsroom.

"I'm going to give it one more shot. I'll take my blouse down a button or two when I stop in his office today to ask him to meet us at happy hour tonight. My boyfriend paid a pretty penny for these girls." She motioned to her gigantic breasts. "I'm sure they will do the trick. They rarely let me down."

Her boyfriend got her a boob job, and she was using them to hit on Jack? Who does that?

"Your boyfriend paid for your boob job?" Bailey asked, her eyes bulging with surprise.

"Of course, he did. He's loaded, and he's very powerful. A total alpha. But he hasn't committed to me just yet, and I have my sights set on our hot boss."

And this is why I prefer to eat at my desk.

"Oh, my," Bailey said, turning to me and smiling. "She's talking about Jack Montgomery. He's so hot, isn't he? You knew him before you came here, right?"

I popped my mac-n-cheese in the microwave and started the timer. "Um, yeah. He's my brother's best friend, so I've known him for a few years."

"Ohhhhh. Good to know. So, you could probably get the deets for us then?" Sabrina asked, moving closer to me, and literally perusing my body from head to toe. She smiled then—an obvious sign that she didn't view me as a threat. Her blouse was gaping between buttons as her gargantuan breasts were obviously tough to contain. She wore a skin-tight black pencil skirt that was far too short to be considered professional, and her heels were a good five inches tall. The girl tried really hard. I'd give her that.

"Um, no, we don't really talk about that kind of stuff, honestly. But good luck with your plan today." I forced a smile and pulled my lunch from the microwave, bouncing it between my two hands so I wouldn't get burned, before setting it in a paper bowl.

"Well, you could ask your brother to find out, couldn't you?" Sabrina pushed. It annoyed me. We worked together. We weren't girl-friends. She'd barely given me the time of day before now. She didn't get to use me for information.

"No, that's not happening. Take care," I said, turning on my heels and getting the hell out of there.

"She's not a girl's-*girl*," Sabrina said loud enough for me to hear once I was out the door. She couldn't be more wrong. I was a total girl's-girl. But I was picky when it came to choosing girlfriends, and I could spot a user a mile away. And Sabrina and her fake knockers were definitely users.

The rest of the day was spent researching local hotspots for first time dates. The irony was not lost on me. I was writing about things that people my age were interested in—yet I wasn't one of them. But I was a capable researcher. I'd never been on a dating site, nor had I had an actual date in a while. I was definitely going through a dry spell, and I was fine with it.

My phone vibrated on my desk and when Becker's picture popped up, I answered. "What's up, Becks?"

"Not much. Just checking in. You want to grab drinks tonight?" she asked.

"I can't, I'm working. But I could go this weekend if you want?"

"All right. I'll call Gwen and Jilly and see if they're free. Ever since Gwen started dating Royce, she's always busy."

I could picture my best friend Becks rolling her eyes as the words left her mouth. Gwen had never had a serious boyfriend in all the years I'd known her, and I was happy for her that she'd found someone. She was all about Royce right now, and I was fine with it.

"Give her some time. It's still really new, and she's happy. She'll come around. I promise."

She chuckled. "Fine. But she better come this weekend or she's getting the wrath."

"I don't doubt that for a minute," I said, shaking my head and smiling. Becks didn't hide her feelings. She didn't have a politically correct bone in her body. She said what she thought, and she was an open book. Most of the time I appreciated it. Unless the wrath was geared toward me, and then I wasn't such a fan.

"So, you've been at Montgomery Media for a few weeks. Give me the lowdown. Any hot guys? I mean, aside from the sexy brothers who own the place," she said with a laugh.

"I don't really know. I'm in work mode when I'm here."

She groaned into the phone. "Come on, girl. You're twenty-three. Get your game on. You're hot, you're smart, and you're funny as hell. You're the whole package, Mon."

"Oh my gosh, what are you, my agent? I'm good. I needed a break from men."

"Because you wasted so much time on that boring bastard, *Thyme the slime.* I told you it wasn't normal to be named after an herb."

I laughed. "His parents are earthy, what can I say? And I've put him in my rearview. Thankfully, I haven't run into him and his annoying girlfriend, which is part of the reason I don't like going out. It would be so awkward to have to see them together."

"Because he's an asshole who couldn't keep his dick in his pants for five minutes. And don't even get me started on that skank, *Sage*. Those two fucking herbs were made for each other. They can run off and have lots of rosemary babies—the backstabbing fuckers."

I fell back in my chair in hysterical laughter. I was finally at a point where it didn't hurt—the reminder that my three-year boyfriend and my coworker had a secret affair for months. Yeah, that one left a mark. Sage and I both interned at CBS at the same time, but she left after I caught them together. At the company Christmas party of all things. They couldn't even make it the three-hour duration of the party without sneaking into a coat closet for a quickie. I mean, who does that? Well, apparently two herbs with a few cocktails in them —that's who.

"They were meant to be—just based on their names."

"And their low hanging morals," she hissed.

My friends had kept me from falling apart the months that followed the breakup. I couldn't even say for sure that I was heart-broken about Thyme, as much as I was devastated by the betrayal. I didn't trust easy, and I'd always been fairly guarded. But Thyme seemed like such a safe bet, and I couldn't have been more wrong. And after everything went down, I'd lost my ability to trust. In hind-sight, I think Thyme and I had just fallen into a routine, one that was safe and passionless. We went through the motions and I was comfortable with it because it meant that I didn't have to put myself out there for anyone else. Thyme never gave me butterflies, nor was I overly excited to spend time with him. And I'd basically handed him Sage on a silver platter as they'd met at a company event, and we'd all joked about how they were both named after an herb, and wouldn't it be funny if they were a couple. Yada, yada. And there you have it.

Two herbs that appear to be living happily ever after.

Together.

"All right, I need to get back to work. Let me know what day this weekend everyone can meet. Love you."

"We're finding you a man this weekend. It's time to come out of the dry spell, Mon. Love you."

I rolled my eyes before ending the call and getting back to work. I spent the next few hours researching information about the club we were going to. It was called The Dark Temptress, and I was on a discussion blog about all the kinky shit that went down there. I needed to make sure I had an out.

I worked late and quickly grabbed a bite to eat before raiding my closet for something that didn't make it obvious that I was undercover. I found some fitted black leather pants and matched it with a black lace bodysuit and sky-high black heels. I'd never worn either of these before, as they were purchased on a drunken shopping trip with Becks who convinced me they were staples.

Thanks, Becks.

Turns out they're perfect for an underground sex operation. I'd bought a black wig and I pulled it over my head. The hair was sleek and shiny and landed just above my shoulder. I tucked it behind my ears. I applied my makeup more dramatically than usual with a smoky eye pencil and red lipstick.

I stood back and looked in the mirror. Perfection. Just the look I was going for. I wouldn't stand out, nor did I look recognizable. The door-bell rang and I grabbed my clutch and hurried to the door. Jack Montgomery stood on the other side and his jaw dropped when he took me in. I frowned. He looked exactly like himself. On a normal day, that wasn't a bad thing. But if anyone saw him there, they would be suspicious. He could blow our cover.

"Damn, girl. You look like you're ready to chain me up and dominate the shit out of me, and I am here for it."

I frowned and placed my hands on my hips. "Don't be a pig, Montgomery. And why do you look exactly like yourself?"

"Looking like myself has always served me well." He winked.

I rolled my eyes and reached for my keys. "You can't come. You'll blow this whole operation."

"Good Christ, woman. Will you relax? My ridiculous disguise is in the car." He held the door for me, and the smell of cedar and citrus wafted in the air around me as I waltzed past him. He was tall, dressed in dark jeans and a white T-shirt. His muscles on full display. His dark hair was tousled on his head, and it was no wonder women dropped their panties at the door. I thought of the conversation I'd overheard earlier with Bailey and Sabrina, and a sharp pain settled in my chest as we slipped into the car.

His driver pulled away from the curb and I couldn't help myself from asking. "Did you go to happy hour tonight?"

"That's random. Nope. I actually went to Napa and had dinner with my mom, my brother Harrison and Laney Mae. Why?"

My cheeks heated at his question. Why the hell did I care what he did or who he did it with? Maybe it was because he was my brother's best friend, or maybe it was because he was my boss. I didn't like the idea of him with a viper like Sabrina. Someone who pulled out all the stops to try to lure men into her web. He was a friend after all.

"No reason. I thought I overheard someone mention that they were asking you to happy hour." I looked up and found his eyes through the dim lighting in the car. Butterflies fluttered in my stomach when I met his gaze. I hated the way my body reacted to him. It was a physical attraction that I needed to control before I embarrassed myself.

"Sabrina? Hell no. She came in, flaunting her tits in my face, but I shut her down." He laughed.

"Why?" Sabrina may be annoying, but there was no denying she was gorgeous.

"Not my type. At. All."

I nodded. Time to get my head on straight. "Okay, what's your driver's name?" I whispered.

"Why are you whispering? He knows where we're going. His name is Big Tony." He smirked.

I shook my head with annoyance. "Um, excuse me, *Big Tony*."

Jack's driver chuckled. "Yep."

"Can you drop us a block from the location and stay nearby in case we need a getaway car?" I asked.

"We aren't robbing the place."

"You've clearly never gone undercover. We may need to haul ass out of there, in which case, the heels will come off and I'll run barefoot. Where's your disguise, Montgomery?"

He laughed and pulled out a baseball cap and some dark shades. "No one is running barefoot through the street. If we need to make a fast getaway, just hop on my back."

"Because that won't draw attention to us at all." I rolled my eyes.

"Blue Jay, if you didn't want to draw attention to yourself then you shouldn't have worn this sexy as fuck outfit. I don't think there will be a man within a few miles' radius that won't be staring at you," he said, and his deep voice sent chills down my spine.

My cheeks heated at his words. "Keep your eye on the prize, Montgomery."

"I'm pretty sure that's what I'm doing." His gaze locked with mine and I shifted on the seat. Jesus. Was he flirting with me now?

"We're here. Just turn right into the alley, and you'll see the door. I'll be right here unless I hear from you to pull in. I can be there in two minutes, so call if you need me." Big Tony got out of the car and opened our door. He offered me a hand and I gaped when I looked up at the large man. I now understood the nickname.

"Thank you. Keep the engine running," I whispered, and Jack laughed from behind me.

As we made our way down the alley, he reached for my hand and intertwined our fingers. I tried to yank it away, but he tugged back.

"We're supposed to be a couple. We're coming to an S&M club to liven up our sex life. I'm guessing we'd hold hands."

"Oh. Good point. Sorry."

When we got to the door, I knocked three times as the lady on the phone had instructed. When the door opened, a woman with a blonde pixie cut and a short leather dress with tall boots looked us up and down. "Melody and Wags?"

"Yep. That's us," I said, sounding a little too eager. Jack squeezed my hand.

"Okay. Follow me." She led us down a long, dark hallway with cement flooring only lit by black lanterns hanging above. "Celine will be with you shortly, to discuss your options."

After she pulled the door closed, he turned to face me. *"Melody and Wags?* You couldn't do better than that?"

"Melody is always my go-to fake name. And Wags was the name of my childhood golden retriever. It was the first thing that came to mind when I thought of you," I said, cracking the door to look out in the hall, before closing it and taking in the room. There were metal brackets hanging on the ceiling, and some sort of cage or contraption on the floor. The walls were lined with all sorts of tools: whips, chains, bands, and muzzles. My heart raced as I realized that we were here, and we might not be able to get out as easily as I planned. Would being restrained by Jack Montgomery be the worst thing? I dropped into the chair in the corner and tried to process our options.

"You a singer, Blue Jay?"

"What, no? Why would you think that?"

"Because you always choose Melody as your fake name. I thought maybe you were a singer," he said, shoving his hands in his pockets and leaning up against the wall like he didn't have a care in the world.

"It was my mom's name," I whispered. It was the truth. I'd always loved her name.

"I didn't know that. She passed away when you were young, right?"

I stared at him for a long moment. "She died while giving birth to me."

I didn't know why I said it. I rarely told anyone what happened to my mother.

The room fell silent before someone turned the handle and entered.

Game time.

five

. . .

Jack

WHAT THE ACTUAL HELL? Buck never told me how his mom died, just that she'd been sick when he was young. But Monroe's words cut me deep. They were laced with sadness and grief—something I recognized immediately.

There was no time to respond, as a woman that stood almost as tall as me walked in the room. She wore some sort of black leather leotard and fishnet stockings. Her hair was white and long, ending at her round ass. Her tits were spilling out of her top, and her features were harsh. Monroe pushed to her feet, her cheeks flushed, and I didn't miss the tremble in her hands. Most wouldn't notice, but I'd been around her enough lately to know she was nervous.

"I'm Celine. I'll be handling you both tonight." She perused Monroe from head to toe and licked her lips, and I moved between them.

"Not so fast. We aren't certain what services we want just yet. I convinced Little Bird to come check this out tonight, but we'd like some time to explore alone at first, if you don't mind," I said, placing one hand behind me and gripping Monroe's wrist in mine.

Celine peered around my shoulder and whispered, "Ah, she is a

Little Bird, isn't she? Oh, how I'd enjoy caging you up and teaching you some tricks."

"Easy there," I said. "She's mine. And I don't share."

"Does she?" she asked, suddenly turning her attention to me, running her hands down my chest and stopping when she slipped just below my waistband. She gripped my cock which was already hard, not because of the she-woman currently stroking me, but because of the woman who was dressed like a sexy little siren tonight who stood behind me. Monroe gasped when she realized what was happening, and I used my free hand to grip Celine's wrist.

"Not just yet. I belong to her. She decides when she wants to share. Give us some time to—explore one another, will you?"

She made a tsking sound. "Such a shame. So much to share here."

"Might not happen tonight, but give us a minute to play around," I said, freeing her hand before she stepped out of the room.

Monroe moved around me and held a hand over her mouth as she shook her head. "Oh my gosh. I, er, I'm so sorry. Um, are you okay?"

I chuckled. "Yeah. Not the first time someone's touched it."

Her cheeks pinked and her eyes grew wide. "Oh. Right. Sure. Okay, then."

"So, what's the plan, Blue Jay?"

"Well, we need to get out of here and try to find Simon Reynolds. This place isn't that big. Should we split up?" she asked, nervously pacing the room.

"No. We stay together."

She stopped and turned to face me. "Why?"

"If we get caught, we can say we were exploring other rooms. If we separate, we're going to look suspicious."

"Good thinking, Montgomery. Let's do this." She cracked the door open and peeked out before motioning for me to follow. She had her phone in her hand ready to snap a photo if the opportunity presented itself.

"What the hell is the plan?" I whisper-shouted as my chest brushed against her back and my overachieving boner reacted once again.

Buck's little sister, dude.

Keep it together.

She turned around and smacked right into my chest before looking up at me and holding her finger to her lips. Hell, I could have just hired someone to follow Simon here, someone who actually followed people for a living. But this was worth the hassle. Seeing her all frazzled and excited. I fucking loved it.

She thrust her thumb at the first room and pressed her ear to the door before shaking her head and moving on. Not sure what she heard, but she seemed confident as we continued to the next door. She listened once again and then her eyes grew wide and she reached for the handle. I gripped her shoulders and shoved her aside.

"Move," I said.

She pouted. Shocker.

I wasn't about to let her walk in on something that could permanently scar her or risk someone trying to pull her in. I cracked the door open and realized very quickly it wasn't Simon Reynolds because a kid who couldn't be more than twenty years old was on all fours on a table getting his ass whipped. The woman stopped mid-beating and her gaze locked with mine before a wicked grin spread across her face.

"Join us," she purred, before I held my hand up in apology and pulled the door closed.

I shot a scowl at Monroe before she tugged my hand and pulled me farther down the hall. After listening at three more doors and walking in on yet another man who wasn't Simon, we returned to our original room and Monroe paced some more.

"Shit. I don't think he's here," she said, tucking the hair of her dark wig behind her ears.

"We can try again another time. It doesn't have to happen tonight."

"I need it to happen," she hissed, dropping to sit in the chair. "Or I'm going to be writing crap my whole life."

I tried to cover my laugh, but I failed miserably. The girl was twenty-three-years old. Where was the fucking fire? "You've got time. Relax."

She pouted and pushed to her feet. "Fine. How the hell are we going to get out of here?"

"I'll handle it," I said, just as someone knocked on the door.

I pushed Monroe up against the wall and covered her mouth with mine just as Celine stepped in. Her lips were soft and plump, and her mouth tasted like peppermint. My tongue dipped in for a little taste. My fingers wrapped around her waist, pulling her closer. Her tits pressed against my chest, while her tongue explored mine. Her body melded to mine like she belonged there. A little moan escaped her sweet mouth, and I nearly came undone. Jesus. I could die a happy man right here.

"Well, well. Looks like the party started without me," Celine said, and I reluctantly pulled away. I missed her mouth the minute I stepped back. Monroe's cheeks were flushed, her chest rising and falling rapidly, and her tongue swiped out to taste her bottom lip.

What the fuck was with that kiss?

"Sure, has. But my girl here isn't quite ready to share. It's going to take some time for her to open up to this."

"That's all right, sweetness. Mmm-mmmm… so damn sweet." She used her thumb and stroked it along Monroe's bottom lip before leaning down and kissing her. Celine moaned against Blue Jay's mouth before pulling away. "Damn, girl. Don't take too long. We could have some fun. Those are some kissable fucking lips. I'll bet Big Daddy here likes those wrapped around his cock."

Monroe's eyes were as wide as saucers and I barked out a laugh before reaching for her hand. "He sure does. Come on, baby. We'll try again next week."

Celine swatted my ass, and I looked over my shoulder and winked at her. I led us both down the hallway and out the door to the alley before calling Big Tony to let him know we were on our way.

"You all right?" I asked when she pulled her hand free from mine and continued to walk in silence.

"I'm fine. Why'd you do that?" she hissed.

"What? Kiss you?"

"Yes."

"Because we're supposed to be a couple. We kicked her ass out of the room and if we weren't doing something when she walked in, we sure as shit would have looked like we were up to something. You don't go to a place like that for conversation, Blue Jay. And it was a fucking kiss. No big deal. Hell, Celine kissed you too."

She groaned. "You don't need to remind me. That's more action than I've had in a year," she said through her laughter.

I looked over at her. The moon was shining down, illuminating her pretty face. Her cheeks were pink, lips plump, and eyes dancing with excitement.

"What do you mean? I thought you had a boyfriend?" I remembered Buck saying she was with a dude that he didn't care for, but he hadn't brought it up in a while.

"Oh, Thyme? No, we broke up last year."

I came to a stop as we turned the corner from the alley. "You're fucking with me, right? His name is *not* Time."

"It's T.H.Y.M.E. Like the herb."

"Who the fuck names their kid Thyme?" I said, barking out a laugh.

"Apparently the ancient Greeks believed Thyme was a source of courage." And now it was her turn to laugh.

"Ridiculous. Good. I'm glad you kicked the herb's ass to the curb."

We continued walking as the car came into view. "Well, I didn't exactly kick his ass to the curb. More like I caught him in the coat closet at my company work party with my coworker."

"Are you shitting me?" I asked, coming to a stop again. The girl was full of surprises. What kind of asshole cheats on a girl like Monroe? Smart, beautiful—she was the whole package. What a douchebag.

"I shit you not. And do you want to know the best part?" She tugged at my arm and started walking again.

"Give it to me."

"He's still with her now. Her name is *Sage*."

I clapped my hands together and howled at the sky, for no particular reason other than that was the only thing I could think to do in this situation. "Shut the fuck up, Blue Jay. Two motherfucking cheating herbs. You can't make this shit up."

She laughed as we stepped into the car and she yanked the wig off her head. Her dark blonde hair was in some sort of braid wrapping around her head like a crown.

"Yeah. Glad I found out when I did before I wasted any more time with him."

"Me too. You deserve better."

"Agreed." She smiled, and my stomach fluttered.

No fucking way. I didn't do stomach flutters or butterflies or any of that bullshit. But Monroe was special.

She was my best friend's little sister.

Definitely off-limits.

Not that she was my type. She wasn't.

I preferred my women less—observant. Monroe didn't miss a beat. She questioned everything. I liked to keep it light. There was nothing light about this girl. But that kiss was—hot as hell. Maybe the best kiss I'd ever had. Could have been the fact that she wasn't expecting it. Hell, I hadn't planned on it either. But when I heard the door opening, I knew I needed to do something. Or maybe I just wanted one taste of those plump lips. Maybe it was the heat of the moment. We were in a sex chamber after all, and my dick was still screaming at me for not giving him any attention as he'd been hard since the minute Blue Jay opened the door tonight.

"Thanks for going with me, *boss*. I appreciate it."

I chuckled. "It pains you that I'm your boss, doesn't it?"

She held up her thumb and her pointer finger about an inch apart. "A little bit. Yes. But don't take it personal. I don't like answering to anyone. I've always worked best on my own. I hated group projects in school, because, well you know—one person ends up doing all the work. And of course, it was always me."

"Group projects were my favorite. I never had to do much. Just show up and look pretty." I winked. "And someone always brought treats. There was great conversation. I think I even got laid a few times after some of those projects. And we always got A's. It takes a village, Little Bird."

She groaned. "Ugh. I hate you."

"You didn't seem like you hated me when I kissed you," I teased. I was actually curious if she thought it was as good as I did. I'd never really cared before, but this was Monroe Buckley. I cared what she thought. Even more so now that I'd gotten to know her.

She shrugged and her cheeks pinked. "I barely noticed."

Big Tony chuckled in the front seat and then tried to cover it with a cough.

"I heard that, Big T."

We all three laughed now.

"Seriously. Who was better? Me or Celine?" I couldn't help but press the matter. That fucking kiss had rocked my world. I needed to know it was amazing for her too. Nothing would come of it, obviously. But it happened, and she appeared to be a straight shooter. I wouldn't mind getting an honest rating. One of my strengths was pleasing women. I liked to think of it as a gift. I prided myself on pleasuring my lady before myself. Always. I was a gentleman after all.

"Hmmm…" She paused to think it over. "Both were unexpected."

"Both were better than that dickhead, Thyme, I'm sure."

She smiled. Her blue gaze locked with mine in the dim lighting coming through the window from the streetlights as we drove toward her apartment.

"Yes. Thyme wasn't much for kissing. He was more of a *wham-bam-thank-you-ma'am type* of guy. I mean, he had sex in the coat closet at my company party."

"With another herb, at that."

Her head fell back in laughter. "Exactly. So, you were definitely better than Thyme, and better than Celine, if I'm being honest. I mean, don't get a big head. She was a bit rough. Our teeth clanked when she forced her mouth over mine and she tasted like pork rinds. And not in a good way. So yes, you win by default."

I nodded. "Okay. I can work with that. I happen to love pork rinds though."

"Of course, you do." She rolled her eyes.

We pulled up to her building and I started to follow her out of the car, but she turned to stop me. "You don't need to walk me to my door. This isn't a date. It was a mission gone awry. But thanks for going with me."

"I'm not walking you up because I think it's a date. I do have manners, you know."

"I couldn't tell with the way you came at me all hungry and needy when you kissed me," she teased as a man held the door to her building open behind her. "Seriously. I have a doorman. Hal's great. I've been walking myself to the door most of my life, Montgomery. See you tomorrow."

"All right, Blue Jay. See you tomorrow. We'll get him next time."

"Yep. We will."

She turned on her heels and paused to hug her doorman. She was much friendlier to him than she was to me. Hell, she was friendlier to everyone than she was to me. But tonight, we'd made progress. And she was Buck's little sister. It would be nice to be friends with her.

She'd told me about her mother's passing, and I wanted to ask more, but I didn't know if she would be okay with it. I'd give it time and bring it up again. I understood what it was like to lose a parent. Miles had been a huge support to me during that time. I wondered who Monroe leaned on for support outside of her brother. Definitely not her piece of shit ex-boyfriend.

Big Tony pulled away from the curb and turned his head to speak to me. "I like that girl."

"Yeah. You and me both, brother."

Maybe a little more than I should.

six

. . .

Monroe

"I LIKE what I'm seeing, Monroe. How are you adapting? Everyone treating you well?" Ford asked. I guess this was my one-month check-in.

"Yeah. It's been a great first couple of weeks. I mean, obviously, I'd like to write more political pieces, but I'll take what I can get for now."

"I can appreciate that. I'm not the most patient man. You know what you want and you're not afraid to go after it. Keep it up. You'll get there. And Jack tells me today is a special day? Happy Birthday."

"Thank you. I appreciate it. And thanks for this opportunity. I won't disappoint you," I said, pushing to my feet.

"I have no doubt you're right about that." He stood and escorted me to the door.

"I saw Harley this morning. She looks like she's about to pop, huh?"

He groaned. "Don't get me started. My wife is a stubborn woman, whom I happen to be crazy about. She refuses to stay home and rest. Thankfully, she's just downstairs."

I laughed. It was sweet, seeing them together. I remember meeting Ford at a few of Miles and Jack's football games in college and he was much colder and more standoffish. Harley was clearly good for him.

You couldn't miss the genuine love that lived between them. It made me long for that type of relationship. Someone who cared so much for you, their own life depended on your happiness. It was something I'd always steered away from, caring about someone that much. The risk. The looming heartache. But seeing it in real life made it all the more appealing.

"I'm sure it's hard to sit still. She needs to keep busy. She was sitting in a chair when I popped in earlier if that makes you feel better."

His lips turned up in the corners. "It actually does. Thank you. I'll run down and check on her now."

"Thanks, Ford. See you later."

He nodded, and we both turned in opposite directions down the hallway. There were elevators on each end of the floor, and I was heading up to the newsroom while he was heading down to the bakery. When I made it back to my office, I found a small cake sitting on my desk with *Happy Birthday, Blue Jay* written on top in pink icing. My stomach fluttered and I scolded myself for reacting that way.

I used the intercom system on my office phone and dialed him.

"Happy Birthday, Little Bird," he purred through the speaker.

"Why must you call me that, and why did you tell your brother it was my birthday?"

"Because *it is* your birthday," he said, like it was common knowledge, and I should know this.

"Well, thank you for the cake." I dipped my finger along the bottom seam and sampled the icing, moaning as the sugary sweetness hit my system.

"Was that moan for me?" he teased, and I startled.

"Oh, no. *No.* I just took a taste of the frosting. Is this a DeLiciously Yours cake?" I cleared my throat and pushed my nerves aside.

"It sure is. She made it just for you."

"That was sweet. Thank you."

"Your brother is going to stop by and see me before you all head to dinner. Have fun tonight. You deserve it."

"You know I'd rather be going to The Dark Temptress to catch that dirtbag in the act than to dinner with Thirsty Thelma."

"Come on. We'll get him next week. Enjoy your birthday. It only comes around once a year."

Jack had such a vibrance for life. I envied it, honestly. I'd never embraced my birthday, for a multitude of reasons. First and foremost, my birthday was also the day of my mother's passing. A blessing and a curse I guess you'd say. She'd traded her life for mine. And I'd spend my entire life trying to make mine worthy of her giving her own in exchange. So, popping the bubbly wasn't high on my list. The second reason was that I despised being the center of attention. Always had. So, this day could pass just as quickly as it arrived, and I'd be fine with it. It was a tough day for my father, though he always tried to hide it. He'd drink a bit too much tonight, and I knew why. He liked to pretend it was in celebration, but we both knew he was numbing the pain of losing the love of his life, all these years later. I was a constant reminder of what he'd lost, and that was a heavy burden to carry at times. So, I'd do my best to make my parents proud, and be worthy of the sacrifice that my mother made for me.

"All right. See you later," I said.

A sadness blanketed my chest, almost suffocating me at times. My brother understood it. Hell, it was the reason he always showed up on my birthday. No matter where we both were, he'd always show up. Miles, Dad, and I had spent every single birthday together since the day I was born. Such a strange day celebrating my birth and the loss of a woman I'd never even known, yet I felt her presence with me always.

The day moved by quickly, as I buried myself in work. I was doing a column on trendy fall fashion which was a bit more fun than any I'd written thus far. Only because I actually cared about clothing. It was a hell of a lot better than researching dating websites and hot spots for meeting your perfect mate. I was all about leggings, cute sweaters, and ankle boots at the moment, so my research was putting a serious dent on my credit card this month. Montgomery Media paid me well, but it wouldn't begin to cover the high-rise that I lived in, nor the amount that I spent on clothing binges. My brother and I had hearty trust funds from both our grandfather and our father. I never took for granted the affluent lifestyle I was born into, but at times I felt like it meant that my life was supposed to be perfect. At least that's the perception from the outside world. I had everything I'd ever want—yet, I'd always had a gaping hole in the middle of my heart, the place that I guessed only my mother would have filled. So, yes. I was thankful for all that I had—but it was far from perfect. If you were able to see into someone's soul the way you gazed through a window, you would most likely find a whole lot of cobwebs and dust in mine. Tattered and bruised. Life was messy, and I did my best to maneuver around it. I was born with a dark cloud surrounding me, and I worked hard to escape it. Throwing myself into work. Striving to be the best at whatever I did to make up for the pain that I'd caused. It was a heavy weight, but I was surviving.

I was a proven survivor.

There was a knock on my open door, and I looked up to see Miles. I pushed to my feet and hurried over to hug my brother. He stood there with Jack right behind him.

"Happy Birthday, sis." He lifted me off the ground and spun me around.

"Put me down, you big buffoon." I laughed as he settled me on my feet.

My office phone rang just then, and I walked back around my desk to answer it.

"Hey Monroe, I have Thelma Buckley on the line. She said it's urgent that she speak to you," Talia, the office manager who handled all incoming calls, said.

My head fell back in irritation, and I closed my eyes as I spoke. "Thank you. You can put her through."

My brother laughed and I put Thelma on speakerphone. "Monroe? Are you there?"

"Yep. I'm here. What's up? Do you need to cancel?" I said, connecting my hands as if I were praying and smiling at my brother and Jack, who covered their mouths to muffle their laughter.

"Don't be ridiculous. It's your special day, *baby girl*," Thelma said. She was only eight years older than me, for the record, so *baby girl* was a bit of a stretch. "No, no. The reason I'm calling is because, well, I know that you and Thyme broke up quite a while ago and you've been single for what feels like—*forever*. Am I right?" She paused to cackle—

her laugh grated my nerves. A cross between the laugh of a chain smoker and an evil witch. Neither appealing. I let my forehead rest on the desk and closed my eyes as I listened. She was obsessed with the fact that I was single. Not that Thyme ever attended family events with me anyway. In hindsight, he was an extremely selfish boyfriend. Thelma acted as if being single were the most pathetic thing she'd ever heard. Mind you, this was a woman married to a man almost twice her age. "So, I'm guessing you're *still single*, right? I just didn't know if I should set a plate for someone, or just seat you solo per usual?"

Well, thanks for that reminder. *Per usual.*

"Um." It's the only word that came to mind as I tried to find a way to tell her it was just me without sounding like a complete loser with my brother and Jack standing there listening to our conversation. Thelma always looked at me with such pity. Sometimes I wondered if it was because I'd lost my mother in such a horrific way—but most of the time I truly thought it was because she really believed that a man defined you. Her entire being was based around being Ryan Buckley's wife. He was a celebrity in this town, and his wife thrived on that attention. My father's fame had never been important to him—Thirsty Thelma was a different story. I believed it was the reason she was with him. I didn't buy into that round of crazy, but it didn't mean that her words didn't get to me sometimes. And I had zero respect for her, so I wasn't sure why I allowed it to bother me.

"Oh, sweetie. It's okay. You can make it your mission this year. You know—start making more of an effort to have a man in your life. They aren't going to find you if you're always working, and most men appreciate a woman who puts a little more effort into fixing herself up, you know? Not that you aren't gorgeous. Of course, you are, baby girl. But you could put some curl in that straight hair of yours and spruce it up. Maybe try some better bras and push those girls up a bit, *what little you have to work with.*" She cackled again and I cringed.

"Actually, Thelma, Monroe hasn't wanted to tell anyone because she didn't want the pressure, being in a new relationship and all," Miles said, holding his finger up to stop me from jumping in, as he winked at me. "She's been dating Jack Montgomery. You remember my best friend, right?"

An indescribable sound left Thelma's mouth as I buried my face in my hands and heard Jack laugh. "Jack Montgomery is dating *our* Monroe? Really? He's so yummy. Wow. How'd she reel in such a big fish? Oh man, is he a big fish. In more ways than one, if you know what I mean."

"I'm still here, Thelma, and I can obviously hear you." I scowled at my brother, half wanting to murder him and half wanting to hug him for rescuing me. I gave an apologetic shrug to Jack, who didn't seem fazed in the slightest by the lie my brother just told.

"Oh, sweetie. I mean no offense. I just, wow. Jack Montgomery. Score, girl. Big score," she said, her tone going from shrieking to serene.

I rolled my eyes as Jack beamed at me, puffing his chest out like the arrogant ass he was.

"He's not that big of a score," I said, trying to hide my smile as my brother laughed. "He's all right though. It's new."

"Hello, Thelma. *Big Jack* here. Grateful that our girl scored and all, but I think I'm the one who scored," he purred, and Miles high fived him.

I shook my head with annoyance. This was going to be a disastrous evening. But I could fake date Jack Montgomery for one night if it meant getting my awful stepmother off my case, couldn't I? I'd have a couple of glasses of wine. Hell, I'd already kissed the man and seen fireworks for days after, so this would be a walk in the park. Maybe he'd fake kiss me once more. It wouldn't be tragic, seeing as this whole thing was Miles' doing, so he couldn't get angry about it. And it was fake after all.

"So, will you be joining us for dinner, Jack?" Thelma asked.

"I wouldn't miss my girl's special day for the world. I'll see you soon." Jack dropped down in the chair across from me and raised a brow as if he were challenging me to join in.

"Yep. We'll see you soon. Goodbye." I ended the call and groaned before reaching for the empty water bottle on my desk and chucking it at my brother. "What are you thinking?"

He caught the bottle and dropped it in the trash before turning to face me. "I'm thinking it's your birthday and you don't need to be harassed by Thirsty Thelma all night, and well, he's my best friend, so I'd like him to come to dinner with us anyway—so I killed two birds with one stone."

"She'll never let this go. Are you sure you're fine with this?" I asked Jack.

"Hell yeah. We already went to the sex den together, so this'll be a cakewalk." He pushed to his feet and laughed.

"Excuse me?" Miles asked, his gaze bouncing between us.

I waved my hand in front of my face. "It was an undercover mission, which someone seems to keep forgetting is supposed to be on the *down-low*. It was nothing. We went to get a picture of someone. And don't ask questions because we've already said too much."

"And did you get the picture?" he asked with a chuckle.

"No. He no-showed that night. We can't go back until next week because of my stupid birthday." I pushed to my feet and reached for my purse.

"Okay. One night of fake dating is harmless. You can tell her you broke up next week." Miles held the door as we all three stepped out and made our way to the garage.

"Fine. But don't overdo it." I shot Jack a look. "I've never been a touchy-feely girlfriend, so she won't expect any of that."

"I'm kind of a needy boyfriend, Blue Jay. You're going to have to deal with it." He laughed and my brother rolled his eyes.

"Keep it light, brother. No handsy bullshit. But the cute nickname is a nice touch. Good thinking." Miles and Jack sat on each side of me. There was no need to tell my brother that the nickname wasn't new. Jack had been calling me Blue Jay for weeks—but we both kept that to ourselves. It was harmless. Jack Montgomery was a flirt by nature. He couldn't help himself.

Big Tony drove us to my family home. The home I'd grown up in. Jack insisted Big Tony pull over in front of a jewelry store in the city and he dashed inside, after mumbling something about not going empty-handed to his girlfriend's birthday dinner.

"Look at the mess you've made. Now he feels like he has to buy me a gift. This is ridiculous, Miles." I huffed in my seat.

"Relax. Jack is a generous guy. Just have fun tonight," he said as he scrolled through his phone like he didn't have a care in the world.

Jack was back within minutes, and I didn't see a gift in his hand, so maybe he'd changed his mind. One could only hope. This was already awkward enough. When we arrived at the house, the door flew open and Thelma stood there clapping her hands.

Let the shitshow begin.

Jack draped an arm over my shoulder, and I tried to slap it away, but he just gathered my hand in his and grasped my shoulder tighter.

"Hey, Thelma. Where's Dad?" I asked, giving her a quick hug. Her gargantuan fake boobs always slammed into my chest, and I swear they hit me hard enough to leave a bruise.

"Happy Birthday, baby girl. Dad's been in his office, so why don't you run and get him?" she said to me, but her gaze remained on my fake boyfriend. "And hello, Jack Montgomery."

I rolled my eyes and took off down the hall. The door was cracked open and I peeked my head inside. Dad sat on his brown leather couch surrounded by floor-to-ceiling bookshelves and a large desk. The smell of cigars wafted around the room. He had his eyes closed, rocks glass in hand, as he tipped the last of his drink back and pushed to his feet.

He turned to see me standing there, and he straightened his dress shirt. "Happy Birthday, sweetheart."

I hurried over and hugged him tight. "Thanks, Dad. Are you okay?"

He pulled away and studied me for a long moment, and I tried to ignore the strong stench of whiskey radiating from him. "Yes, angel. I'm good. Come on. Let's go join the party. I hear you have a date tonight. Jack Montgomery? Great guy, but I can't believe Miles is okay with this." He chuckled.

He isn't.

seven

. . .

Jack

"SO HOW LONG HAVE YOU and Monroe been dating?" Thelma asked as she stroked my arm. She wore a low-cut red dress, leaving very little to the imagination. Her tits were large for her frame, but I'm guessing that was intentional.

"We've been together for a few months now," I said, sipping my wine and turning as Monroe and her father entered the room. Her blue gaze locked with mine and she raised a brow as if questioning how I was surviving my visit with Thelma.

"Jack here is just telling me that he and our baby girl have been dating for a few months. She's kept this little secret awfully quiet. And he was quite the football player in college, if memory serves. She found herself a guy just like her daddy," Thelma said, walking toward her husband and wrapping her arms around him.

"Yeah, well, it's all right to keep your private life quiet. I'm just surprised you've been able to get approval from this one," Ryan Buckley said, as he thrust his thumb toward Miles.

My best friend chuckled. "Well, it's not too serious yet, and I'm just happy if they're happy."

"And yes. Jack was one of the best college quarterbacks I've ever seen play," Ryan added.

48

"He was all right," Miles snorted as he elbowed me in the side.

"Well, us girls sure do love a football player. Let's continue this conversation in the dining room. Petra has prepared a delicious birthday feast. I requested all your favorites, baby girl," Thelma said, leading us all toward the dining room.

"Thank you," Monroe said as she walked between her brother and me. I reached for her hand and she slapped it away. I couldn't help but laugh. She was so fun to mess with. Miles glanced over at me and gave me his infamous warning stare. I'd seen it many times over the years when we were considering doing something stupid. Which we both did often in college. I'd seen it out on the field when I went for risky plays—but this time, there was a bit more seriousness behind it. I rolled my eyes. I was just playing, so he needed to chill. After all, this was his idea.

We took our seats in the oversized dining room. Monroe sat between Miles and me and Thelma and Ryan sat across from us. The tall dark mahogany chairs looked more like individual thrones than they did dining chairs. Thelma had redone the place, and it was a bit gaudy if you asked me. Red and gold wallpaper covered the walls and a similar print hung in long panels on the windows. Hey, maybe regal, over-the-top décor was in these days. Wasn't really my thing, as I preferred a home to look like a home. My mother always managed to create that in our homes, and I appreciated it. They were grand, sure, but they were comfortable because actual people lived in them.

The platters set before us overflowed and my stomach rumbled with anticipation. Filet mignon, ribs, sweet pork. I leaned into my fake girlfriend. "I thought you were a vegetarian?"

We'd had a few working lunches at the office, and I paid attention. She turned to face me. "I am."

This was her birthday dinner? Food that she wouldn't eat? She reached for the salad and Miles passed her the bowl of pasta. Thelma dove right into an enormous rib as her husband sat beside her quietly sipping his cocktail. What was up with him tonight?

I remembered Monroe telling me their mother died during child-birth, and I imagined this day might be tough for Ryan Buckley. Losing the woman that you love but gaining an amazing daughter. That's a bag of mixed emotions right there.

"No meat for you, baby girl?" Thelma asked, as she set the oversized rib down on her plate. A large dollop of barbecue sauce landed between her giant tits, but there was nothing sexy about it. She tried too hard to pull off the whole sex kitten vibe, and it wasn't working for her. And why in the hell did she call Monroe *baby girl*? I could see that it grated Blue Jay's nerves and even Miles appeared annoyed by it.

"Nope. Still a vegetarian."

"Oh, that's right. How long has this trendy little phase been going on?" Thelma paused and sucked down all the liquid in her wine glass and we all three gaped as we watched her wipe her mouth with the back of her hand.

"A little over a decade, so I'd say it's a bit more than a trendy little phase. It's an actual lifestyle choice." Monroe's words had some bite behind them, and I put an arm on her shoulder before I could stop myself. She needed the comfort, and I'd be damned if I wouldn't give it to her. It was her goddamned birthday after all.

Ryan Buckley looked up as he set his glass down and waved over one of the three servers who hovered around us and requested a refill.

"I remember that day vividly. My little girl came home from fifth grade after doing a report on the meat industry, and she told me she'd never eat meat again," Ryan said, his words slurred a bit.

Monroe smiled. "It's a promise I kept."

"Yeah. And you tortured my ass all through middle school and high school for eating meat. Printing out those pictures of little chicks and baby cows and setting them on my plate every night before dinner." Miles' head tipped back as he laughed.

"Just trying to help you see the benefits of a plant-based diet." She smirked at her brother. They were like my brothers and me... they could communicate with just a look. It was impossible to miss their bond.

"So, do you eat meat, Jack?" Thelma purred before her gaze locked with mine and she stuck her pointer finger in her mouth and sucked on it slowly before pulling it out and licking off the remaining barbecue sauce, all while watching me with an intensity that made my skin crawl. Jesus. This woman had no shame. Her husband sat beside her completely disinterested in her antics. My hand still rested on Blue Jay's shoulder, and it surprised me that she hadn't slapped it away. Although we were supposed to be dating, so I assumed a little contact would be acceptable.

"I do," I said around a mouthful of meat and Monroe chuckled beside me.

Ryan Buckley's phone rang on the table startling all of us from the conversation. "Excuse me. I have to take this."

"Awww… I want to give baby girl her birthday gift during dinner," Thelma whined. Her long blonde curled hair was stiff with hairspray and every time she moved it looked more like a wig than her own hair.

"That's fine. You can go ahead. I'll be back." He pushed to his feet and left the room, and I didn't miss the way Monroe's shoulders sagged in defeat.

"Okay, here you go, baby girl. I just can't wait one second longer." She reached across the table and handed me the envelope to pass to Monroe.

"There's really no hurry. We can wait for Dad to get back."

"No. I want you to open it now. I've been so excited about this. I put a lot of thought into your gift this year. And well, I think it will bring you and I even closer together."

Monroe stiffened at her words. Closer together? There was obviously no love between Thelma and her husband's children. They couldn't stand her. It was impossible to miss.

"Just open it, or this will never end," Miles mumbled to his sister as Thelma requested another refill of wine.

Monroe opened the envelope and froze as she read the card. "Oh my gosh. I, um, wow. I don't know what to say."

Miles and I shared a glance before we both leaned forward to look at the card. He closed his eyes and shook his head as I tried to make out what it was.

"You can just say thank you, baby girl."

"Thank you for the generous gift of *plastic surgery*?" Monroe said as she broke out in laughter. It wasn't the kind of laugh that caused others to join in. It was laced with disdain and hurt. I was good at reading these things. My sister-in-law, Laney Mae, claimed it was because I thrived in the area of *emotional intelligence*. And for whatever reason, it pained me to see Blue Jay upset.

"You got it. Anything you want. But I've already met with the doctor, and he is best known for his boob jobs. He did mine. So, if I were you, I'd take advantage of his skills." Thelma winked before reaching for another rib.

Monroe set her wine glass down after taking a sip and coughed uncontrollably. I patted her back and she gaped at her stepmother with disbelief. "You want me to get a boob job?"

"Honey, no. I mean, only if you want one. He's the best in the city. Look at mine." She ran her hands down the sides of her oversized breasts and her eyes locked with mine before her tongue slowly dipped out and traced her bottom lip. Miles choked on his cocktail before breaking out in laughter. I didn't know if he was laughing at her offensive gift or at the fact that she was shamelessly trying to flirt with her stepdaughter's boyfriend. Well, fake boyfriend, but she didn't know that. Either way, it was all disrespectful and I didn't like it. I wasn't okay with the way Monroe slumped in her seat or how this woman belittled her.

"Absolutely not." My harsh words surprised everyone, including myself, and both Monroe and Miles turned to face me. "She's perfect just the way she is."

"Of course, she is. But are you going to tell me you wouldn't mind her, um, enhancing a few *lacking areas*?" Thelma tipped back yet another glass and held her hand in the air, snapping her fingers for a refill.

Monroe groaned beside me. "All right. I'm kind of over this conversation. It's not up to Jack, nor is it up to you. I'm quite content with my boobs, but thanks for the *thoughtful* gift."

Her lip trembled as she spoke, and it pissed me off. It was her fucking birthday. I reached over and tugged her onto my lap, catching her off guard as she let out a gasp. I wrapped my arms around her as she squirmed, and I held her tight. "You're fucking perfect just the way you are."

She stopped fighting me and her head fell back in laughter. The smell of lavender and honey surrounded me, and I reveled in it. In her. I liked seeing her all light and happy. She deserved it. And no woman should be made to feel bad about her body *ever*. And Monroe Buckley was the last person that should be lacking confidence.

The girl was fucking gorgeous.

Fucking perfect.

"Thanks. I'm fine, *boyfriend*." She dug her nails into my hand which rested on her thigh and turned, patting my cheek with her palm.

"Well, aren't you two adorable." Thelma held her phone up and snapped several pictures of the two of us together, and I didn't mind it one bit. The woman needed to back the fuck off Monroe, and if dating me made her do so, I was fine with it.

Miles growled beside us. "Okay. Enough PDA at the table."

Monroe moved back to her seat, and I didn't miss the pink hue covering her neck. Adorable. Whether she liked it or not, I'd always have her back. She was Buck's little sister after all. And I liked her.

Ryan Buckley returned to the table, and he asked Thelma if she gave Monroe her gift yet. When she nodded, he reached across the table and handed her a package. "I got you a little something just from me."

She pulled the ribbon off the box and lifted the top before pulling out a small pendant with a heart. She opened the heart and her eyes watered. "Thanks, Dad. I love it."

Miles and I both leaned in once again to see a small picture of the three of them tucked inside. She unclasped it and reached behind her neck and I moved to my feet. She startled when I grazed her fingers and took the chain from her hand. She held her hair up and I clasped it behind her neck. I lingered there longer than I should, for no particular reason other than I wanted to. Her skin was soft, and she smelled fucking good, and I was only human.

"Thanks," she said, brushing my hand from her shoulder and raising a brow as her gaze locked with mine.

I dropped back down in my seat.

"Well, take some time with the other gift, and think about what you'd like to do. You know, starting young is a good way to be proactive in the aging process," Thelma said with a wink.

"Got it. I'll take that into consideration." Monroe tensed beside me.

"I have a little something for you," Miles said, reaching in his suit coat pocket and handing her a card.

She opened the envelope and laughed at the picture of the little boy and girl on the card. The boy was smashing a cake in the girl's face and she read the card aloud. "I hope you have a smashing good birthday. Don't get any ideas there, brother." She laughed. There was some sort of gift card inside. "Thank you. I could use a good massage."

Monroe leaned over and hugged Miles, and I reached in my suit jacket and pulled out a little black box. "Happy Birthday, Blue Jay."

Her cheeks pinked, and I covered my mouth with my hand so I wouldn't laugh. She didn't like the attention which only made me want to pour it on even thicker.

She opened the box to see the diamond stud earrings I got her. They may be a bit over-the-top, but fuck it. She was supposed to be my girlfriend, and I was a giver. And it was Monroe. I wanted to give her something nice.

"Oh my gosh. They're gorgeous. Thank you," she said, cocking her head to the side and waiting for me to meet her questioning gaze.

"I'm glad you like them. I wanted to get my girl something nice." I kissed her cheek and felt the warmth of her skin on my lips.

"Dinner table," Miles reminded me once again. The dude was such a buzzkill. He was the reason we were even in this situation, but he sure didn't like me acting like she was my girlfriend.

"Ooh, girl. And he's a good gifter. I'll bet that's not all he's good at." Thelma winked at me, and Monroe burst out in laughter.

"Are we having cake, Thelma?" Ryan turned to face his wife. He showed no emotion where she was concerned. Like he'd completely checked out.

"Oh yes. Let me run in the kitchen and tell them to get your cake ready. It's your favorite, baby girl." She pushed to her feet and turned to the two ladies standing off to the side of the dining room and snapped her fingers. "Let's get this cleared off. Now. We're ready for dessert."

"Wow. Thelma's really on one tonight," Miles said, facing his father.

"She means well." He tipped his head back and finished his drink.

"You sure you're okay, Dad?" Monroe asked, and the tenderness in her voice caused a sharp pain to settle in my chest. She loved her father and her brother so much, and she'd been dealt a shit hand losing her mom during childbirth. Hell, I missed my father every day, as losing him in that car accident had been life-altering for me. But at least I'd gotten the first twenty years with him. She'd never even gotten to meet her mother.

"I'm good, sweetheart."

"Okay, cake time." Thelma used her hands to fluff her hair before taking a seat beside her husband.

Petra set a large cake down in front of Monroe and we all sang "Happy Birthday." She laughed and waved her hands in front of her face, anxious to have the moment end. I'd quickly learned that Monroe Buckley didn't like being the center of attention.

But she should revel in it.

Because she was the kind of girl that deserved to be the center of someone's whole world.

eight

. . .

Monroe

I WOKE up to several texts and missed calls, which wasn't the norm. I frantically read through the messages, anxious that something had happened to my brother or my father.

I couldn't have been more wrong.

Holy hell.

This wasn't happening.

Fucking, Thirsty Thelma.

There were a slew of texts from Becks, Gwen, and Jilly all asking for details about Jack Montgomery. The phone rang, and I picked up on the first ring.

"Hey, Becks."

"Um, '*hey, Becks*?' That's all you have to say, Mon? You're going viral on social media. What the hell is going on? I can't believe you didn't tell me."

I ran a hand down my face. Thelma had posted a picture of Jack and me on both her Instagram and her Facebook, as well as my father's social media. She'd outed us as a couple. Only we weren't dating. And my father had a couple million followers, so word spread fast.

Hence the nickname. Thirsty Thelma. She lived for this shit.

"Oh my gosh. I'm going to kill the woman."

"We can verbally abuse Thirsty Thelma later. What's going on with you and Montgomery? And seriously, Miles is okay with this? I know how protective he gets when it comes to who you date. His best friend? A well-known playboy?" She barked out a laugh and I rolled my eyes as I carried the phone into the bathroom.

"We aren't dating. It was Miles' stupid idea because Thelma was going on and on about me still being single. And Jack was there. So, he just said we were dating, and we figured we'd tell her we broke up in a few days."

"Mmm-hmmmm, that picture sure doesn't look fake. Let's take a moment to appreciate the way he's looking at you. And you appear remarkably comfortable sitting on his lap, smiling at your fake boyfriend, like you can't wait to get him home and jump on his—"

"*Stop!* Oh my gosh. No one is jumping on anything. I haven't even seen the picture yet." I scrolled to my father's Instagram and groaned. "Dear God. Why would she post this?"

"Because it's hot. And you look like a couple in love, which is why it's going freaking viral. I've gotten all sorts of texts this morning from coworkers asking why I kept it a secret. You know, my best friend is dating the city's hottest bachelor." She laughed.

"I'm going to vomit."

"Good attitude, Mon. Now put on something sexy and go to work. You're dating your boss after all."

I dropped to sit on the toilet as the reality set in. People at work would think we were dating now. No. They wouldn't be trolling social media. This would go away, and no one would be the wiser.

"I'll call you at lunch. I need to get to work."

I quickly showered and got ready, praying that no one at Montgomery Media would get wind of this ridiculous story. We covered the news, not trivial gossip.

My brother phoned me as I walked toward the building and I answered with a less than charming greeting. "*I hate you.*"

He laughed. "It'll blow over. Jack sure played his part though. I think Thelma was drooling over you two."

"She was not. She was drooling over him. Did you see her licking her lips and pushing her ridiculous boobs toward him? The woman has no shame. Oh my gosh, can we even talk about the worst birthday gift ever? *A boob job?* What is wrong with her? How is Dad even with this woman?"

He chuckled once again. "I don't know. Dad seemed pretty checked out. Sorry for getting you in this mess. Just tell her you broke up in a day or two and everyone will forget about it."

"All right. I'm at the office. I need to go."

"Love you, sis."

"Love you, idiot head. And you can take all the calls from Becks about this. Goodbye."

I heard him laughing as I ended the call and stepped in the elevator as a few people turned and stared once the doors closed. I rubbed my nose to make sure nothing was there and looked down at my dress to see if I had toilet paper stuck to me. Why were they looking at me like I had three heads?

I hurried off the elevator and down the hall to more ogling eyes. What the actual hell was happening? When I approached my office, Ford, Jack, and Harrison Montgomery were already there. Ford paced the room as Jack sat in a chair eating a cupcake and Harrison sipped his coffee.

"Um, hey. Am I late for a meeting?" I asked, dropping in my chair across from them.

"Good morning, schmoopie. We've got quite the shit storm going on," Jack said with a smirk.

"This is not fucking funny, asshole," Ford hissed, and I straightened my posture at his tone.

"Relax. It's going to be fine. Monroe, Jack filled us in on the misunderstanding from last night, but unfortunately, your stepmother posting the pictures has caused a whole lot of havoc for the company. We've covered quite a few *Me Too* stories in this paper over the past few months and outed several large corporations for this type of practice. Having one of the owners of Montgomery Media dating a new employee who happens to work for him, not to mention the fact that you're younger than him, well, we're opening ourselves up to a lot of criticism." Harrison was the middle Montgomery brother. From what I'd heard he was the most even-keeled and level-headed.

"I'm sorry about that. I should have anticipated that she might do this."

"It's fine, Blue Jay," Jack said, popping the last of his cupcake in his mouth. He really was beautiful to look at. His dark hair was tousled on his head, and dark scruff peppered his chiseled jaw. Golden whiskey eyes locked with mine and butterflies swarmed my belly. I shifted in my seat.

Focus.

"It's actually *not fine*, Jack. Every paper in the city is going to run with this story, just to poke at us. You own the company. You're dating an employee. That's not okay." Ford's tone was harsh and angry, and I reached for my water to calm myself down.

"We'll break up this week. It's not a big deal." Jack pushed to his feet and walked over to stand beside the window.

"It is a fucking—" Ford shouted, and Harrison held his hand up and pushed to his feet.

"Relax, brother. Listen, we need to release a statement. This is how it's going to play out. We're going to say that you two have been dating for a while. We brought Monroe on and kept your relationship under wraps for privacy issues. So, you won't be breaking up anytime soon. We need to let this blow over. And hopefully, neither of you have had any public, er, dalliances over the last few weeks, or you're going to be called out for cheating."

"That just might work," Ford said.

"Wait, what? We have to pretend to date? For how long?" I gasped.

Jack smiled. "Come on, Little Bird. I'm not that bad, am I?"

"Um, yes. You are. For starters, you sleep with everything that moves, so people will think you were unfaithful. I don't want to be the victim. Jesus. I'm going to kill Miles. And Thelma."

"At least I won't be able to testify against you, because we're dating." Jack laughed.

"Do you have a serious bone in your body?" Ford snapped at his younger brother.

Jack gazed down at his crotch. "Just the one. And he's got a mind of his own."

I rolled my eyes. "Have you been out in public with anyone recently? I don't want to start this fake relationship off looking like the poor pathetic girlfriend who's being cheated on."

"Nope. I keep my relationships private. I'm not having sex in store-front windows. Unless that's your thing? So, do we get to have any fun while we're fake dating?"

"Jack." Harrison gave him a warning look. "Monroe, I'm sorry about this. But we can't have people saying that he started a relation-ship with an employee *after* we hired you. And we need to keep this as close to the chest as we can. You can't tell anyone it isn't real. It will run its course in a couple weeks and this will all be behind us."

"Wait. So, this is for show and it isn't real, but you're saying I can't sleep with anyone privately? I'm supposed to go with no sex for several weeks?" Jack's face suddenly turned to stone. No happy-go-lucky smile in sight.

"That's exactly what we're saying. Keep your goddamned dick in your pants." Ford stormed to the door.

"What's his problem?" Jack dropped back down to sit in the chair and ran a hand through his hair, as the realization set in. We'd made a mess for Montgomery Media and it was my fault we were even in this situation.

"He'll be fine. Let him cool down." Harrison turned to me. "You going to be okay with this?"

"Yeah. Of course. I'm really sorry to have caused so much trouble."

"It's all right. You've got to love social media. Nothing's sacred anymore," Harrison said, clapping a hand over his brother's shoulder. "Don't antagonize Ford today, he's got a lot on his plate. He's worried about Harley working, he's got two little girls on the way, and a bit of a shit storm with the press over this situation. So, stay out of trouble, got it?"

"Got it, Har bear. I'll see you, Laney Mae, and Mom for dinner tonight. You want to join us Blue Jay? We are supposed to be dating." I knew that Laney Mae was married to Harrison, as my brother Miles had attended their wedding not too long ago.

"No. I'm not going to start spending every evening with you. I'm not that kind of girlfriend." I rolled my eyes.

"Well, I've got bad news for you. I'm a very needy lover. I like a lot of affection, a ton of attention, and whatever else you want to throw in. I will not have the press thinking my girlfriend doesn't want to spend time with me."

Harrison's head fell back in laughter before he turned to give me an apologetic shrug. "He is who he is. It might not be a bad idea to be seen out in public a few times, and I know Mom and Laney would love to see you."

I closed my eyes for a minute, processing the shitshow I'd created. Miles was going to pay for this. "Okay. Let me see if I can get all my work done today and maybe I'll be able to squeeze in some time with my fake boyfriend."

He chuckled. "You two need to be aware that people around the office are watching. So, for all intents and purpose, you're dating. Leave the disdain for one another behind closed doors. Obviously, Mom and Laney will know the truth so you can be more relaxed tonight, but when you're in public—you're a couple. Got it?"

"Yes. I'm totally fine with it. I was thinking I should settle down soon anyway," Jack said with a wink.

I threw a pencil at him, and he caught it midair.

"I'll write up the statement today and release it to the press. I'll get you out of this as soon as I can. See you both later." Harrison left the office and closed the door behind him.

I dialed my brother immediately and put him on speakerphone.

"What's up, Mon?" he said.

"I'll tell you what's up. You've created a literal disaster for Montgomery Media. Now we have to pretend that we've been dating for a while. This is a mess, Miles." I buried my face in my hands as I waited for his response.

"You there too, Jack?"

"Yep. I'm fine. Your sister looks like she's about to lose her shit. I've never met anyone so upset about dating me. Everyone wants to date me."

Miles barked out a laugh. "Easy, brother. You're not dating my sister. You're fake dating."

"Potato, po-tot-o." Jack chuckled.

"Shhhh… no one can know this isn't real. Oh my gosh, Miles. What have you gotten me into?" I rubbed my temples.

"I hate seeing my girl upset." Jack smirked.

"You're enjoying this way too much," I groaned.

He laughed and pushed to his feet. "I need to get to work. I'll see you tonight. I'll call you later, Miles."

"You still there?" my brother asked on the other end of the line, as we sat in silence after Jack left the room.

"Yes. And I still hate you."

"I think we should focus all of our energy on hating Thirsty Thelma."

"I hate her too," I whined, resting my forehead on the desk.

"There are worse things than fake dating San Francisco's most eligible bachelor, you know?" he said.

"Name one."

"Dinner with Thelma. Running into your least favorite herbs… Thyme and Sage."

"Touché. You win."

"Sorry I got you into this mess. Where do you have to go tonight?" Miles asked.

"Harrison thinks it's a good idea for us to be seen out a few times, so I'm going to Napa for dinner. But at least his family knows it isn't real."

"Just do it for a few weeks. Hell, it's good for you to get out a little and have some fun."

"I'm hanging up on you now because I have to go to work. And fake dating is exhausting. Goodbye."

"Love you," he said before I ended the call.

I wasn't happy about any of this, but I was in it, so I'd have to deal with it.

How hard could it be to fake date the hottest guy in town for a few weeks?

Painless, right?

nine

. . .

Jack

"YOU NEED TO RELAX. It's just dinner."

"I don't like lying and all of this is based on a lie," Monroe said as the helicopter settled on the ground in Napa. The flight from the city to my mother's home was a quick up-down, and my brothers and I used the helicopter to commute back and forth often.

"My mom and Laney Mae have already been informed that it's for show. It's no big deal. You need to eat. I need to eat. We'll be at my mother's house for dinner, so there won't be any pressure to act like we're together. And I saw a dude outside of Montgomery Media snapping pictures of us as we exited the building. That's all we need. Now we can relax for the rest of the night."

She walked in silence until we stepped into the car I kept parked at the helicopter pad to commute to and from the winery.

"Okay," she said as she buckled herself up before turning to face me. "I'm sorry for dragging you into this mess. I'm sure this isn't going to be the most pleasant experience for you either. You know, depriving all the women in the city of all the sex."

My head fell back in laughter. "What? I'm not a prostitute. Just a normal man with a healthy libido."

She rolled her eyes. "Spare me the gory details."

"It wouldn't hurt to know a little about one another, seeing as we're kind of in a relationship for the next few weeks. Fake or real—we're going to be spending time together."

"True."

"So, you haven't dated anyone since Cilantro?" I said, knowing it would lighten the mood. I knew his name. He just didn't deserve to be mentioned.

"*Thyme,*" she said through her laughter.

"Ah, yes. The heroic herb."

"After we broke up, I've just sort of taken a break from dating. So, this fake relationship works well for me because I was due for one." She shrugged.

"You shouldn't feel pressure to date. Do what feels right. Trust your gut."

"Tell that to Thirsty Thelma. She acts like something's wrong with me because I don't have a boyfriend. But I'm not just going to date a random guy so that I can say I have a boyfriend."

"Nor should you."

I pulled in the long driveway leading to our family home. I led her inside, and Laney Mae hurried to the door to meet us. It smelled like warm bread and garlic. My mother was an amazing cook, and my stomach rumbled with anticipation.

"Well, if it isn't the happy couple," she said, as her laughter echoed around the foyer. "Hey, Monroe. I'm Laney."

"She's *Laney Mae*. She just likes to act all adult these days." I wrapped an arm around her neck and kissed the top of her head.

"I've been Laney since second grade, Jack-ass. You and Ford just refuse to drop the middle name."

"Nice to meet you, *Laney,*" Monroe said, making it obvious whose side she was taking on the name game.

"I already love you. Any chance this fake relationship could secretly be real?" she asked as we followed her in the kitchen.

"No chance," Monroe said, and I rolled my eyes.

The girl acted like dating me was the worst thing in the world. There were a shit ton of women who would disagree, but no sense pointing that out for the millionth time.

"Monroe, hello. It's such a pleasure to see you again. It's been a long time." My mother had met Monroe at a few college football games when Miles and I played back in the day.

"It's so nice to see you as well. Sorry for the unusual circumstances, and for dragging your family into this little mess my brother created."

"Don't be silly. I'm happy to see my Jackie boy in a relationship, whether it be fake or real." Mom winked and I rolled my eyes.

"Jesus, Mom. I'm not a whore," I hissed. I was a normal mid-twenties dude who liked to date. I wasn't banging multiple women in the same day or going to The Dark Temptress for twisted shit. I liked sex. And women enjoyed having sex with me. Sue me.

"I know, sweetie. But I've told you I'd like to see you settle down."

I wrapped my arms around her from behind and leaned forward to kiss her cheek. I couldn't be mad at her for wanting the best for me. I loved the shit out of her. She was my pulse, my reason to be better. After losing our father a few years ago, Mom, Ford, Harrison, and I really relied on one another even more so than we had before. Losing Dad had caused the earth to crumble beneath my feet. Family meant everything to me, and I knew my mother wanted my brothers and me to find what she and Dad shared. Ford and Harrison already had. I wasn't quite there yet. But I wasn't complaining. In all honesty, I preferred to keep my relationships light. I knew the pain of losing someone you loved. Loving someone meant that you had something to lose. I already loved my family so there was nothing I could do about that, but I wasn't looking to add more people to that list.

Casual worked for me. Fun conversation. Great sex. No strings. Nothing to lose.

Harrison waltzed in from the backyard. "Ah, San Francisco's favorite couple is here."

Monroe laughed and I flipped him the bird. "Nice press release, brother. Now the whole city wants to know our story."

"Hey, I had to clean up the mess, and it wasn't that far-fetched. You have known one another for years. You are her brother's best friend. I just added the part that you couldn't fight your love for one another any longer." He laughed.

"It was sweet," Laney Mae said, pushing on her tiptoes to kiss his cheek.

"It would make for a good story if we actually liked one another," Monroe said.

I bumped her with my shoulder and scowled. "Hey. I do like you."

"Oh. Sorry." She burst out in laughter as did everyone in the kitchen before we made our way to the dining room.

No one made penne pasta in vodka sauce better than my mother. It was my favorite. A large salad sat in the center of the oversized farm table along with a basket of garlic bread, and I carried out the bowl of pasta and set it beside the salad.

"Wow. This looks delicious," Monroe said.

"Thank you. It's my specialty." Mom passed the garlic bread to Harrison. "So, tell me, do you still run? I recall you were quite the running superstar in college."

"Not competitively, but yes, I still run daily."

"Didn't you win nationals your senior year?" Harrison asked. "I read something about you being an Olympic prospect back then."

"Jesus, dude. Did you stalk her?" I spewed, and everyone chuckled. I didn't like that he knew more about her than I did. Harrison was an attention to detail guy—I wasn't. But for some reason, when it came to Monroe Buckley, I wanted to know everything. I wanted to know things that no one knew.

"It's called research. We hired her. It's all available on this thing called the internet, dufus."

Monroe finished chewing and dabbed at her mouth with her napkin and chuckled. "Yes, I won nationals my senior year, and I did think about training for the Olympics. But I also had this burning desire to start my career. Training for the Olympics is a full-time job, and there're no guarantees. I realized I'd lost some of that passion after all those years of competing. I wanted to start living my life, I guess."

"I get that," Laney Mae said. "I imagine it takes a lot of discipline. You and Jack actually have that in common. As goofy as he is, he was the most disciplined athlete I've ever known."

Atta girl. Laney Mae loved to pump me up, and damn if I didn't love it.

I winked. "Thanks. It wasn't hard to be disciplined because I loved it."

"And I loved watching you play. But I will admit I was relieved that you didn't pursue going pro. It was hard to watch you take a beating out on the field over and over again," Mom said, tilting her head and smiling at me.

"Thanks, Mama," I said around a mouth full of food.

"Was it hard for you to walk away?" Monroe asked, studying me like she genuinely wanted to know the answer.

"Oddly... no. I knew that my family needed me, and I knew that's where I wanted to be." It was the truth. Everyone thought I would regret it. Hell, I wondered if I'd have a change of heart after I walked away from football. But I never did. I'd enjoyed it for the years that I played, but I was where I wanted to be now. "Do you ever regret walking away?"

"Nope. I'm happy that I get to run for myself now. Not against a clock or another person. No expectations or disappointments about how far or how fast I run. It's just for fun. Just for me."

I nodded. I understood it. Competitive sports were great and rewarding, and they could become a huge part of your identity. But I was more than football, and obviously, Monroe was more than a runner. And it wasn't always easy to separate.

"Good for you. Maybe we can go for a run sometime. I'm sure we'd push one another," I said, my gaze locking with her deep blues. I still trained every day like I had in college. I needed the outlet.

"We could give it a try. You know, you're not so bad for a fake boyfriend, Montgomery." She smiled and my stomach did some sort of bullshit flip.

What the actual fuck? Maybe it was the pasta?

"Ah, you two make the perfect fake couple, if I do say so myself," Laney Mae said before scooping salad onto her plate.

The rest of the night was spent laughing and talking, and Monroe fit in just perfectly with my family. She and Laney Mae were fast friends. And Monroe and I were forming a friendship as well, even if she didn't want to admit it.

———

I dropped in the chair in Ford's office and he sat behind his desk.

"So, what's the plan? Those babies going to come out anytime soon? Seems like they've set up permanent residence in Harl's belly." How long was she supposed to carry them around like that? It was ridiculous. Her stomach was far too large for her small frame, and she waddled around trying to balance her own body.

He rolled his eyes. "That's not how this works. They stay in as long as possible. Thank god she finally decided to stay home and rest a little. Not that she had a choice. Once the doctor said she shouldn't be working, she had zero chance of fighting me on it."

"Such a barbarian," I said, popping a cookie in my mouth. "Thankfully, she baked enough ahead of time to be gone for a while. I wouldn't survive without her pastries."

He smirked. "Yeah. She sure is talented, huh?"

"Yep. She's the best."

"How are things going with Monroe? The press is really eating it up. How do you want to play this?" he asked.

"Play what?"

"You'll need to keep it going for a few weeks, and then we can release a statement that you broke up, or something. We'll let Harrison come up with the wording for it."

"Yeah. There's no hurry. I needed a break from going out anyway."

"Is that so?"

"Did I stutter?" I asked.

He smiled. A rare occurrence in my brother when his wife or our mother wasn't around. "What does Buck think of this?"

"He's the reason we're even in this situation. He apologized, but he also warned me that if I touched her, he would kill me." I chuckled. But Buck wasn't kidding, and I knew that. Not a line I'd ever cross. Not that she would want to anyway. The girl could barely tolerate me. It bothered me because I actually liked her. Liked being around her. And she didn't seem to be warming up to me in any way, shape, or form.

"Don't fuck it up, brother."

"No one is fucking anything up," I said, pushing to my feet slowly.

"What's with you? Why are you walking so slow?"

"I ran six miles this morning with Blue Jay. Quite possibly the toughest workout I've ever done." I hobbled to the door.

He barked out a laugh. "She kicked your ass, didn't she?"

"Nope. I held my own. I may have vomited in my mouth twice, but I kept up with her. She talked the whole fucking time too, and I was gasping for every breath."

He shook his head. "You're ridiculous. Don't forget you have the Simon Reynolds charity event this weekend. Take Monroe. There will be lots of press."

"Sometimes I feel like you're just using me for my good looks. You know there's more to me than just this strikingly handsome face and chiseled body."

"Yeah, yeah, yeah." He waved me out the door as his phone rang.

I limped back to my office and found Monroe sitting in the chair behind my desk. I shut the door behind me and studied her.

"Nice to see you, darling," she said through her laughter.

"What are you doing?" I rubbed my lower back before stumbling to a chair and dropping to sit.

"Ah, a little sore, are we? Mr. Badass Football Player."

I rolled my eyes. "I'm fine. Why are you behind my desk, and what's with the evil smirk? What are you up to?"

She pushed to her feet and came around the desk. "I just thought I'd sit here with the door open, because I assume if we were actually dating, I would do that, right?"

"Good thinking, ole wise one."

"This is why I get paid the mediocre bucks." She used her pointer finger to tap her temple and smiled. "Don't forget, it's Tuesday. We're going back to The Dark Temptress tonight. Operation Dirty Reynolds is on."

I nodded. I had a private investigator following Simon, but I wouldn't tell her that just yet. I knew she wanted to do this on her own, and I didn't want to ruin all the fun. No one liked a buzzkill.

"Don't forget, we have the fundraiser at his house this weekend. You'll go as my date."

"No duh. We're dating. I have no choice." She rolled her eyes.

"As if you aren't dying to go," I said, trying to stand and wincing because my muscles were screaming like little bitches.

She patted me on the back, just enough to make me flinch. "Buck up, buttercup. You've got a couple more weeks with me if you're lucky."

She waltzed out the door, and I stood frozen in my office. Partly because I had physically taken an ass-kicking this morning—but also because she was right.

I was lucky.

And I was in no hurry for my luck to end.

ten

· · ·

Monroe

"LISTEN, there's something I should tell you," Jack said when he arrived at my door.

I put my finger to his lips to silence him, but also because I'd been staring at his plump lips for days and just wanted to touch them any way I could.

I'd never felt that way about Thyme when we dated. Like I wanted to touch him or press my lips to his just because I could. Obviously, I'd already dated a crappy herb... so it was only fair for me to be physically attracted to the best looking guy I'd ever laid eyes on, who was also pretending to be my boyfriend. It didn't hurt that he was attentive and thoughtful—not at all what I'd expected. But his smooth talking was not going to deter me from my investigation. I knew he was sore from our run this morning. I'd poured it on and ran harder than I'd run in a long time, but he'd bragged so much about his training he left me no other choice. But sore or not—we were doing this.

"If you are going to come up with a reason not to go—save it. We're going. Take some ibuprofen and suck it up." I walked out ahead of him and we made our way to his waiting car.

"You're a real peach sometimes, Blue Jay." He held the door open and slid in behind me.

"I've been called worse. Hey Big Tony," I called out to his driver.

"Look how friendly you're being to Big T. Why the hell are you always so irritated with me?"

"Fair question." I looked up at the ceiling as my fingers drummed along my jaw as I thought it over. "I think you annoy me more than most."

"I annoy you?"

"Yes. Is it that hard to comprehend?"

"Nobody's annoyed by me. People love me," he insisted, and it took all I had not to laugh. The truth was, he didn't annoy me. I actually liked him, maybe even too much—and *that* annoyed me.

"Then you have nothing to worry about. Okay, we're here. Focus. We'll see you in a little bit, Big Tony. Stay close." I hopped out of the car as Jack slipped on his sunglasses and baseball cap.

I wore my same get-up, the wig, the hot pants, the whole nine yards. I would be lying if I said I wasn't dying from this morning's run. I'd killed myself to prove a point, and I was feeling it in these sky-high heels.

I knocked three times and the door swung open. The woman on the other side had a lavender, blunt cut bob that rested on her shoulders. She wore a black leather catsuit, and she was strikingly beautiful. Her gaze perused Jack from head to toe, and she barely gave me the time of day. Jealousy crept in and I reached for his hand.

"Come on, baby," I purred, surprised that those words left my mouth.

He chuckled and pulled me close, tucking me beside him. "I'm right here, Blue Jay. Let's go."

The lady appeared miffed, but she walked us to our room.

"We're going to need a little alone time, so hold off on sending anyone in," Jack said, reaching his hand to hers and sliding her something.

"Mmmm, you sure you don't want company?" she purred.

"Not now. We'll let you know."

She left the room and he turned to face me. "Was that jealousy back there, Little Bird?"

"What? Don't be annoying, you pompous ass." I placed my hands on my hips before storming toward the door.

"You sure seemed jealous," he said from behind me, his lips grazing my ear as he spoke. "And I love that you're wearing the earrings I gave you."

I turned around fast. My chest slamming into his. I did wear the earrings that he gave me. So what? It didn't mean anything. He had good taste in jewelry. "What did you give her anyway?"

"A hundred bucks."

"Pfft. Focus, *moneybags*. We've got a senator to find." I yanked the door open, desperate for some freaking space from this man. My breaths were labored. His nearness was making me crazy.

I hurried to the first door, and he pressed his chest to my back as he attempted to listen as well before whisper-shouting in my ear, "Sounds like some girl-on-girl action going down in there. No pun intended."

I turned around and slapped his chest. "You're disgusting. Let me guess, you'd like to go in there and join them."

He was the ultimate playboy. I'd be wise to remember that.

"Believe it or not—I have no desire to go in there. I'm completely content out here with you abusing me, even if we're wasting our time." He towered over me now, his whiskey gaze locked with mine.

"Well, lucky me. My fake boyfriend wants to spend time with me. Throw me a ticker-tape parade. And how exactly are we wasting our time? We're here for a job, remember?"

He brushed a piece of hair from my wig away from my face, and his fingers grazed my cheek, sending chills down my spine.

Damn you, Jack Montgomery.

"Reynolds is not here."

"How do you know that?" I asked, whipping my head around to make sure no one was coming. A few moans came from the room we were standing by, and I tugged his arm to pull him into the corner.

"I have an investigator following him. He went to his kid's school function."

"What? When did you find that out?" I huffed, folding my arms over my chest.

"On my way to pick you up."

"Why didn't you tell me? Why the hell are we here?"

"Because you told me not to speak, remember?" A wide grin spread across his handsome face.

"I told you not to speak if you were going to try to talk me out of coming. Not if you were going to tell me he wasn't here. I could be soaking in a tub with a hot tea, but I'm at this creepy sex den because you didn't speak up."

"You told me not to speak," he repeated, cocking his head to the side as he studied me.

My stomach flipped, and I sucked in a long breath to pull myself together. Why did he have to be so damn good-looking?

"You should have insisted. I think you wanted to come here, you big perv," I said, poking my finger into his hard muscled chest.

He caught my finger in his hand and smiled as he held it there. "Is that what you think?"

My breath caught in my throat, and I froze until a voice startled me from my Jack Montgomery trance.

"What are you two doing out here?" a woman I'd never seen asked. Her black hair was slicked into an oversized bun on top of her head, and her lacy dress clung to her voluptuous body.

"My girl's got a jealous streak. We need to leave. I don't think she's cut out for this," Jack said, grasping my hand in his and tucking me behind him.

"What a shame. Well, don't be a stranger. I'm sure she'd under-stand if you came back by yourself. I think we could have some fun." She ran her fingers up his torso and my hand fisted at my side. She moved closer, grazing his lips with hers. "Think about it."

"He doesn't need to think about it. Back off," I hissed before moving beside him and staring her down.

The other woman chuckled. "So salty. I like it. That's good—protect what's yours. If he were mine, I'd do the same thing."

I tugged at his hand. "Let's go."

He followed me out the door and broke out in a fit of laughter once we were outside. "You go, girl. That was badass. Turned me on a bit, if I'm being honest. The way you staked your claim."

I rolled my eyes. "Hardly. Just playing the part."

"You sure? You seemed a little bit jealous back there."

"You wish."

I'd been unsettled all night. There was a force that drew me to him, and I fought it every chance I got. The last time we'd been here, he'd kissed me. It was a kiss that I couldn't seem to wipe from my mind. It stayed with me. Consumed me. I liked it, which horrified me. Being near Jack was not easy. He was a touchy guy, and I found myself longing for the contact. Maybe I'd hoped he'd have to kiss me again tonight as part of our undercover operation. What was wrong with me? Why was I attracted to the most unattainable man?

I was relieved when I spotted Big Tony up ahead and I pushed away my crazy thoughts.

The drive to my apartment was silent until we pulled in front of my building. "Next time tell me that he isn't going to be there, please. And since when do you have an investigator following him?"

"Since our last visit to The Dark Temptress. He's just looking for anything out of the ordinary. Although I think he stopped going there, because according to my guy, he hasn't been back once since he's been trailing him."

"Damn it. He's probably aware that he's being followed," I huffed.

"Very doubtful. My guy is a pro. He's a retired Navy SEAL. Slick as fuck. No way Simon saw him."

I thought it over. "Fine. He did just announce his intention to run for president. He is probably being more careful now. I'll reach out to my contact and ask her if she's seen him."

"Your brother's, uncle's, mechanic's, dentist?"

I chuckled and rolled my eyes. "Whatever, Montgomery. I'll see you tomorrow. We have the fundraiser coming up. We can keep our eye on him there."

"Sounds like a plan, Blue Jay."

I jumped out of the car when Big Tony opened my door and held my hand up when Jack tried to follow me out. "I can walk myself to the door, remember?"

He nodded, and I turned on my heels. I needed a break from the guy. We were working together and spending too much time outside of work trying to keep up appearances for our fake relationship.

I needed to cleanse myself of all things Jack Montgomery.

eleven

. . .

Jack

WORK HAD BEEN CRAZY, and Ford was on edge as Harley was scheduled to give birth to the twins in a week. Tonight, we had the fundraiser at Simon Reynolds' home, and I was looking forward to taking Monroe. I hadn't seen much of her the past few days. She appeared to be avoiding me, which wasn't a great idea seeing as we're supposed to be dating. But I understood it. Lines were getting a bit blurred with all the time we spent together. And I had a wicked case of blue balls, as it had been too long since I'd been laid. It had to be some kind of record.

I popped in the bakery for my morning pastry and was surprised to see my very pregnant sister-in-law behind the counter.

"I thought you were on bed rest?" I said, coming around the counter and giving her a hug. I loved everything about Harley Montgomery, and all the ways she'd changed my broody brother's life for the good. I couldn't wait to meet the babies, and I knew she'd be an amazing mother.

She rolled her eyes and shook her head. "The doctor never said *bed rest* or that I couldn't go to work. He said for me to take it easy. I'm nesting, so I just came in to check the count in the freezer and snatch a few cookies."

"Does Ford know you're here?"

"No. But I'm going to go upstairs and surprise him. Laney and Harrison picked me up. Har had a meeting with Ford, and Laney came to check on me."

"Where is she?"

"In back in the freezer taking inventory for me," she said, moving around the counter and dropping to sit in a chair.

"Laney Mae," I shouted before taking a bite of the world's best red velvet cupcake.

"What's up, Jack-ass?"

"Not much. Just dropped in for a sugar boost and a cup of coffee. Where's Kourtney?" Kourtney was working full-time to cover for Harley while she was out on maternity leave and she'd been promoted to manager per my brother's urging.

"I'm in back making a few batches of butter cookies," Kourtney said from the back room.

Laney Mae handed me a coffee and we both pulled up a chair to sit with Harley before I had to head upstairs.

"You do realize Kourtney's my first employee that you haven't hooked up with, which is why she hasn't had a meltdown and quit yet."

"Give her time." I laughed before holding my hands in the air. "I'm kidding. I'm in a relationship, remember?"

Someone cleared their throat from behind me, and I turned to see Monroe moving past me and walking toward the counter. Her shoulders were stiff, and she barely gave me a side glance. Had she overheard our conversation? She was pissed because I *used to hit on girls* before I started fake dating her. Are you kidding me?

"Hey Monroe, good to see you." Harley pushed to her feet and hugged her. "You look gorgeous today."

She did. She always did. She wore dark jeans, a pink blouse, and sky-high heels. Her hair was in some sort of twist, and she looked fucking beautiful.

Laney Mae moved around the counter and grabbed a muffin and a coffee for Monroe before hugging her goodbye as well.

"Do you want to join us?" I asked, pulling up another chair.

She scowled at me. "I know you like to hang out and hit on all of the employees here, but the rest of us have actual work to do." She turned to my sisters-in-law with her friendly smile. "Have a great day. Thanks for breakfast."

She glared at me one more time before leaving the bakery.

Jesus. I couldn't win with this girl.

"I have to say, I'm on the fence with this whole fake relationship," Harley said with a laugh, dropping back down to sit beside me.

"What do you mean?"

"I don't know how fake it is, honestly. Maybe it's my hormones, but there is some serious sexual tension between you two." Harley raised a brow at me before rubbing her oversized belly.

I rolled my eyes. "Did you just witness the same thing I did? The girl hates me ninety percent of the time."

"Um, that was not hate. That was pure jealousy. I think she heard Harley talking about you dating her staff. Fake girlfriends don't care if their fake boyfriend is hitting on other women. Trust me, Jack-ass, there's something there and I'm totally down with it. I like her for you. She holds her own and doesn't have patience for your shit," Laney Mae said, groaning as she took a bite of the brownie she'd chosen from the display case.

I rolled my eyes. "You're insane. We have the fundraiser for Simon Reynolds tonight, so she'll need to put on a smile and act like we're together."

"I'm with Laney on this one. There's something there," Harley said, reaching for her water.

"You're both crazy. But I still love you." I pushed to my feet.

"So, you have no feelings for her. None at all?" Harley pressed.

"Sure, I like her. She's Buck's little sister."

"That's not what I asked. Do you like her, or do you *like her*?"

I rolled my eyes. "Of course, I like her. What's not to like? She's smart, she's funny, she's gorgeous."

"I knew it." Laney Mae fist-pumped the sky.

"Knew what? She's a friend. Nothing could ever come of it."

"Because she's Buck's sister?" Harley asked.

"That among other things."

"So, what if she wasn't Buck's sister? Would you ask her out?" Laney Mae pressed.

I thought about it. And the answer was easy. "Yeah. I would."

Harley clapped her hands together. "Like you'd want to date her?"

"I am dating her."

"You're fake dating her," Laney said. "And you like it, don't you?"

I chuckled. "It's fine. It can't go anywhere, and she hates me, trust me."

"She definitely does not hate you," Laney Mae said.

"How do you know?"

"I just know. I see the way you look at one another. The playful banter. The jealous outbursts. It's impossible to miss."

"I'm leaving. This is ridiculous. You're trying to prove that I like my fake girlfriend who I could never date, so the conversation is pretty pointless."

"Jack," Harley called out.

"Yeah?"

"I think Buck would understand, you know, if you ever wanted to date her for real." Harley pushed to her feet and braced her hands on her lower back.

"You couldn't be more wrong. Would you want your little sister to date me?"

"I don't have a sister," Harley said.

"Neither do I. But if I did... you'd be my pick for her to date, Jack-ass. If you were into her, that is." Laney Mae winked before tossing her napkin in the garbage.

"I'm out, girls. See you later."

"Love you," they both called out and I laughed as I made my way to the elevators.

I thought about our conversation. Did I like Monroe? Sure. I liked her. More than just as my fake girlfriend. I liked being around her. Hell, I didn't even mind going without sex, because she preoccupied my thoughts.

Would Buck ever be okay with me taking her out for real?

Hell no.

I knew the answer before I even had to think about it.

Not to mention, she dated boring herbs. She was annoyed with me more than she wasn't. It would never work.

Didn't stop me from wondering what she'd wear tonight.

Nor from getting excited that I'd be alone with her in a few hours.

———

I couldn't take my eyes off of her. Monroe Buckley was gorgeous on a normal day, but tonight... tonight she was breathtaking. She wore a black spaghetti strap satin gown that clung to her body, with a low plunging front. Her perfect tits hid behind the thin silk, and I couldn't stop staring at them. At her. At all of her. The dress hugged her feminine curves in all the right places, and my dick was on high alert. Eager and observant and needy as fuck.

But she was off-limits.

Try telling him that.

Our fingers intertwined between us as I led her through the crowd. Several heads turned to stare as we walked through the packed party. Our photos had been splashed all over social media as this was the first time I was seen out consistently with the same woman. I didn't mind it at all. Her floor-length gown blended with the other dresses in the room, but Monroe stood out. Just like she always did. Her hair was pulled back in a low twist at the nape of her neck, and I'd been lost in the smell of lavender and honey on the drive over.

"There he is," she whisper-shouted before tugging on my hand to make sure I heard her.

I beelined for Simon, and he looked up to see me coming and turned his attention my way.

"Jack Montgomery, so nice to see you. I have a few calls in to your brother, but he can't seem to find time for me. I want to make sure I have the support of Montgomery Media behind me moving forward with the election. How about we grab lunch this week?" He reeked of bourbon. Surprising, seeing as this was an event for his campaign. He was obviously feeling the heat right now, and not handling it well. At least that was my observation as he appeared more frazzled than usual.

"Call the office and we'll get you on the schedule. This is my girl-friend, Monroe Buckley."

She extended her hand, but she didn't smile. "Hello, Senator Reynolds. I believe we've met before when I was interning at CBS."

"No, I don't believe I'd ever forget meeting such a beautiful lady. Your relationship is making quite the splash on social media. You must be some woman," Simon said, licking his lips, and his gaze ran the length of Monroe's body, zeroing in on her chest. My free hand fisted and I squeezed her hand in mine with the other. Before I could stop myself, my hand slid down her body and wrapped around her hip caressing it as I pulled her closer. Tucking her beside me.

Mine.

"Get your fucking eyes off of her tits before I lose my shit," I said, surprising all three of us by the anger in my voice.

"Montgomery," she whisper-hissed, her gaze searching mine.

But Simon didn't miss a beat as his head fell back in laughter. "You always were the fun Montgomery brother. You're actually my favorite. Your brothers are a bit uptight for me. And you know me well, don't you, son? If she doesn't want me looking at her perfect tits, she shouldn't wear a dress like that."

"Ah, I see. You think she's asking for you to take her in like she's your next meal, you sick fuck. That shit might work with everyone else, but she's off-limits, do you hear me?" The man was old enough to be Monroe's father, yet he was taking her in like he was ready to devour her. But this wasn't some dark sex club, and she wasn't avail-able. My blood boiled and rage coursed my veins with fury.

"Loud and clear. You've got a live one here, young lady. You best rein him in. And now you've got my number when you get sick of him," Simon said, handing her a card, leaning close to Monroe and keeping a fake-ass smile plastered to his face.

"If we weren't in public, I'd knock you the fuck out," I hissed, looking around to make sure no one was listening.

"And if we weren't in public, I'd have your girl in the bathroom where I'd be banging her brains out."

That was it. I swung before I could stop myself. Simon flew backward with disbelief and Monroe gasped. This was about Monroe's honor—hell, women everywhere shouldn't have to put up with this womanizing bullshit.

He crashed into a group of men, who helped to stop him from hitting the ground. He burst out in laughter and waved his hands in the air as he wiped the blood from his lip. "It's all in good fun. I'm fine."

Monroe tore his card into tiny pieces and tossed them in the air. "If we weren't in public, I'd be backing up my boyfriend while he knocked your ass out, you asshole."

"Damn straight, Blue Jay."

I took her hand and led her out of the stuffy, haughty joint, and made our way out to where Big Tony stood outside the car.

"Short night, boss?"

Monroe and I hadn't said a word yet. "Something like that, Big T."

We slipped into the car and Monroe burst out in laughter. "Well, that was a bust."

"He's a fucking piece of shit."

"He's not going to make it as the front-runner come election day. He's coming apart at the seams already," she said.

"You're right about that. I don't even know what the hell just happened. The way he looked at you. Jesus. The man has no shame. He sure as shit didn't hide the fact that he wanted you. And his wife and kids were in the room. What the fuck is wrong with him?"

She shrugged. "Thanks for defending me. My boobs have never garnered so much attention. Thirsty Thelma would be so proud."

She laughed.

I didn't.

"He shouldn't have spoken to you that way. Hell, he shouldn't have looked at you like that. I'll fucking knock him out next time I see him, and he won't get up so easily."

"You're an awfully good fake boyfriend, Jack Montgomery."

"You're not so bad yourself, Little Bird."

My phone buzzed, and I knew who it was before I looked at it.

"Ford," I said, leaning back in my seat as Monroe instructed Big Tony to take us to In-N-Out burger for some food.

Damn, this girl was perfect.

"Did you seriously just punch out a presidential candidate?" Ford asked. My brother had eyes and ears all over the place. I guess it came with owning a media company. He had a pulse on the entire city at all times and he rarely missed a beat.

"Simon Reynolds is an asshole. You should have heard the shit that came out of his mouth," I said.

"I forgot to give you a heads-up. I was asked this afternoon if we were going to support him as the presidential candidate—I told them he wasn't someone I could give my support to, nor did I believe my brothers could. Word must have traveled fast. What did he say?"

"He talked about Blue Jay's tits and how he'd like to bang her in the bathroom."

Monroe covered her ears and shook her head. "Not anything I ever want to think about."

"That piece of shit. At a fucking campaign party with his wife and kids there? What the fuck is wrong with this guy?"

"You name it. He's a twisted fuck. I think it's safe to say that everyone now knows that the Montgomery family will not be supporting Simon Reynolds come election day, not that I think he's going to even make it that far." The guy was a loose cannon. He was going to blow himself up long before votes were cast.

"Sorry for putting you in that situation. Is Monroe all right?"

"Yeah, she's not too fazed by it."

"Okay. Send her my apologies and I'll see you in the morning."

"In-N-Out for a vegetarian?" I asked once I ended the call.

"I get the burger without meat. It's like a grilled cheese. And they have the best fries."

I laughed. "You sure you're okay?"

"Relax, Montgomery. This is not the first slimebag I've dealt with. I'm fine."

I filled her in on what Ford said, and we sat in the back of the car eating burgers and grilled cheese and reminiscing about the night. Big

Tony's order was double both of ours, but he was part of the family and I enjoyed his company.

Fake or real, being with Monroe was the best relationship I'd ever had.

And I wasn't in any hurry for it to end.

twelve

. . .

Monroe

THE PRESS HAD a field day with photos from the campaign party for Simon Reynolds. Fortunately, Jack's interaction with him barely made the evening's highlights. Simon's wife was caught in the pool house with her trainer, and the pictures did not leave much to the imagination. His son had been arrested for a DUI only a block away from their home during the party, and Simon was caught with his pants down in the kitchen pantry with his daughter's best friend.

If you looked up *shitshow* in the dictionary, I was fairly certain you'd see a photo of the Reynolds family the night of the campaign party.

My phone buzzed on my desk and I picked it up.

"Get your ass down to the conference room, Blue Jay," my fake boyfriend said, and my heart rate picked up at the sound of his voice.

"There must be a more polite way to ask me."

"Reynolds is about to make an on-air statement. So, like I said, get your ass over here," he said before ending the call.

So bossy.

I jumped to my feet and ran down the hall. Ford and Jack both stood in the back of the room staring at the TV, and Dan Arbor followed me in.

"I'm guessing he's going to try to do some damage control from the disastrous weekend, but I don't see how he can fix it at this point." Dan moved to stand beside Jack.

"I think he's way past damage control," Ford said.

"Come here, Blue Jay." Jack stepped back so I could slide in beside him. Ford turned to study us, and I stiffened beneath his watchful gaze. We were supposed to be dating, but Jack wanting me beside him had very little to do with that, and I think Ford knew it. We'd grown close. We were friends. He wasn't as annoying as I'd once thought. And the way he'd stood up for me at Simon Reynolds' home had not gone unnoticed. There were very few people that I let into my circle, but Jack Montgomery had made his way in.

We all turned our attention back to the television, as Simon Reynolds took to the podium. He wore a sharp navy suit and looked the part of the perfect future leader. But we all knew differently now. He definitely had makeup covering his altercation with Jack, but I noted the slight bruising around his lip.

"I'd like to apologize to the people of San Francisco, and to my supporters. My actions were reprehensible, and something that I plan to work on in the future. At this time, I would like to take my name out of the running for the office of president in the next election. My family and I ask that you respect our privacy at this difficult time as we focus on rebuilding the strong family unit that we once were, and hope to be again. Thank you."

At least I wouldn't have to make any more visits to The Dark Temptress, as this story had come to an abrupt end. I didn't get an article out of it, but I wasn't going to give up that easily. There were always more stories, and the next one would not be far off.

"That might be the fastest fall from grace yet," Dan said with a chuckle.

"Nah. He's been on a slippery slope for a long time. It all just caught up with him." Ford looked down at his phone when it buzzed. His face visibly paled. "I have to go. Harley's on her way to the hospital. Her water broke."

Harley was scheduled for a C-section tomorrow, so her timing was spot on. I clasped my hands together and smiled. I was happy for them. And the poor girl was ready to burst, so I knew she was ready.

"Coming with you, brother. Call me later." He leaned down and kissed my cheek, running his knuckles over the spot where his lips had just been as his gaze lingered there. My legs wobbled at the contact and my mouth went dry. I nodded because I couldn't speak and he walked out the door.

I might actually miss Jack Montgomery when this was all over.

"It's nice to see him this way," Dan said as we walked toward the door.

"What way is that?" I teased.

"Well, Jack's the happy-go-lucky Montgomery brother for sure, but seeing you two together—I don't know. He's different. He seems so... happy and content. More at peace." He laughed.

I rolled my eyes. "He was born happy."

"Maybe. But something's different. In a good way. It's okay to say you're happy, Monroe. It doesn't make you less human," he said, bumping me with his shoulder.

I shook my head and laughed. "Yeah, yeah, I'm happy."

"It looks good on both of you. Good work on the Reynolds case. Thanks for sharing your lead about his visits to The Dark Temptress. Your time is coming. I had to write all sorts of bullshit about hotspots in the city, and what men found interesting in women for years. It'll come. Be patient. And I'd be happy to have you on my team when the time comes."

I couldn't wipe the goofy smile from my face if I tried. "Thanks, Dan. I appreciate it."

I'd taken what I knew about Reynolds going to the seedy club to Dan, per Jack's encouragement to do so. I was glad I did. He hadn't felt threatened, the opposite in fact, he brought me in and shared what he knew about the man, and we'd worked well together.

"See you later. Keep your head down and stay out of crazy sex dens," he said with a wink before turning the corner to go to his office.

I spent the rest of the morning working on a new story about how soon is *too soon* to have sex with your significant other. *Riveting stuff, right?* But this is what I was hired to do, and I needed to remember that. My column was gaining a following already and people were tweeting about it. I couldn't ask for more. Well, I could, but it would all come in good time. I was willing to put in the work, and I would get there.

Did it bother me that some people at Montgomery Media now thought I'd been hired because I'd been dating the boss? Not really. I'd never spent much time in that world, worrying about what others thought of me. I knew who I was, and I'd show that through my work ethic. No one seemed to look at me differently aside from Sabrina who had made a point to come see me as soon as the story broke about Jack and me dating. She apologized profusely for talking about him in the lounge, but she went on to make a few snide comments about the perks of dating the boss, and I made an effort to avoid her as much as possible. I found her hovering around Jack's office several times since, and it got under my skin. We weren't really together, but she didn't know that. And I didn't like the idea of him with her. Hell, I didn't like the idea of him with anyone. This was a problem and I needed to snap out of it.

This was temporary.

It wasn't real.

I made my way a few blocks down to North Street Bistro to meet my friends for lunch. I hadn't seen them since our last happy hour a few weeks ago, and the photo of Jack and me hadn't gone viral yet. My best friend Becks was the only one who knew that my relationship with Jack was fake. I'd sworn her to secrecy. Gwen and Jilly were happy to hear that I was finally dating someone. I felt horrible for lying to them. I insisted it wasn't anything serious, and we'd left it at that. This whole thing would end soon, and things would go back to normal.

"Mon." Gwen waved me over as the three of them sat at a corner table.

"Hey," I said, dropping to sit beside Becks. Her blonde bob sat just above her shoulders, and she wore a sleek white button-up to complement her black pencil skirt. She was gorgeous, and men were always staring and gawking.

"Did you see Simon Reynolds dropped out of the running this morning?" Jilly asked as she pushed her auburn locks off her shoulder.

"Yes. I can't say I'm too surprised. The man is shady. He had no business running for office."

I perused the menu as I spoke.

"So, how is it going with Jack? Are things getting serious? Seems like you spend a lot of time together," Gwen said. "I would love if we could do a double date with our guys."

"I'm sorry. I just vomited in my mouth." Becks waved the waiter over and ordered a gin martini. Dry. Two olives. I laughed. It was noon on a Monday. Hardly the time for a cocktail, but Becks beat to her own drum and that's what I loved about her.

The rest of us ordered iced tea and we all got salads and a big side of fries for the table.

"Don't hate on Royce," Gwen said, staring hard at Becks. Gwen's brown hair was pulled in a long ponytail, and her natural beauty was impossible to miss.

"I'm not hating on Royce. The man is beautiful, no doubt. I'm hating on *your relationship* with Royce. I find it very annoying."

My head fell back in laughter as they bantered back and forth about why Becks had such an issue with it. My phone buzzed and I looked down to see a text from Jack. I'd asked him to keep me posted about Harley.

Jack ~ Hey. Harley is in surgery or whatever it's called to have those two little humans taken out of her stomach. Everything is going smoothly, with the exception of Ford losing his shit every two minutes. Take the rest of the afternoon off and come to the hospital after your lunch.

Me ~ I'm excited for them. Really? You want me to come to the hospital?

Jack ~ We're supposed to be dating. Wouldn't a girlfriend come sit at the hospital with her boyfriend? No one likes a selfish lover, Blue Jay.

My head fell back in laughter and all three heads turned to face me.

Me ~ I'll be there in an hour.

I responded quickly and dropped my phone in my purse.

"Was that Jack?" Gwen asked.

"Yes. Harley's in labor and he wants me to come to the hospital after lunch."

"Those two are going to have some ridiculously good-looking children," Becks said about Ford and Harley as she sipped her martini.

"Wow. Going to the hospital to meet the family is serious. Things are moving fast, huh?" Jilly asked.

I shook my head. Guilt flooded as I tried to spin this the best way I could. "No. I mean, he's my brother's best friend, so we have a bit of a family connection, that's all. I've met his family over the years, so it's not that big of a deal."

Becks barked out a laugh. "When do we get to meet the guy?"

I shot her a look. She knew I didn't want to lie to Jilly and Gwen and having them meet Jack would be digging myself into an even deeper hole.

Gwen clapped her hands together. "Yes, please. I mean, I've seen all the Montgomery brothers in the media, and they're all three beautiful, but personally, I think Jack's the best looking. What if you bring him to my opening at the gallery next week?"

"I think that would be a great idea," Becks said with a wink.

Asshole.

Gwen ran an art gallery in the city, and she loved discovering new artists. "Yeah, sure. I'll see if he can make it."

We finished lunch, catching up on one another's lives. Becks had a new Australian lover on the rotation because she didn't believe in dating one person and thought monogamy was overrated. Gwen was ridiculously happy with Royce and things were going well, and Jilly told us about a new dating app she was trying after reading my article about the best options out there.

When I arrived at the hospital, there was security near the lobby screening people. I had to remind myself that the Montgomerys were a famous, often stalked family, which was why my photo with Jack had gone viral in the first place. I spotted Big Tony up ahead and he winked before waving me over and pointing to a set of chairs where Jack was sitting.

I took Jack in for a moment. I rarely got to look at the man without him moving or distracting me. He was sitting in a chair with Laney Mae and Harrison beside him, and his mother across from him. His arms were flailing, and everyone was laughing as he just had a way of telling a story that enraptured all those around him. His dark hair was tousled on his head, his chiseled jaw and perfectly angular nose made it difficult to look away. But his best feature was his smile. It always reached his eyes and lit up his entire face. His whiskey-colored gaze danced with mischief as he bellowed out in laughter and Laney Mae fell forward in her chair as Harrison and Monica erupted in laughter.

As if on cue, he glanced my way. "You made it, Little Bird."

He pushed to his feet and walked over to me, wrapping his arms around me, and kissing the top of my head. Normally this would annoy me, but for whatever reason, when my fake boyfriend was affectionate with me—I liked it.

More than I should.

"Is there an update?" I asked, working hard to control my racing heart at his nearness.

"Nope. We're still waiting." He led me back to the chairs and I dropped to sit beside Monica.

Jack's mom pulled me in for a hug and everyone chatted at once, filling me in on Ford threatening to shut down the hospital if they didn't relieve Harley's pain at once. We all shared a laugh at how protective he was. The double doors swung open, and all of our attention turned toward Ford Montgomery, standing tall and proud in light blue scrubs. His smile stretched from ear to ear and his gaze was wet with emotion.

"She did it."

Harrison, Jack, and Monica rushed toward him and Laney and I stood right behind them as they patted him on the shoulder and pulled him in for a bear hug.

"I knew Harls could do it." Jack beamed, looking over his shoulder and winking at me. He was ridiculously adorable. Like, of course she could do it. Women had babies all the time. But Jack had a way of making everyone he interacted with feel like they walked on water. I wondered if he treated his one-night stands this well. The thought made me sick to my stomach. The man got around, and everyone knew it. He would go back to business as usual the minute this charade ended. His life would change immediately, as he'd return to wining and dining his ladies while mine would remain the same—sans Jack Montgomery.

Work. Books. Bubble baths. Netflix.

Rinse and repeat.

I'd return to my boring existence.

Maybe it was time for me to get back out there and start dating. It had been a year since Thyme stabbed me in the back. I could do this, right?

"Come on. Let's go check these little angels out," he said, reaching for my hand as Ford led us all to the nursery.

"Do we have names yet?" Monica asked, because they'd kept the names a secret up until now.

"Yep. That little cherub right there, with the little rosebud lips, her name is Penelope Rose Montgomery. And her sister right beside her, with the perfect button nose, her name is Everly Mae Montgomery."

Laney Mae clapped, and Harrison pulled her into a hug. I turned and caught all three men, large in stature, with tears streaming down their faces as they watched these two little angels sleeping through the glass. Monica swiped at her face and nodded. "Beautiful names, for beautiful princesses."

"They own me. I'm going to spoil the shit out of them. What can I bring them? Do they eat treats or read or do anything yet?" Jack asked, and Monica, Laney, and I burst out in hysterical laughter.

"They're babies, Jack-ass. They just want to be held and loved," Laney said.

"Well, I intend to do that too." His gaze never left the window.

"Okay. I need to get back to Harley. Why don't you guys head home and tomorrow you can come back and hold them in our room if all goes well." Ford took one last glance before thanking us all for coming.

They all agreed to meet back the following morning and we made our way out of the hospital. We said our goodbyes and I grabbed my phone to call for an Uber. I'd come straight here from the restaurant.

"Hold up. Where are you going?" Jack asked.

"Um, home? It's a work night."

He chuckled. "Come to my place. We can order dinner."

"And do what exactly?" I folded my arms over my chest.

"Eat. Watch a movie. Talk about how fucking perfect those babies are. You can fill me in on what I need to do to be the best uncle."

I glanced at my phone to check the time. "Well, I guess I do need to eat."

"Come on. How does pizza sound?"

"Good," I said as I smiled at Big Tony before getting in the car.

Jack called in the order, and I sat back and wondered how I was going to feel when all of this came to an end.

And a sick feeling settled in my stomach.

thirteen

. . .

Jack

IT HAD BEEN a week since the twins had come home from the hospital, and I'd gone over every day. I couldn't get enough of them. Of course, it was disappointing to learn that they didn't eat cupcakes yet or respond when I spoke to them... but that would all come in good time.

Tonight, I was going with Blue Jay to her friend's gallery opening, and she was very uptight about the whole thing. We spent a lot of time together, so I didn't know what the big deal was. She said she felt guilty for lying to her friends about our relationship. Hell, the truth was—we basically *were* dating, minus the no sex rule that she had. When we were together, it was impossible to keep my hands to myself. I'd find any reason to touch her. Even just to tuck her hair behind her ear or pull her close to me in the car. She didn't fight it anymore. She'd touch my arm or reach for my hand when we stepped off the elevator without thinking. It had all just become natural. But this was the longest I'd ever gone without sex in my adult life, and I was feeling it. I wasn't proud to admit that I'd rubbed it out to visions of my fake girl-friend every single day since she arrived at Montgomery Media. Buck would fucking kill me. But fantasies were okay—as long as you didn't act on them.

It wasn't that difficult to pretend to be her boyfriend. I'd grown comfortable with our set-up. I actually preferred being in public with her because it meant I could hold her hand and show some affection. She'd rested her head on my shoulder when we watched a movie the night the twins were born, and I'd wrapped her in my arms like it was totally normal. I think we'd both forgotten the fact that we weren't in public and no one was watching. She'd caught herself and quickly made up an excuse to head home. The crazy thing? I didn't want her to leave. I liked touching her. Making her laugh. Holding her hand. All the things I'd never wanted to do with other women.

I liked doing those things with Monroe Buckley.

My best friend's little sister.

I needed to pull my shit together. The fallout we'd anticipated from the photo of Monroe and me going viral had never come. In fact, it was the opposite. A few competing papers had tried to stir up drama online about it, but people had responded positively to us announcing that we were a couple. I'd been single so long that apparently news that I'd committed to someone had worked in our favor. So, there was no pressure to keep up the charade, as no one took issue with it. But surprisingly, calling it done was not an option for me. Not now at least. I wasn't ready for it to come to an end. For her to go back to ignoring me, and me to return to my meaningless romps. And it was completely fucking selfish that I wanted to keep this going for my own personal reasons. The thought of Monroe with someone else made me physically sick. The girl would not stay single forever, and I couldn't allow my mind to wander there. But being in a constant state of *want* wasn't conducive either.

Maybe I should just get laid, and I'd be able to get her out of my head. But I wouldn't cheat on her, whether this shit was real or not. I couldn't do that to her. Maybe I would see how she felt about us just testing the waters with one another. You know, physically, so we didn't have to suffer during this fake relationship. She had needs. I had needs. Why not fulfill them during this time? We'd get one another out of our systems and then return to our regular lives. We wouldn't have to tell Buck because it wouldn't be a *real* relationship. We could fake date and have real sex. Fabulous fucking sex, I'm sure. Let's just say I was gifted in that department, so I'd be doing her a favor. And for whatever reason, the thought of pleasuring Blue Jay did crazy shit to me. I wanted to see her come undone, wild and free and sated. And I wanted to be the one to do that to her.

What the fuck was happening to me?

The knock on my door startled me from my X-rated thoughts about Monroe Buckley.

"Hey, I'm heading out." Ford sauntered in and dropped in the chair across from me. He looked a little frazzled, but happy. I liked seeing him this way. Like a man who had everything he ever wanted. Sure, he and Harley were tired, and definitely lacking sleep, but he came into the office for a couple hours a day and underneath it all, I knew he was happier than he'd ever been. And I was trying to pick up the slack where I could.

"I may come by with Monroe on our way to her friend's gallery opening. I know she'd like to see the babies, and I don't want them to forget about me if they don't see my handsome face every day."

His head fell back in laughter. "Hell, unless you've got a nipple with a hearty supply of breast milk, I don't think they give a shit if you come by."

I closed my eyes for a brief moment. "Don't talk about nipples, please. It's been a while, you know?"

He studied me and a wide grin spread across his face. "You're fucking sexually frustrated, aren't you? I'll bet you've never gone this long without sex."

"That doesn't make you a rocket scientist, dude. Obviously, I've never gone this long before, at least not since I started having sex."

"Manage yourself. Can't you take care of business for a couple weeks?" He rolled his eyes and shook his head with disgust.

"Trust me, I am taking care of business... more than once a day most of the time," I said, and he rubbed his temples like he couldn't bear to listen to what I was saying. "What? I have a healthy libido. I enjoy sex. Fucking sue me."

"Well, you and Monroe have been together long enough at this point, it would probably be fine to call it done. Surprisingly, no one gave a shit that you were dating an employee. Obviously, we don't want it to look like it was fake, but at this point, you gave it a good run. We can have Harrison release a statement that the relationship ended amicably, and she will continue to work at Montgomery Media. I'm sure she's ready to get back out there too."

A growl escaped before I could stop it. "Shut the fuck up. Don't say that."

"You jealous little prick. Don't be a hypocrite."

"I'm not. I, well, I just think it's too soon. I don't want people thinking I didn't give it a fair try. I'm certainly not a quitter. We should probably wait a few more weeks. I'll just have to slap the salami often until then."

"Jesus. Don't even tell me that. Those are the hands you hold my daughters with, you dirty asshole." He pushed to his feet and continued laughing. "Maybe you ought to consider the fact that you seem to really like your fake girlfriend. You could do something about that, you know?"

"I don't think she'll be on board for sex. I've already considered it."

"Oh my god," he groaned and ran his hands through his hair. "I'm not talking about propositioning her for sex. I'm talking about actually dating her."

"Buck would kick my ass."

"But he'd be fine with you sleeping with her?" He raised a brow in challenge.

"Of course not. *I'd* be fine with me sleeping with her though, and maybe we could just keep it from Buck. But that would mean convincing Blue Jay it was a good idea, which is unlikely. This is why I don't date. I'm no fucking good at it."

"Neither was I, brother. Until I met Harley. Think about that. I'll see you later."

I sat back in my desk chair and thought about it. I sucked at relationships, what more was there to think about? I'd only had two and neither had gone well. I was a terrible flirt and no woman had ever managed to hold my attention for long… at least those were the things that Marin and Ashley told me after we'd ended things.

I focused on work the rest of the day and stopped at Monroe's office just as she was getting up from her desk.

"Hey, I was just coming to see you," she said. Her pink dress clung to her body like a second skin and ended just at her knees. She wore sky-high heels and her hair fell in loose waves over her shoulders. Fucking gorgeous. Full kissable lips, dark blue eyes, and legs for days.

"I came by to see if you wanted to run by Ford and Harley's to see the babies with me, before we head to the gallery." I shoved my hands in my pockets to keep from reaching for her.

"Oh, sure. I'd love to see the girls. You sure it's okay with them?"

"Yes. I'm positive. You ready?"

"Yep." She reached for her purse and we made our way down to the car.

When we arrived at Ford and Harley's penthouse, they both looked like they'd been roughed up and left for dead. My god... these were two tiny humans. Harley refused to hire a nanny and insisted she and Ford spend every minute with the girls. I respected it. My parents were the same way. They had enough money to bring in a team of help, but my mother had refused, and I know having three boys close in age wasn't easy. Monroe and I washed our hands the minute we stepped in the penthouse per Ford's insistence. He was a protective little fucker.

My brother handed me Everly who was a little tinier than Penelope, but they were both small enough to fit in the palm of my hand. I loved everything about them. They smelled like... baby powder and sour milk. They cooed and their innocent little gazes searched mine, and it made my heart squeeze.

"I need to go clean up. Can you hold her for a few?" Ford undid his tie and headed for the master bedroom.

"You look sexy with baby puke on your dress shirt," Harley called after him, smiling down at baby P and turning her attention to Monroe. "You want to hold her?"

"Sure. Yes. I'd love to." Monroe held out her arms and scooped her up.

"Maybe you should take a minute to clean up too, Harls. You smell like baby puke, and I think you have some sort of goop in your hair." I raised a brow at my sister-in-law.

She laughed. "Really? You don't mind?"

"Not at all. We don't have to be at the gallery for an hour. Go take a shower—and use soap," I teased.

"Okay. I'm going to take you up on that. We'll be out in a bit. Just shout if you need me."

"Don't worry, we've got this," Monroe called out, as she dropped to sit on the couch and looked down at Penelope. "Wow. They're so pretty. I thought babies were wrinkly and splotchy. These two are so perfect. Dainty and feminine. Just gorgeous, right?"

"They look like pretty little birds, too," I said.

She chuckled. "You and your fascination with little birds is something, Montgomery."

Maybe this would be a good time to broach the topic of sex. I mean, we were holding two perfect little humans that came from the act, after all.

"I am fascinated by *you*, Blue Jay. There's actually something I wanted to talk to you about."

"Okay. I'm all ears," she said, making little noises at my niece as she stared down at her.

I dropped to sit on the couch and popped Everly over my shoulder, feeling her little breaths against my neck. She was a sleepy little one, and rarely stayed awake long enough for me to take her in.

"So, this thing we're doing, how do you think it's going?"

She pulled Penelope against her chest and watched as the little angel's eyes slowly closed. "I think it's going well. It's sad really, because our fake relationship is better than my last real relationship was, if I'm being honest."

Well, this was a good start.

"Agreed. Same here. You aren't clingy, hell, most of the time I'm not sure you can even stand to be around me." I laughed and Everly squirmed on my shoulder.

"Most of the time I can't," she said with a smirk. "I'm kidding. You're not as bad as I thought. I don't mind hanging out with you. So, what is this? Is this the breakup speech? You wanted to do it in front of the babies to soften the blow?"

She had a smile on her face that didn't reach her eyes. Her shoulders tensed, like she was preparing herself for something.

"No. I think it's too soon to break up. It'll look fake if we don't give it a fair amount of time. But I thought, I don't know, maybe we could add in a few, er, benefits, as long as things are going so well already." I didn't look at her, because I was afraid of what I'd see if I met her gaze.

Her head tipped back, and she barked out a laugh, rocking Penelope back and forth as she shifted in her arms. "What kind of benefits are you offering?"

"Well, you've been dating me for weeks, whether it be fake or real, it doesn't really matter. I'm sure you have needs, as I know I do, and I thought maybe you'd appreciate being on the receiving end of what I have to offer."

Her mouth gaped open. "You're going to grace me with your amazing sexual skills? Is that what this is about?"

"Listen, Blue Jay, I'm dying here."

"So, if I don't sleep with you, you're going to cheat on me? Is this an ultimatum?" A wide grin spread across her pretty face. I couldn't read her. She just might be the only woman on the planet that I couldn't read. I couldn't tell if she was on board or if she was about to slap me across the face.

"I'm not going to cheat on you."

She laughed and popped baby P up on her shoulder, caressing her little back. "Oh my gosh, Montgomery, I'm kidding. I kind of assumed you were discreetly cheating on me, you know, since we *aren't actually dating*. I just didn't want you to do it publicly and humiliate me."

"I wouldn't cheat on you. I respect you too much."

"But we aren't really dating, so would it be cheating?"

"Yes."

Everly shifted and I kissed her temple and rubbed her back until she settled back down.

"Well, we could break up, you know, so you could get back to business as usual?" Her tone hardened.

"No. It's too soon. If you want to just keep things going as they are, I'm in. I'm not offering an ultimatum. I'm offering to take things in a new direction. I mean, you must have needs?"

She rolled her pretty eyes. "Please. You aren't doing this for me. I haven't had sex in over a year, which is long before this arrangement—and I'm doing just fine."

Over a fucking year? No wonder the girl was on edge most of the time. "Jesus, Blue Jay. You're going to explode. And I am doing this for you too. Believe it or not, it would make me happy to pleasure you."

"Oh my god," she gasped. "Stop talking. Someone might hear."

"Well, Ford and Harls have obviously had sex," I said, glancing at the two babies in our arms.

"Okay. You've made your point. I'll think it over."

"We also need to discuss the elephant in the room," I said.

"I would have thought sex was the elephant in the room, but let's hear it." She chuckled.

"I don't want to betray my best friend."

She rolled her eyes. "You're propositioning me for sex, but you're worried about how my brother will feel? You're kidding me right now?"

"You don't think we should factor that in?" I shrugged, how could we not?

"Um, no. I'm a grown woman. Miles is not a factor in this conversation. Obviously, he wouldn't need to know. It would just be a fake relationship with benefits. But take my brother out of the equation. I'm not a child and I don't appreciate being treated like one."

She didn't look at me. I'd offended her. But of course, Buck was a concern for me. He'd never forgive me if he found out. But this wasn't a conquest for me. I liked Monroe. Maybe too much. And I'd been fighting this attraction for a while now, and I didn't see the harm in acting on it if we both wanted the same thing.

"He'd kill me if I hurt you."

"And what if I hurt you, Montgomery? Have you ever thought about that?" Her gaze locked with mine and she raised a brow in challenge.

"No. I don't get hurt." Because I didn't get close enough to people to allow it.

"Well, I'm not worried about getting hurt. You have to have actual feelings for someone to get hurt."

Ouch. That stung.

"Wow. Tell me how you really feel."

She chuckled. "You know what I mean. This is fake. We'd be acting on a physical attraction. Not an emotional one. No one gets hurt. Miles never finds out. It's sort of a win-win."

I ran my free hand over my jaw. I was a loyal fucker through and through. I'd never broken my word. But I was hanging on by a thread, spending every day with her, and needing her more than I ever knew possible. But crossing the line meant betraying Buck, which I didn't want to do. I was trying to find a technicality to get around it. The dude called me every day, and he always ended our calls with a warning about Monroe.

"He did put us in this fucked up situation, so he is partly to blame." That's the best I could come up with to justify what I wanted to do.

"I don't need permission from my brother regarding who I sleep with. If you do, then that's something you need to figure out."

I nodded. "Fair enough. We could have our own relationship separate from my friendship with your brother."

"We already do," she said.

"I can't tell you how much better I feel," Harley said, coming down the hallway. Her long hair was wet and brushed away from her face. She wore black leggings and a T-shirt.

Their home was immaculate, which was surprising, considering the condition they were in. Ford had a housekeeper that he'd had for years that spent her days keeping this place pristine. Harley appreciated the help so she could focus on the girls.

"I'm happy to come hold them any time. They're so—perfect," Monroe said.

"They really are, right?" Harley ran her finger gently over the back of Penelope's head.

"I feel like a new man." Ford waltzed out behind her, wearing gray sweatpants and a white T-shirt. Family life looked good on him. It was nice to see him so happy.

"You ready for a crazy Friday night with the girls?" Harley teased as she reached for Penelope and Ford came around and scooped up Everly.

"I was born ready, baby," he said.

"And that's our cue. We're out of here."

Monroe moved to her feet and kissed the top of each girl's little head before walking toward me.

"You guys saved us. Thank you," Harley called out.

"I'll come by tomorrow and give you a break, okay?" I said, as I reached for the door.

"Thank you," they both said as I pulled the door closed.

"You impress me, Jack Montgomery," Monroe said as we stepped into the elevator.

"How so?"

"Well, you're not as selfish as I thought you were. You're phenomenal with babies. You're just full of surprises, I guess."

My chest puffed up with pride. "You want to make a baby with me? Imagine how fucking beautiful our kid would be?"

Her head fell back with laughter, and I just took her in. Her face bright and eyes full of mischief. "Easy there, fake boyfriend. The jury's still out if I'm going to sleep with you. But having a baby would be awfully hard to hide from my brother."

She continued laughing as we walked toward Big Tony who stood outside the car.

But I didn't laugh once.

Because having a baby with Monroe Buckley didn't sound that ridiculous to me.

fourteen

. . .

Monroe

THE GALLERY EVENT WAS PACKED, and Jack and I made our way inside. My head was still spinning at the thought of having sex with him.

Did I want to?

Yes.

Was it a smart idea?

Absolutely not.

I had played it safe my entire life. A part of me wanted to break the rules for the first time. He just might be worth breaking them for. I'd only had sex with two guys in my life, and neither were anything spectacular. My high school boyfriend and I were one another's first, so we didn't know what we were doing. And no one was to blame for that. We broke up shortly after I went to college and then I met Thyme, who was probably the world's most selfish lover. He was always in a hurry, chasing his pleasure, and not concerned about me or making sure I enjoyed it as much as he did. I sort of just figured that was how sex was supposed to be. I mean, aside from Becks, my girlfriends had similar experiences. Becks claimed she wouldn't waste her time on a selfish lover. Maybe there was something to be said about that philosophy. Jack Montgomery was a lot of things, but I knew in my gut, in my soul—a selfish lover wasn't one of them.

And the way he'd spoken about giving me pleasure—I didn't even know how to process it. No one had ever spoken to me like that, nor had anyone ever stated that it would make them happy to give me pleasure. But no one had ever propositioned me for sex and been concerned about what my brother would think either.

This was a first.

But the thought of having sex with Jack Montgomery.

Oh my.

I fanned my face and Jack chuckled beside me before he spoke. "What I wouldn't give to be able to read your thoughts."

My stomach flipped. Lines were getting blurred. We were playing a dangerous game. And there was no doubt in my mind that if I wasn't careful, I would end up hurt when all was said and done. I'd acted like it wasn't a possibility, but I knew it was. I just didn't want him to know that. This relationship wasn't real. I needed to remember that.

So, would it be the worst thing in the world if I allowed myself to benefit from all of this? I mean, the world's most beautiful man was offering himself up to me on a silver platter. How could I refuse? The thought of his lips on mine again—my heart raced. The way he felt. The way he tasted. And that was just a kiss. Was I awful for wanting more?

Buck would never be okay with me having a casual fling with his best friend. Hell, I would have never considered it before. But now that I knew him, it didn't seem like a bad idea. I liked Jack Montgomery. He was a good man. An honest man. And a beautiful, sexy man at that.

I bit down hard on my bottom lip. I needed to pull it together.

"Just thinking about work," I lied as we stood in front of the sexiest portrait I'd ever laid eyes on. A man and woman lying naked looking at one another like they couldn't exist without the other, sketched in pencil.

"Sure, you were." He took my hand and led me to the next room.

"There you are." Becks walked up beside us. "You must be Jack. I'm the bestie, Becks. I'm happy about this, whatever this is, and you just may need to pour it on real heavy in about two minutes."

Jack reached for her hand. "Nice to meet you. What's going on?"

"Not sure if you told him about the *herb assholes* yet, but they're here. Gwen just asked me to find you and give you a heads-up. Apparently, Sage is a friend of one of the artists on display tonight."

A waiter walked over to us and I reached for a second glass of champagne, and Jack studied me before turning back to Becks. "I know about them. And we won't have any problem giving them a good show, will we, Blue Jay?"

I chugged the glass of bubbly and Jack took it from my fingers, his touch lighting my entire body on fire as he grazed his hand along mine. He set the empty glass down and I looked between him and Becks.

"No. It's fine."

"Good, because they just walked in this room," she whispered.

"That's him? That's the guy who cheated on *you*? He's scrawny and has gelled, stiff hair. And she has nothing on you, Little Bird," Jack whispered and Becks and I both chuckled.

I tried to calm my racing heart. I hadn't seen either of them in over a year. And I had no desire to see them together now.

Thyme wore navy fitted dress slacks and a pink button-up. His blonde hair was cut close to his head, and he looked—nervous. The gallery was buzzing with people, moving from room to room, and he and Sage maneuvered through the crowd and made their way to us.

"Monroe, Becks, wow. I didn't expect to see you here," Thyme said, wrapping one arm around my ex-friend Sage's shoulder. My eyes bulged out of my head when I looked down to see her blossoming stomach. She'd either put on a quick twenty pounds or she was growing a human in there.

That was fast.

"Really, herb boy? It's our best friend's gallery. You didn't think Monroe would be here? As usual, your choices are repugnant." Becks scowled.

"I forgot Gwen ran the gallery. Kind of had my hands full these days." He glanced at me and shrugged.

"Hey, Monroe. It's good to see you." Sage cocked her head to the side before perusing Jack with curiosity.

My boyfriend.

Without me even realizing it, Jack had moved behind me and wrapped his arms around my middle, holding me close. My back resting against his front. I could feel how much he wanted me because now that I was pressed against him, it was impossible to miss.

"Sure. And I guess congrats are in order." I used my hand to motion to her stomach before placing it back on top of Jack's. "This is my boyfriend, Jack Montgomery."

"Yeah, Sage is pregnant. It came as a surprise to both of us." Thyme's gaze locked with mine and he shrugged. "I heard about your new relationship in the press. Surprised your brother was okay with it. I know how protective he is. Hell, he barely tolerated you dating me." His awkward humor was even more annoying now than ever.

"Her brother, my best friend, doesn't want her dating dickheads. That's why he never liked you," Jack said, and Becks put her hand over her mouth to cover her laughter.

Thyme nodded, and Sage stared at Jack as if she were in awe of him. She licked her lips as her eyes perused his body.

Not this time, girl.

I tipped my head back and Jack leaned down and grazed my neck with his lips. The feel of his mouth on my skin had my body going into overdrive. I'd never wanted anyone the way I wanted him, and I didn't know how to stop it. I didn't know if I wanted to stop it anymore.

"Well, I'm glad to see you're happy, Mon," Thyme said. "I've been worried about you."

I narrowed my gaze, trying to think straight with Jack's nearness. "You're worried about me? It's a little late for that, isn't it?"

"I always worry about you."

Sage stiffened beside him before crossing her arms over her chest and narrowing her gaze at Thyme. He was a douchebag, no doubt about it.

"You don't need to worry about her anymore, buddy. That's my job. And I assure you, she's in *very good hands.*" Jack chuckled before tugging me closer. My ass was pressed against his erection and I couldn't think straight.

Becks squeaked next to me, like she could barely handle how much she was enjoying seeing Jack put Thyme in his place. And the weird thing—I didn't care. I didn't feel anything for him. Seeing him and Sage, I thought it would hurt, but it didn't. Not even a little. All I felt was—relief.

"You guys take care," I said, before turning in Jack's arms and telling him what I needed with just a look. His mouth covered mine, and everyone and everything disappeared around me. His tongue dipped in, and I couldn't get enough. I tangled my fingers in his hair and urged him closer. He growled against my mouth when he pulled away.

"Holy shit. That was abso-fucking-lutely amazing," Becks said, shaking her head as she watched Thyme and Sage walk away. "I think you and I are going to get along just fine, Jack Montgomery."

He smiled, pulling me against him once again. I was more than aware that he only kissed me to get back at Thyme, but something about it felt—real.

And I wanted more.

I wanted more than I should because it could never go anywhere. This was just the perfect storm. We were forced together temporarily, and he was offering me to take what I wanted for a short time.

"The guy is an asshole. And we'll get along well, Becks, because we both want the best for Blue Jay."

"Damn straight. And I'm totally digging the nickname," Becks said, waving the waiter over as we both reached for another drink, but Jack did not. My head was already buzzing. I rarely drank, but tonight, there were a hundred and one reasons why I wanted to throw caution to the wind.

"I can't believe she's pregnant," I said, shaking my head before I tipped my head back and chugged the whole glass down.

"Does that hurt you?" he asked as I looked up at him. The look in his eyes nearly brought me to my knees. This big strong man was such an anomaly. He was arrogant and cocky, yet he was all heart. Tender and sweet. Genuine and real. All wrapped up in a sexy-as-sin package.

"Actually, no. It doesn't. I thought it would. Honestly, I can't believe I ever dated that guy."

"Well, I couldn't believe it even when you were dating him." Becks rolled her eyes. "He's the worst. You were way too good for him, Mon. But I wish you could have seen his face when you two kissed. It was priceless. He was one jealous douchey herb, that's for sure."

"Looks like he and the missus are over there arguing. I say we go flaunt our shit in front of them. You down?" He raised a brow and smirked.

"I'm down."

Becks led the way, and we spent the next hour working the room. I downed more glasses of champagne than I could count, and every few minutes Jack would press me up against a wall and kiss me senseless. He kissed me like he'd die if he didn't, and I responded the same way.

"I think he's actually following us now, which is starting to piss me off," Jack said, pushing me up against a wall in the final room and dipping his head down to cover my mouth with his. Every room we walked in, Thyme would enter shortly after. Sage had fled the gallery after they'd had a public argument, and a tiny part of me felt bad for her. He wasn't an attentive boyfriend, and I couldn't even fathom how she felt being neglected when she was carrying his child.

"I don't care about him," I said, my words slurring a bit as I brushed Jack's hair away from his handsome face. My thumb tracing his bottom lip, begging him to kiss me again.

"What do you care about, Blue Jay?"

"Lots of things." I tugged him back down to me, and he pressed his body against mine letting me feel everything.

And oh my, was there a lot there.

Holy hardness.

I nipped at his bottom lip when he pulled away before speaking, "Follow me."

"I'd follow you anywhere, Little Bird."

I led him into the storage room in back of the gallery. Gwen had given me a tour a few months ago. It was dark, with just a little moonlight coming through the high windows. I stumbled a bit, as all the champagne had gone to my head.

I turned around, holding his hands and walking backward until my back hit the cement beam and I stopped. I tugged him closer.

"I want you," I said, barely recognizing my own voice. It was raspy and needy. Laced with desire and desperation. I couldn't believe I'd said those words. But it was the truth. I did want him. I had for a long time. And I didn't want to wait one more second.

"No one's watching. It's just you and me back here. No ex-boyfriends. No press. No curious employees."

"Just you and me," I whispered.

His mouth crashed into mine. His tongue exploring my mouth as he pressed himself against me. I couldn't stop myself, my fingers tangled in his unruly hair and my hips started moving of their own volition. Grinding against all his hardness. His desire impossible to miss. A burning need lit inside me, and I tugged him closer.

Wanting more.

Needing more.

"Please," I said against his mouth when he started to pull away.

"Jesus, Blue Jay. Not here. Not like this. You're drunk. I need you clear-headed. I don't want you to do anything you're going to regret." His voice was gruff, his breathing labored.

"Please. I need you. I need to feel—something. Anything." The words were leaving my mouth before I could stop them. Before I could process what I was saying.

I'd never begged a man to touch me before. But I didn't want him to stop. I'd never felt so much desire and need for another person.

He tucked a loose strand of hair that had broken free behind my ear. His mouth covered mine as his hand slipped beneath my dress, stroking the thin lacy fabric that I wanted him to tear away. He pushed the fabric aside, allowing his fingers to tease my most sensitive area.

"Jesus, you're so wet for me."

I whimpered as one finger slipped inside and I could no longer keep it together. I arched my back as my hips moved rapidly, grinding against his hand, desperate for release. His mouth never lost contact, and his tongue dipped in and out in the same rhythm. A moan left my lips, a sound I'd never heard before, and my breathing was out of control between kisses.

"Oh my god," I whimpered as his hand moved faster and faster and I lost all control.

"Let go, Blue Jay," he said against my neck as he kissed his way down and my entire body started to implode.

I gasped and shook and trembled. My legs unsteady, he used his free hand to hold me there as the best orgasm of my life ripped through my body.

"Oh my god," I shrieked again, fighting to catch my breath. Fighting to come back down to Earth.

Jesus. We hadn't even had sex, and he'd managed to rock my entire world. My head spun, and I couldn't see straight.

He steadied me on my feet and removed his hand from beneath my panties and slipped his finger into his mouth, sucking it slowly. He closed his eyes and groaned as he did.

"Fucking perfect, Blue Jay."

Oh. My. God.

I couldn't speak.

I was drunk and sated and floating on air. And I knew I'd regret it in the morning, but for right now, I was going to enjoy the moment.

He adjusted my dress back into place before leading me out to the gallery.

"Let's get you home," he whispered, his lips grazing my ear, and I was still tingling and dazed by what had just happened.

"Okay." I squeezed his hand and smiled at him.

Even though I never wanted this night to end.

fifteen

. . .

Jack

WHAT THE ACTUAL fuck was I doing? I'd taken Monroe home last night and carried her to her bedroom. She'd had way too much to drink, and I'd had a moment of weakness. I couldn't deny her what she wanted, and hell, I wanted even more.

I wanted everything.

Especially now that I'd had a taste. Literally and figuratively.

Jesus. What was this girl doing to me? And how the hell was I going to stop now? I'd never wanted anyone the way I wanted her. What was happening? She was all I could think of. I didn't notice other women anymore. My eyes never wandered when I was with Monroe, because she was all I could see.

All-consuming.

I'd kissed her goodbye, and I swear it took every ounce of restraint not to climb in bed with her. Make her mine. The way she had sprawled out on her bed, looking at me with those deep blues.

Fuck.

I was in deep shit.

But I certainly wasn't going to take advantage of her when she was drunk. That's not what I was about. If she didn't want this to happen when she was sober—then it wasn't going to happen at all.

I rolled out of bed, irritated that my dick was rock hard—per usual these days. I reached for my phone to see what time it was and saw the notifications lighting up my screen.

I opened to see a screenshot that Harrison had sent me. It was a photo of Blue Jay and me, in the back room of the gallery. Thankfully, I was blocking her with my big body, but my face was buried in her chest. Someone had fucking been back there? Watching us?

I shook my head.

I'd been reckless. Sloppy. And now this picture was going viral on the internet and apparently was on the cover of one of my least favorite smut papers.

The headline: *Sorry ladies... San Francisco's favorite bachelor can't keep his hands off his girlfriend!*

Motherfucker.

Miles would not be okay with this.

I scrolled through the numerous texts informing me about the article and the photo. Nothing from Miles. Maybe he hadn't seen it. He did live in Los Angeles, and I wouldn't think this trivial shit would make its way to other cities.

I shot Monroe a text to give her a heads-up. I'm sure she wouldn't be feeling on top of the world this morning anyway. The girl had downed more glasses of champagne than I could count.

I jumped in the shower and quickly made my way to the office.

My phone buzzed and Laney Mae's face lit up my screen. That was one call I wanted to take this morning. I asked Big Tony to drop me a block from the office so I could get some fresh air before spending the rest of the day in my office.

"Hey, girl," I said, jumping out of the car and tugging my peacoat closed. There was a chill in the air, which wasn't uncommon now that fall was approaching.

"You've got some explaining to do, Jack-ass." She giggled through the line, and I couldn't help but smile.

I groaned. "Jesus. It was a moment of weakness. I don't know how the fuck someone got a picture. We were in the back room. No one was there."

"Well, it sure seems like someone was there, because the two of you had your hands all over one another, so you definitely weren't holding a selfie stick." Her laughter gave me no choice but to hold the phone away from my ear.

"I get it. It's not as bad as it looks."

"It doesn't look bad. It looks like you're crazy about one another, which I already knew. What's the big deal?"

"The big deal is that she's my best friend's little sister. And for the record, I don't think she likes me that way. Sure, she's attracted to me, because, well, who isn't?"

"Sure, Miles is going to be pissed if he thinks you're using his little sister. But if you like her, that's a different story."

I ran a hand through my hair. "I don't know. We've never talked about it. She's made comments that we don't have anything in common before, so it's a good thing this is a fake relationship."

"Then convince her it's worth fighting for. Come on. You're Jack fucking Montgomery," she said.

"Atta girl. You've always got my back, don't you?"

"Damn straight. And I always will. Find things you have in common. Show her what it could be like."

I entered the lobby of Montgomery Media and made my way to the elevator. It was early so the place was still fairly quiet.

"All right, girl. I'll talk to her today. Thanks for the tips. Love you."

"Love you, Jack-ass."

I chuckled as I made my way down the hall. Monroe's office light was on which surprised me, so I pushed open the door to find her slumped over her desk. She looked up and her cheeks flushed pink the minute she saw me.

She covered her pretty face with her hands. "Oh my god, Montgomery. I'm so sorry. I don't know what happened. But I'm pretty sure I begged for it—and I have no excuse other than I was drunk and maybe emotional after seeing Thyme and Sage together. And Sage is pregnant," she groaned.

I made my way around her desk and pulled her hands away to see tears streaming down her face. "You have nothing to apologize for or to be embarrassed about."

"I threw myself at you. I don't know what's wrong with me? And someone photographed us." Her words broke on a sob, and a sharp pain landed in my chest.

The door flew open out of my peripheral and my best friend charged me. He grabbed my shoulders and thrust me against the wall. I'd never seen Miles so angry. The veins on his neck bulged, and his face was bright red.

"What the actual fuck, Jack. You're my best fucking friend, and you fuck over my little sister? Really? Is this your idea of a fucking joke?"

"Miles," Monroe shrieked and yanked at his shoulders to pull him away from me. "It's not what you think."

"Really, Mon? I'll tell you what it looks like. A fucking photo of my best friend and my baby sister is going viral, and his head is buried in your fucking chest, and God only knows what is happening elsewhere. Thankfully, we aren't able to see that." He ran a hand through his hair and directed his anger at me. His face was inches from mine, and I didn't try to push him away. I deserved this. "You're in a back room obviously, so this wasn't a show you were putting on for the public. And now here you are, crying the morning after this fucker took advantage of you. How could you, man? I fucking trusted you."

"Oh my god, you are ridiculous," she shouted, stepping away to close her door.

How the hell did he get here so fast? Obviously, he saw the picture and got his ass on a plane. The Buckleys had access to private planes, so I wasn't completely shocked. But damn, the disdain in his eyes left me feeling like the world's biggest dick.

"Sit your ass down, Miles. You are so off base. Obviously, someone was there, as the picture wasn't taken by us. It was Thyme. He followed us in the room." She led him over to the chair across from her desk and he dropped down to sit.

"Your ex-boyfriend?"

"Yes. He was at the gallery, with his new girlfriend, who also happens to be very pregnant at the moment. It was humiliating to see them, and well, Montgomery here made it look like I wasn't still single and helped me not feel so pathetic. Thyme was following us around, so we put on a little show. It was harmless. Nothing happened." She kept her face completely even and reached for my arm and pushed me over to the chair beside her brother.

"So why are you crying this morning?" Miles asked, shifting in his seat, clearly uncomfortable with the fact that he'd overreacted. But he hadn't. Monroe was covering my ass.

"Um, because my asshole ex-boyfriend is having a baby with the woman he cheated on me with—who also happened to be a friend of mine. I'm hungover as hell and feel awful. A rather inappropriate photo of me is circulating. And I just called the vet, and they think I need to put Mr. Boots down today. He hasn't eaten in over a week. Is that *not* reason enough?"

He cleared his throat and glanced at me before returning his attention to his sister. "It is. I'm sorry, brother. I just saw the picture and saw red. And then I walked in and she was crying, I don't know, I just thought you'd fucked her over."

"I wouldn't do that," I said, pushing to my feet and pulling him in for a bear hug. That part was true, but I felt like shit not telling him the whole truth. "Who the fuck is Mr. Boots?"

"Her cat, who has to be as old as Mon. We got him when she was a little girl, and he was already old then."

She swiped at her eyes to clear away the last of her tears. "It's been a crappy morning."

"I'm sorry," I said, wanting to walk over to her and wrap her in my arms, but I didn't dare in front of Miles. His shoulders relaxed and he sat back in the chair.

"It's okay. Jack has actually been very decent to me, Miles. But I think this whole thing has run its course. I texted Harrison this morning. He's going to make a public statement that this relationship is done. He'll say the photo last night was a drunken, emotional moment of weakness. So, we can finally put this behind us."

"Shit. I'm sorry, guys. I got you into this mess and then attacked you for playing your part." Miles ran a hand over his face, and I saw the distress. Monroe was his weakness. He loved his little sister and just wanted to protect her. Hell, I understood it now that I knew her. I wanted to protect her too.

And the fact that she'd fast-forwarded our breakup. It stung. I wanted to give this a real try, and she couldn't get out of it fast enough.

"Dude, don't beat yourself up. I saw the photo. It looked bad. I'm sorry that I put you through that."

"Don't be. I'm fucking glad you stuck it to that asshole. I hate that dude."

"You and me both," I said, and we laughed as he clapped a hand over my shoulder.

"Okay. Are we all good now? I need to call the vet and make arrangements, prepare for my fake breakup, and get to work." Monroe pushed to her feet, her back stick straight as she made her way to her brother. "Thanks for flying in here like the giant asshole you are. I love you for it. But I'm a big girl and you need to get to work, and so do I."

"Love you, Mon. I can stay if you want me to, you know, to help you with Mr. Boots later. I can work remotely today."

She waved her hands in front of her face. "You have to stop treating me like a child, Miles. I've got this."

"And you have to stop thinking you have to handle everything on your own," he said.

"I can go with you tonight if you want?" I said as we made our way to the door.

"Oh my gosh, you both need to stop. Go to work." She put her hand on my back and guided me to the door, before pushing her brother out in the hallway as well. "Call me later, Miles."

And she shut the door in our faces. She was done with us.

Done with me.

Panic flooded, but I focused my attention on my best friend. "Are we good, brother?"

"I'm sorry, Jack. I jumped the gun. It's just—I feel so fucking protective over her. I always have. Maybe it's because we lost our mom in such a tough way, I don't know if I ever told you what happened?"

"Monroe told me. She died during childbirth. That's just not right, man."

"Wow. I'm shocked she told you about that. We never talk about it, and I know she isn't quick to share what happened, which I understand. Maybe I've misjudged this friendship you have with her, and

I'm sorry about that. I just know that one woman isn't ever going to be enough for you. Hell, I get it. Before I met Sierra, I was the same way. But I can't have anyone fucking over Monroe, you know? But if you two are friends, I'm all for it. And I'm sorry for ever thinking you'd cross the line. I know you better than that. You're the most loyal fucker I know. I'm sorry for doubting you."

Guilt flooded me, but I kept my face straight. I hadn't totally crossed the line, had I? I wasn't using Monroe, I actually really cared about her. Why the fuck does the first girl I actually want to take things further with have to be Buck's fucking sister? What are the chances?

"Stop apologizing. She's your sister. I get it."

"Thanks, brother. You want to go grab breakfast before I fly my ass back to LA?"

"Sounds good." I liked hanging with Buck, but anxiety coursed through my veins and my chest was heavy. Monroe was ready to announce our breakup. I wasn't there yet.

Not by a long shot.

And I was all about long shots.

sixteen

. . .

Monroe

THERE WAS a knock at my door, and to my surprise, Becks waltzed into my office.

"What are you doing here?" I asked as she plopped down in the chair across from me.

"Hello to you too." She raised a brow and chuckled. "I just had lunch with Tabi up the street and your breakup is all the word right now. You didn't tell me you were ending it so quickly. Things seemed awfully hot and heavy last night."

Tabi was Becks' little sister whom I adored. She attended art school in the city.

"It's a long time coming. We let things go on too long," I said, and a sick feeling settled in my stomach. How could I be grieving the end of a relationship that wasn't even real?

"Who decided to end it?" Her gaze narrowed as she studied me.

"Me. You saw that picture currently going viral. Miles lost his shit and went after Jack this morning. Things are just too out of control. I needed to put an end to it."

"Why? Because you were actually enjoying yourself?"

I sighed and shook my head. "I can't keep living in a fantasy world. It wasn't real."

"It looked awfully real last night, but maybe you two are both Academy Award-winning actors," she said, sitting back in the chair and looking around my office.

"Yep."

"This is nice, Mon. Look at you, being all official. So, I have something to tell you that I think you are going to want to hear."

"Is that so?"

"Yep. And I don't want to betray my sister, but I think gossiping with my best friend about her juicy relationship is allowed. I have no control over what you do with it. Let's just pretend I don't know about your anonymous column." Becks was the only person outside of the Montgomerys, Miles, and my father that knew about the column.

"Is something going on with Tabi?" Becks' little sister made my best friend seem mild. She was a wild and free spirit to the nth degree.

"Yep. She has a boyfriend. First guy I've seen her serious about… ever. You know, with my dad being the drunk, cheating bastard that he is, we're both slightly damaged." She chuckled, tucking her blonde sleek cut bob behind one ear. "So, of course she's with someone whose family is also fifty shades of fucked up."

"Is it someone I know?"

A mischievous grin spread across her face. "She's dating Lyle Labrith."

"The governor's son?"

"The one and only."

"How is that bad? His family was just featured on the cover of TIME magazine for their philanthropy work. His father is considered one of the most brilliant minds of our decade," I said through my laughter. Melissa Labrith was our beloved governor and her husband, Professor Labrith taught history at the most prestigious university in the city.

She shook her head. "Apparently it's a real shit show over at the mansion. Lyle attended boarding school on the east coast during high school because he hates his father so much. The professor is a shady little fucker. Big into drugs and throws these parties that turn into orgies right under his wife's nose. He doesn't give a shit. I guess the boy wonder wants his mom to leave his father, but she won't because she's up for reelection next year, and her work is all she has. You see, there's no such thing as a fairy tale. Men are ruthless pigs."

My head fell back in laughter. "Not true. My dad and Miles are good guys. Jack and his brothers are also impressive. They're out there. You just have to find one. But I am shocked to hear this about the Labriths. And since my dirty Reynolds story was a bust, I haven't been able to write a single thing yet for my column. How do we know this isn't just a spoiled rich kid trying to create daddy issues?"

"I know it seems like a stretch, but Tabi is pretty good at reading people's bullshit meters, and she said this kid is really worried about his mom. He wants to turn his father in, but he doesn't want to hurt his mother. Apparently, the bastard throws one of his orgy fests every New Year's Eve. Tabi wants to go to see what he's talking about, but Lyle refuses to go. He said the party starts out fairly normal but when the bulk of the guests leave, the *real party begins*. His mom apparently goes to her room, as they've had separate bedrooms for years. Anyway... *you're welcome*. Look into it. Keep Tabi and Lyle out of it. Do your thing, girl."

"Wow. I'm shocked. They seem like the perfect family. I mean, lots of people put on facades, look at the Reynolds. But I can usually see through it. The Labriths genuinely seem like the all-American family. And she's one of the few politicians that I absolutely love."

"Well, you've got your work cut out for you. I've got to get back to the office for a meeting." She pushed to her feet and made her way to the door just as Jack barreled through as if the building were on fire.

"You got a minute?" Jack asked as he high fived Becks on his way in. "What's up, girl?"

"Just stopped by to see where my girl works. Sorry to hear about the breakup."

"Yeah. You and me both," he said as my best friend waved and turned down the hallway.

I rolled my eyes to feign irritation, but my heart sped up with excitement to see him. It had been a few hours since our little show this morning with my brother. How could I miss him in that amount of time? This was not good. Exactly why I needed to end this charade now before it went any further.

"Sure," I mumbled, trying to avoid looking at him because that's how the lines got blurred in the first place.

I was still horrified by what happened last night. I'd begged him to touch me. Does it get any more desperate? My brother showed up at my workplace like a bat out of hell and was ready to fight his best friend. I'd made a mess of things, and now it was my turn to clean them up.

He shut the door and took the seat across from me, sitting in silence until I looked up and met his gaze.

"So, you can't look at me now?"

"What? No. I'm just working on something," I said, clearing my throat, desperate to push my nerves away. I couldn't stop thinking about how he made me feel. How commanding he was when his lips covered mine. The way he took control.

Those whiskey eyes waited for mine to find his. "Don't be embarrassed about what happened. Hell, I'm not."

I covered my face with my hands and shook my head. "You weren't the one begging for it."

He leaned over the desk and his hands wrapped around my wrists, tugging mine away from my face. I looked up to find him hovering over me. His nearness made my mouth go dry instantly.

"I begged for it earlier that night, and I'd beg for it any day of the week. But not when you're drunk. And what happened last night was just as good for me as it was for you."

My breaths came hard and fast. I couldn't think straight. Had I missed something? I remember him giving me the world's best orgasm and then taking me home and putting me to bed. How was that good for him?

"How do you figure?" I whispered.

"Because pleasuring you was amazing. I liked seeing you come undone. Maybe too much."

I let out a long, slow breath. "Okay, you need to sit back down. I can't think straight with you this close."

"And that's a bad thing?" he asked with a chuckle before dropping back in the chair.

"Um, yes? We just broke up. Whatever this is—it's over."

"What if I don't want it to be?"

"I don't know what that means," I said, reaching for my water and trying to slow my racing heart.

"What if I want what happened to happen again?"

"It can't."

"Why? Because you got scared and told Harrison to release a statement?"

"It's run its course. You saw my brother this morning. This is way too messy."

"What if it doesn't have to be? What if we dated for real, you know, like what we were doing before, but we add in sex? Lots of sex."

Holy hell. Was this happening?

I rubbed my temples. "Listen, Jack, as tempting as that sounds, I'm a relationship girl. What happened last night—*that's not me.*"

"What? Having orgasms in dark storerooms?"

"Um, yes. I don't do the whole friends with benefits thing. I drank too much and lost control. And almost ruined your friendship with Buck in the process."

"Let me talk to Buck. Hell, I wanted to tell him the truth at breakfast today, but after you denied that anything happened, I didn't want to throw you under the bus." He stretched his long legs out in front of him, crossing them at his ankles. I wanted to run my hands down his muscular thighs.

What. Is. Happening?

"The truth? What's that?"

"That I like you, Blue Jay. I like you a lot. I'm not suggesting that we're friends with benefits. Let me prove it to you. I want to take you out for real." His tongue darted out to wet his bottom lip, and I gripped my hands around the arms of my chair to keep from lunging forward.

"No, you don't. We have sexual chemistry, that's it. We have nothing in common."

"I disagree. We were both athletes, and pretty damn talented ones. We both love your brother. And we both love cats," he said, looking like he was deep in thought.

I laughed. *"We both love cats?* Bullshit. You've probably never held a cat in your life. You're making this up."

"Ye of little faith. I actually have a cat, Little Bird."

"Is that right?"

"Yep." A wide grin spread across his face. "Let me take you to dinner tomorrow night. I know you have to put Mr. Boots down today, and I'd happily join you, but you already shut me down." He leaned forward, resting his elbows on his knees, and stroked his bottom lip with his thumb.

I reached for a tissue and dabbed my forehead. I couldn't help it. I was sweating profusely now.

"We can't go to dinner. We just publicly broke up. How would that look? And my brother would freak out if he saw us together after the breakup announcement." I rolled my eyes.

"I don't give a fuck how it looks. And I told you, I'll speak to Buck about how I feel about you."

I pushed to my feet. This was crazy. I leaned over my desk, locking onto his intense gaze. "Do not talk to Buck about this. First off, I'm a grown woman. Secondly, this has very little chance of survival, so why risk your friendship over something that probably won't go anywhere? If I agree to go out with you, it's just me and you. We don't involve anyone. And we can't go in public because it will be all over social media the following day."

"You want to get me alone, don't you?" He wriggled his brows.

I dropped back down to sit and closed my eyes. I didn't know what to say. My head was still pounding from my enormous hangover, and my desire for Jack Montgomery was out of control.

Dangerously out of control.

These were two unfamiliar feelings for me.

"We can't be seen out in public."

"Great. I'll make you dinner at my place."

"You're going to make me dinner?"

"Yes. Did I stutter? I won't talk to Buck until we know where this is going."

I couldn't hide the smile on my face, but I tried. "It's going nowhere. We're playing with fire."

"I'm fine with that. Big Tony will pick you up at seven tomorrow night. Wear something sexy." He smirked, but the heat in his gaze told me he was serious.

"Fine. See you then."

"Looking forward to it, Blue Jay." He moved toward the door.

"Hey, Montgomery," I called out.

"Yeah?"

"I'm looking forward to hanging out with your cat tomorrow. What's his name, anyway?"

He looked up at the ceiling before speaking. "You'll have to come over to find out."

"I'll believe it when I see it."

He waltzed out the door, and I laid my forehead down on the desk. What a day. I had just gotten the lead on a story that could be huge in the political arena, and I was going on a real date with my ex-fake boyfriend.

I left work at a normal hour for the first time and sat on the couch with Mr. Boots for an hour before there was a knock on the door. His frail body was a sign that his health had deteriorated, and I'd tried to pretend he was fine for far too long.

I opened the door and invited Dr. Roberts in. He'd been a family friend since I was a little girl, and house calls were one of the perks of knowing your vet personally.

"How are you doing, honey?"

"I've been better," I said, swiping at the tears streaming down my face.

"Have you said your goodbyes?"

"I have." The words were barely audible.

"He's had a good run, Monroe. He's got to be in his late twenties. He's had a happy life with you. But he's suffering now, so you're doing the unselfish thing," he said. He'd been Mr. Boots' vet since the day we brought him home from the rescue.

"I know. It just makes me sad. We've been through so much together."

"He's part of the family. I understand." He reached over and scratched the top of Mr. Boots' head. We sat like that for another hour before I gave him the okay to proceed.

Mr. Boots passed away peacefully in my arms, and I swear he took a piece of my heart with him when he took his last breath. Dr. Roberts wrapped him in a blanket and patted me on the shoulder before leaving my apartment. I curled up on the couch and sobbed until there was a call from my doorman to let me know I had a delivery.

It was awfully late for a delivery. It had to be from Buck or Dad. They both knew how difficult it would be for me to put Mr. Boots down.

The delivery guy knocked on the door and I couldn't even see him behind the enormous arrangement. I chuckled and swiped at my eyes as I took it from him and thanked him for delivering at such a late hour.

"Don't worry. The guy paid me five times the normal rate to deliver it tonight. Have a good evening."

I set the colorful arrangement full of peach and white peonies, hydrangeas, and roses on the dining table and reached for the card.

Blue Jay,

I'm sorry about Mr. Boots. Looking forward to cheering you up tomorrow night, Little Bird.

J.M.

Well, this was unexpected. I reached for my phone as the tears continued to fall. I stopped swiping at them, and just let them run their course. Losing Mr. Boots was an enormous loss.

And I was definitely feeling it.

Me ~ Just received an obscenely large floral arrangement. Thank you. Very thoughtful.

Montgomery ~ I told you, I'm full of surprises. How are you doing?

Me ~ I'm sad.

Montgomery ~ That's good. It means he was important to you. It's okay to grieve. You loved him.

Me ~ Thank you, ole wise one.

Montgomery ~ I lost my dad in college, and I know what it's like to lose someone you love. And you need to let yourself feel it, otherwise it will just be waiting for you later.

Me ~ Is that what you did? You felt it?

Montgomery ~ Every fucking day. I still do. But that's just because he was such a good man. Not feeling his loss would be a shame. So, I feel it. All the fucking time. And that's okay, because it doesn't hurt as much as it used to.

Wow. I was stunned by his honesty. There was a lot more to Jack Montgomery than I ever expected.

And I wanted to know everything.

seventeen

. . .

Jack

I SNUCK AWAY from work and took the helicopter to Napa after lunch, making my way to Laney Mae's office. Harrison sat behind her desk with his arm wrapped around her as he held her on his lap.

"Jesus. Get a room already. You're married, and you live together. This is a place of work, for god's sake," I said through my laughter.

I'd caught my brother and Laney Mae in inappropriate positions for as long as I could remember. They'd never been able to keep their hands to themselves, and since finding their way back to one another after a few years apart—they were like two lovesick teenagers. And I fucking loved it.

"Shut it, Jack-ass," Laney Mae said as a wide grin spread across her face and she kissed Harrison one last time before pushing to her feet.

"I hear you got yourself in a sticky situation. *Shocker*." Harrison moved to stand and wrapped his arms around her waist, guiding her to the door.

"It's Laney Mae's fault." I shrugged. "She told me to find things in common with Monroe."

Her head fell back in laughter. "Find things in common does not mean to lie about having a cat. It means that if she likes to read, you pick up a book so you have something to discuss. If she likes a Netflix series, you give it a shot so you can share that with her. Lying about owning a cat—that's not the same thing."

"Potato, po-tot-o. You should have been more clear. She was devastated about putting Mr. Boots down and she seemed so certain that I wouldn't own a cat."

"And she'd be right," Harrison said as he shook his head.

"It's only a lie if I don't own a cat." We made our way down the hallway and my brother stopped at his office door.

"You don't own a cat, brother. It's a lie."

"I will own a cat today. I just exaggerated the details about when I got him. And it cheered her up that he'd be there tonight, so it's worth getting myself a pet in the end. Win, win."

He studied me for a long moment before speaking. "You really like her."

"Of course, I like her."

"He means you *like her*, like her," Laney Mae said, kissing Harrison's cheek. "I'll be back."

We hopped in my truck, and Laney Mae directed me to make a few turns as we made our way to a woman's house that she claimed rescued tons of local cats. As usual, Laney Mae was saving my ass. I'd called her in a panic last night, and she told me to meet her this morning and we'd figure it out.

"So, Velma said she just got this cat in a few days ago. He needs a home. The family divorced and neither were able to have pets in their new place. Apparently, he's having a hard time with the separation."

"What the hell does that mean?"

"I have no idea. But he needs a home, and you need a cat. So, let's go meet your new addition." Laney Mae and I hopped out of the truck and made our way up the cobblestone walkway. "What are you making her for dinner?"

"I can't cook. Sarah is going to make one of her specialties and leave it in the oven for me so it will look like I cooked." Sarah had worked for me for two years. She cleaned, she cooked, she took my clothes to the dry cleaner and she basically kept me in check.

"Look at you, Jack-ass... you're really trying to impress her. I love it. And Monroe is fabulous. I hope she doesn't kick your lying ass to the curb when she figures all of this out. Hopefully, she'll find the effort endearing." She laughed as she knocked on the door.

"This house has got a *Silence of the Lambs* feel, right? And I'm not lying. I said I had a cat and he was old. I will have a cat today and he sounds old. I also told her I'd make her dinner, and I am. Dinner will be there when she arrives. I wasn't specific that I'd be the one cooking said meal, just that I would have it at my house. So, there you go."

She rolled her eyes just as the door opened. A tiny woman that looked no less than one hundred and fifty years old stood on the other side. She wore a pink nightgown and white slippers. Her skin resembled a dried apricot with all the deep lines and grooves. Her gray hair was wrapped around little pink rollers, and she looked me up and down like she was sizing me up.

"Mmmm-mmmm. Good to see you, Laney Mae, and thanks for bringing this eye candy to my doorstep. Glad I fixed up today." Her voice made it clear that she'd likely been sucking back a carton of smokes for more decades than one could count, and her blue eyes danced with mischief.

Fucking adorable.

"Thanks for helping me out, Velma. I'm Jack." I extended my hand and she pulled me into a hug.

"I haven't been in the arms of a man in years. This will keep a woman young," she said through her gravelly voice.

Laney Mae barked out a laugh while I wrapped my arms around the fragile woman and patted her back. She smelled like a mix of cigarettes, lemons, and vodka.

"Okay, handsome. Let me go get Pussy for you." Velma pulled away and shuffled her feet down the hall.

"Pussy? What kind of rescue is this anyway?" I glanced around the room and spotted a dozen cats in random places from the windowsill to the top of the dining cabinet. There were faded floral velvet couches that looked to be as old as the woman who lived here, and stacks of books on the coffee table. Sunlight flooded the space, highlighting a layer of dust that covered every surface in sight.

"It's the kind of rescue that gives you a cat on a moment's notice.

Maybe that's just a nickname for her cats?" Laney Mae could barely contain her laughter.

"Okey dokey, here he is. This is Pussy. He's a big fellow. A lot of heart, but right now he's scared shitless because his parents just jumped ship on him. He doesn't get along with the other cats, so I can't keep him. I think he'll do better being the only cat in your home. You don't have any others, right?"

I cleared my throat as I took in the gargantuan four-legged creature. Jesus. He was larger than any cat I'd ever seen. He'd give a medium-sized dog a run for his money. He'd obviously been well fed. His coat was tan and black, and his eyes were yellow. Velma held him in her arms like a baby, and I was surprised the petite woman could support his weight. I glanced down to see the large heart that hung from his collar with PUSSY spelled out in black letters.

What the actual fuck?

"Nope. He'll be the only one. Is Pussy his name, or just a cat reference?" I asked, clearing my throat as Laney Mae covered her mouth with her hand.

"A cat reference? No, don't you see the tag here, Sonny boy? It's his name. The only one he's ever known. Pussy, meet your new daddy, Jack."

She went to hand him to me, and the crazy son of a bitch hissed and screamed out like a tiger. Laney Mae and I both stumbled back, and Velma chuckled.

"What the fuck is wrong with him?" I asked.

"Don't use the harsh language in front of Pussy. He's a sensitive kitty. He just doesn't know you yet. He'll warm up to you. Do you have a crate with you?"

"No. I didn't know I'd need one."

"Well, lucky for you, I have a crate and a starter kit you can purchase here. I've got a week's supply of food and a kitty litter box for you as well."

"Thank you. You, uh, you sure he'll be okay with me later?"

"I think anyone would be okay with you, Sonny boy. He'll warm up to you in a couple of hours. How far of a drive down the road do you have?"

"I actually live back in the city. Can he go in a helicopter?"

"A helicopter? Hell no. That'll scare the bejeezus out of Pussy. You'll need to keep him in the kennel and drive him back."

I sucked in a long breath. This was turning into much more of an ordeal than I'd expected. I thought cats were supposed to be easy. Like having a stuffed animal. So far Pussy was proving to be a big pain in the ass.

"Fine. I'll drive him back. Is it possible to change his name?" I asked, as she turned to go get the supplies, holding the four-legged tiger in her arms.

Velma whipped around to face me. "No sir. Would you appreciate it if someone started calling you Walter? I don't think so. He's been Pussy for more than a decade. Can't change it now. And what do you have against Pussy?"

Laney Mae's head fell back in laughter. "I think she's right, Jack-ass. You love Pussy, don't you?"

"Shut up, Laney Mae," I grumbled under my breath. "Pussy's fine, Velma. Sorry for asking."

"All right. I just want to make sure Pussy's going to the right home." She shuffled down the hall.

"Please make her stop saying *Pussy*. And what the hell am I going to tell Monroe? I've got a cat named Pussy and he wants to kill me? And why the fuck does he look like he ate his brother? He's a fat fucker, isn't he?"

Tears ran down Laney Mae's face as she tried to speak through her laughter. "He is rather large and slightly terrifying. But she said he'll warm up in no time. And just tell her that you named him that because you like Pussy."

"Oh sure. That'll win her over."

"I think Monroe just might be your Har-bear," she said, wrapping her arms around my middle and hugging me tight. "My little boy is all grown up."

I chuckled and rolled my eyes. "Don't get ahead of yourself. It's dinner."

"Well, I've never seen you make such an effort for anyone before."

She was right. What the hell was I doing? Getting this ridiculous cat to cheer her up. Risking pissing off my best friend. This wasn't me. I'd never tried this hard for a woman. But Monroe Buckley was special. Different.

Everything.

I closed my eyes for a minute and thought it over. "I hope I'm not making a mistake?"

"About adopting the fat cat or making dinner for the Little Bird?" Laney Mae whispered, before she burst out in laughter. "Don't overthink it. Follow your heart. You're here for a reason. She must be important."

There was no doubt about that.

Velma came around the corner carrying a kennel with Pussy inside. He looked a little large for the space, but at least he wasn't hissing. She set him down and grabbed a bag full of supplies before telling me I owed her two hundred bucks. For a scary cat and a bag of crap. I handed her the cash, and she gave me a piece of paper with her phone number on it.

"Call me if you have any problems," she said, waving as we stepped out the door.

We both thanked her and made our way to my truck.

"I can't believe I have to drive back to the city," I groaned.

"You must feel like such a peasant. Driving one of these old contraptions to get to your destination." She smirked before a wide grin spread across her face. "You'll be fine. It's not that long of a drive. You can come up with a plan for tonight. And I want text updates throughout the evening."

"That's what Harley said. I can't be texting you two while I'm on a date."

Once we were buckled up, and on the road, she said, "Yes, you can. Sneak in the bathroom. And don't try to sleep with her. It's the first date."

"Have you always been this bossy?"

"Sure have. Call me later, Jack-ass. Good luck with Pussy," she said when I dropped her off at the winery. She shut the door and I glanced in the back seat at the odd creature before pulling his crate up front on the passenger seat.

"You're going to need to be nice tonight, Pussy. You and I are going to be fast friends." I stuck my finger in the grid and the bastard hissed and nipped and broke the skin on the tip of my finger. Jesus. How the hell was I going to make her think this cat was mine?

I spent the next hour driving back to the city, singing along to the music filtering through the speakers and talking to my new best friend who hadn't hissed at me again since we'd pulled out on the road.

I carried him up to my apartment and found Sarah in the kitchen cooking. It smelled like heaven and I dropped Pussy on the counter and grabbed a bottle of water.

"Oh my. What is that?"

"It's my new cat, Pussy. What do you think?"

She raised a brow and walked closer, opening the door to check him out before I could stop her. He sprung from the kennel and landed on the floor before taking off to check out the place. Well, I guess he'd need to make himself at home, so better now than later.

"Why in the world would you name him that?" she balked before returning to the counter to chop mushrooms.

"That's the name he came with, so I'm stuck with it. What are you making? I see the flowers arrived." I glanced around, seeing the arrangements I'd ordered in the dining room and living room.

"Yes, they arrived an hour ago. I'm guessing you cleaned out the florist." She paused and chuckled. "You seem to like this girl. It's about time."

"Yeah, yeah, yeah." I snatched a slice of cucumber and popped it in my mouth. "You spoil me, Sarah. She'll be here in thirty minutes. I'm going to go grab a shower. Thanks for everything."

I set up the litter box in my laundry room and put down some food and water for my new roommate. I walked into my bedroom and found Pussy sprawled out on my bed.

"Make yourself at home, big P," I said, reaching my hand out to pet the top of his head as he snarled and scratched me like a goddamned tiger.

Let's hope he wasn't setting the tone for the night.

Hopefully, Monroe wouldn't be hissing at me and pushing me away.

But she sure as shit wasn't going to believe he was my cat if he didn't change his tune soon.

"Pull your shit together, Puss. This is a big night for both of us."

I heard him hiss behind me as I walked into the bathroom and laughed. I wanted tonight to be perfect, and a fat cat with a bad attitude wasn't going to deter me.

Not by a long shot.

eighteen

. . .

Monroe

"THANKS FOR THE RIDE, Big Tony. You know I could have driven myself," I said as I sat in the swanky black SUV. Jack had offered to come pick me up with his driver, but it seemed silly. And he sounded a little distracted. I needed a few moments to pull myself together anyway. I didn't know what we were doing. I assumed he was as attracted to me as I was to him, and the sexual tension was heavy when we were in a room together.

But were we really going to act on it? I mean, we already had just two nights ago, or at least *I* had. And I couldn't get it out of my head. Talk about a fantasy come to life. Jack Montgomery was my living, breathing fantasy. But where could this go? The guy didn't date, he was an infamous playboy, and he also happened to be my brother's best friend. Not that I was worried about Miles. I wasn't. I was a grown woman, and my brother needed to respect that. My concern was that Jack was allowing it to be a huge factor, which made me apprehensive. I didn't want things to get weird when all of this came to an end. Which it would.

I was a realist. I wasn't disillusioned into believing this could actually be something. It couldn't. We're talking about Jack freaking Montgomery, after all. He was *every woman's* fantasy. And he lived up to the reputation. He was gorgeous and charming and sexy as hell. But he definitely wasn't mine. At least not long-term. But maybe that was okay. The ache between my legs sure wanted to believe so. And after what he did to me just two nights ago—it left me wanting more. As shameful and desperate as that sounded, it was the truth.

I knew it would hurt when he tired of me, so I was going to force myself to live in the moment. Be present. Enjoy this and not overthink it. At least that was the plan.

"Are you kidding? He wouldn't allow you to drive yourself." Big Tony stepped out of the car and came around to open my door.

"So, you just run around and pick up all his ladies, huh?"

He offered me his hand. "You'd be the first. I probably shouldn't say this, but in all the years I've worked for him, I've never brought a woman here for dinner."

I laughed. He obviously felt obligated seeing as I was Miles' sister and all. "Thanks. I'll see you in a few hours."

His doorman assisted me to the private elevator and typed in a code. I made my way to the top floor. The elevator opened into his apartment, and I was immediately hit with the smell of garlic and lemon and my stomach rumbled with anticipation. There were candles lit around the space and pretty pink and white floral arrangements caught my eye.

An oversized cat moseyed over to me. Wow. He was large. He rubbed up against my shin and I laughed.

Me and cats… we were one.

I hadn't believed that Jack really had a cat, so he was already proving me wrong.

"Hey there," I said before I leaned down to scratch the top of his massive head. He purred, and I scooped him up into my arms. He nuzzled his nose beneath my chin, and I chuckled.

"Dear god. You're holding him? He doesn't usually allow that. And wow, you look gorgeous." Jack's gaze studied me with concern. The air left my lungs at the sight of him. Dark jeans that showed off his long legs, and a white button-up exposing just enough skin to tease me. His hair was damp and tousled on his head, and cedar and citrus engulfed me at his nearness.

"Thank you. You look nice too. You didn't have to do all this." I bit down on my bottom lip and glanced around the room at all the bells and whistles. We were about to cross the line. It wasn't about flowers and candles, but about going in knowing what we were doing. We were going to have sex. And I'd agreed to come here, so obviously I was on board with the idea.

"You don't like candles and flowers?" he asked as his cat poked at me to continue rubbing his belly.

"Of course, I do. But it's not like you're trying to date me. We're sort of doing this backward, right? We fake dated first, and now we want to have sex. You don't need to make this more than it is."

He walked toward me, and his cat surged upright and hissed. "Jesus. Put the fat bastard down, would you?"

"Please tell me that isn't his name." I glanced down at his collar and my head fell back in laughter before I set the big guy down on all fours. "You did not name your cat *Pussy*?"

"Of course not. I rescued him, and he came with the name. Come here," he said, leading me to the large gray velvet sectional surrounded by a wall of floor-to-ceiling windows that overlooked the city. It was breathtaking. His penthouse was classic and elegant with black and white prints on the walls and modern décor.

He faced me as we dropped to sit, and he took both of my hands in his. His whiskey gaze locked with mine. "You told me you don't do casual sex, remember, Blue Jay?"

"Yet here I am." It was the truth. I couldn't resist him. I didn't want to. So, I came here with my eyes wide open.

"I told you I wanted to give this a try. For real. This is not about just having sex for me. You don't believe me?" His voice was gravelly, and something in his gaze pulled at my heartstrings. He appeared hurt? Vulnerable?

I shook my head. "You don't need to tell me what I want to hear. I know who you are. And you need to remove Miles from the equation. I think you feel like you need to do all of this out of obligation. I'm never going to tell him about what happens between us, if that's what you're worried about. We're two consenting adults."

Without warning, he pulled me onto his lap and wrapped his arms around me, hugging me close to him. "You think I'm doing all of this for Miles? This is for you. I wasn't just saying I wanted to give this a try to get you in bed. I really want to give this thing between us a chance. Our fake relationship was better than anything real I've ever had. That's why I wanted to talk to Miles. To tell him how I feel about you."

My heart raced and my mouth went dry. I wanted to jump in the deep end with Jack, but I knew better. This man could wreck me, and I needed to proceed with caution. I turned in his arms and faced him. His warm breath tickled against my cheek and I reached up to brush back the dark flock of hair that tumbled down his forehead. "How do you feel about me, Montgomery?"

A wide grin spread across his handsome face, and my stomach fluttered.

Damn traitor.

We came here for sex, nothing more.

"I like you, Little Bird. I like you more than I ever knew I could. I like being around you and I miss you when you aren't there. Hell, I miss you every time we say goodbye. So, all of this," he said, holding his arms out and staring at me. "This is my way of telling you that I'm crazy about you."

I sucked in a long breath and shook my head. "You'll tire of me. You can have anyone, why even go there?"

"Because I only want you."

"You're confusing your feelings. You want to have sex with me. There's a difference."

He studied me, moving his face closer. His lips grazed my ear as he spoke. "What are you afraid of?"

"I'm afraid of what everyone's afraid of. *Getting hurt.* I've had a lifetime of hurt, I'm not looking for more." My words surprised me. My voice was hoarse and raw, and the truth floated between us like an invisible barrier.

"I'm not afraid of getting hurt. I trust you."

"That's because you'll be the one doing the hurting. Look at your track record. Why do you think my brother was worried? You're a playboy through and through. One woman will never keep your attention." I closed my eyes as his lips teased mine.

"Wrong, Little Bird. No woman has kept my attention before, because I was waiting for you," he whispered.

I pulled back and my breath caught in my throat. I needed to clear my head. My gaze locked with his. My fingers found his jaw and slid across his peppered scruff, loving the rough contrast against my skin. "How do you know?"

"Because I know. I wouldn't bullshit you. I've been feeling it for a while. I'm just asking for a chance." His finger circled around one of the diamond stud earrings that he'd given me for my birthday, and he smiled.

Gold flecks sparkled in his gaze as the moonlight flooded his grand living room. I leaned forward.

Wanting and needing him in a way I'd never known before.

These feelings of desire were so foreign I didn't know if I could make a rational decision.

My lips found his and this time the kiss was slow.

Cautious.

Curious.

His hand tangled in my hair and he pulled me closer as his tongue explored my mouth. "I'll never tire of you, Little Bird. You're all I think about."

I was lost in the moment. Lost in this man. This need. This burning desire.

He pulled away, and the loss hit me like a freight train slamming against a brick wall. He held my shoulders, keeping me just a few inches from his face. "Let's have dinner."

Dinner? I forgot he'd invited me here for a meal.

"Oh. Um, okay." I pushed to my feet, my face flush with embarrassment. What was it about Jack that made me lose control? Every. Single. Time. This wasn't me. I didn't even like sex with Thyme. In fact, I used to dread it. But Jack… he was different.

He linked his fingers with mine and led me to the dining room. "Don't be embarrassed. I feel it too. But I want to show you that there's more here than just an intense attraction."

I nodded as he pulled out my chair. "So, you feel it too?" I whispered.

"Fuck, yeah." He kissed my mouth and walked toward the kitchen just as Pussy came around the corner and hissed at him, lunging just enough to scratch his calf which was thankfully protected by the denim barrier. "Jesus. Why is he such a dick to me?"

I chuckled and studied his jumbo kitty who watched him cautiously. Jack walked out carrying two plates and I didn't miss the fact that he walked a bit faster when he moved past Pussy this time. The dining room table was a sleek glass table with a modern crystal chandelier hanging above.

"Has he always been like this with you?" I asked.

He dropped to sit, leaning forward to fill my glass with a bottle of Montgomery wine. He set the bottle down before taking his seat.

"Um. Yeah. He's never liked me."

I knew it hurt him to admit because everybody liked Jack. He was that guy. I wasn't buying it.

"Look at me," I said, setting my fork down. "How long have you had him?"

He searched my gaze and sucked in a long breath. "A few hours."

My head fell back in laughter and it took me a minute to contain myself. "What? You got him today?"

"Yep."

"Why?" I asked, shaking my head.

"I wanted to impress you." This man was causing all my walls to crumble to the ground and I was frantically trying to keep them in place.

I pushed my plate across the table and made my way over to him. He set his fork down and looked up at me. I moved to sit on his lap and tipped his head back to look at him. "That might be the sweetest gesture anyone has ever done for me. Thank you."

"Wow. If I'd known getting that fat bastard would get you to sit on my lap, I would have brought the fucker home weeks ago."

I chuckled, and reached for my plate, taking an oversized bite. I took my time chewing and savored all the flavors bursting from the white wine sauce generously poured over the pasta. He remembered that I was a vegetarian and made an effort to cook something that I would eat. No one had ever done that. With Thyme, I was used to just eating the sides of whatever he'd prepare. He'd never taken what I wanted into consideration, in fact, we always went to a steak house on our anniversary. I wasn't used to a man being this thoughtful. Hell, he'd brought home a cat that clearly hated him, just to make me feel better about losing Mr. Boots.

That was sweet.

Jack Montgomery was sweet to the core.

Under all that charming sex appeal, was a warm, considerate man.

We sat this way for the next hour or so. Talking and laughing and eating. With me in his lap and him snagging bites from my plate once he'd finished his.

"So, who made the meal?"

His chest rumbled beneath me. "Damn, Little Bird. You don't miss a beat. Sarah made it. She works for me, and she's a hell of a lot better in the kitchen than I am. But I told her what to make because I know what you like."

"I couldn't quite picture you mincing garlic and lemon and making a homemade white wine sauce from scratch," I teased, turning to look at him. His tongue swiped out and licked my bottom lip and my body heated instantly.

"You had a little sauce there," he said, his voice gruff.

"Let's go sit on the couch and introduce you to your cat." I pushed to my feet, trying to control the ache between my legs.

I grabbed our plates and set them in the kitchen sink before we walked to the couch. Pussy followed me and lingered beneath my leg.

"I don't know what his problem is. I didn't take him on the helicopter, I drove his ass back so he wouldn't freak out. And still, the dude hates me."

Our knees were touching, and we sat facing one another. I reached down and pulled his gigantic cat onto my lap. "Cats sense fear. He knows you aren't comfortable. He just needs to get to know you."

"Kind of like you," he said, a smile growing on his face.

"Did you just compare me to Pussy?" I covered my mouth to mask my laughter, as his cat settled on my lap.

"I think you hissed at me the first few times I tried to pet you too."
He smirked. The man was ridiculously sexy.

"Give me your hand." I reached mine out for his and rested our
hands on the cat currently setting up residence on my lap. My hand
looked so small on top of his. I moved our hands slowly over the back
of his head. My fingers laced with his, as I moved them across the
soft fur.

Pussy purred and tilted his head into Jack's palm for more love.
"This is progress, but I'd rather have my hands on you."

"Yeah?" I asked, continuing to move our hands in sync.

"Always. I want you to spend the night with me. No sex. I don't
want you thinking that's what I'm after. We'll take it slow."

I pouted. "I thought I was coming over for my first booty call."

"If that were enough for me, I'd take you up on it. But it's not, and
I'm going to prove it to you. Now get fat bastard off your lap, so I can
have you on mine."

"So bossy," I said, moving the cat to the floor, and he whined a few
times before walking away.

Jack pulled me on his lap and kissed me hard. He tipped me back
on the couch and propped himself above. "I'm going to take my time
with you, Little Bird."

My breaths sounded like little pants, and I didn't even care. I was
well beyond hiding my attraction to him. "I thought we weren't
having sex."

"We're not. But I plan to worship every inch of you tonight. Make
you cry out my name over and over from the earth-shattering orgasms
I give you, just like the one I gave you the other night. I want you
naked in my bed, in my arms, so I can touch you any time I want."

I couldn't speak, which was a first. My mouth hung open and his
whiskey gaze locked with mine. This was too much. And not enough. I
wanted more.

I wanted things I'd never wanted before.

I wanted everything.

nineteen

. . .

Jack

I CARRIED her to my room. I'd thought about Monroe Buckley naked and sprawled across my black silk sheets more times than I could count. I'd tortured myself for weeks every time I fantasized about her —torn between the guilt of betraying my best friend and the desire to make this woman mine.

Because she was mine.

There was no if, and, or but about it. Now I just had to convince her of that and then speak to Buck calmly and get him to believe that I wasn't fucking around.

Because I wasn't.

I understood why Buck would be concerned. I wasn't this guy. I didn't get invested in women. But I was all in. I barely recognized myself.

My need for her.

My desire for her.

I dropped her on my bed, and her petite frame bounced a little before she settled on the gray comforter. Her light brown hair spread all around her and she looked like some sort of goddamn angel lying there.

"You're so fucking beautiful," I whispered as I propped myself above her.

She shook her head and chuckled. Monroe wasn't used to being fawned over. She put on a tough front, but she was soft and tender beneath that strong exterior she portrayed.

"You're too much, Jack Montgomery," she said, reaching up to run her fingers over the scruff covering my jaw.

"*Not too much*. Just honest."

I leaned down and took her sweet mouth. I wanted to explore every inch of her. I moved my way down, kissing her jaw, her neck, her shoulder. She moaned and arched into me, and my hand slipped beneath her shirt. I paused and sat back on my heels, reaching for the hem of her top and pulling it over her head. I'd been wanting to see her—all of her, for so long.

So, fucking long.

Too fucking long.

"You're stunning," I said, grazing over the lace of her pink bra with my fingertips. "Do you know how long I've thought about this?"

"Since this morning?" she teased, but I didn't miss the hoarseness in her voice. The desire in her gaze.

"Since the day you walked through the door for your interview, and every day since."

"Jack," she whispered, squeezing her eyes closed. She was scared. Hell, I understood it. My track record sucked. But I'd never wanted anyone or anything as bad as I wanted this girl.

"I'm right here, Little Bird. I'm not going anywhere." I leaned down and covered one lacy breast with my mouth. I reached behind her and unlatched her bra, tossing it to the side. "Too much fabric. I want to feel you. All of you."

"Oh my god," she whispered as I took turns licking and kissing and sucking her perfect tits. Jesus, I couldn't get enough of this girl.

I made my way down her stomach, lavender and honey flooding my senses. "So sweet. Every goddamned inch of you. Pure goodness."

I paused when I reached her skirt and she pushed up on her elbows so I could shimmy it down. Her matching pink lace panties the only thing between us. I used my teeth to pull at the edge of the lace, and she gasped. I tugged them to the side and buried my face between her legs and she tangled her fingers in my hair, urging me on.

I took my time, tasting and exploring. Teasing and taunting. Bringing her just to the edge and keeping her there until she begged for more. And that's exactly what I gave her. She cried out her release, and I swear to fucking God it was the best feeling in the world.

"Oh my, I, I..." was all she said, and I chuckled against her sweet spot and she tugged my head up and I met her gaze. "Wow."

"I guess Ole Thyme wasn't much of a lover. And you've only had my hands and mouth on you so far. I haven't even pulled out my best feature yet," I said, raising a brow as I sat back on my heels and she watched me.

She reached up and tugged at the hem of my shirt and I yanked it over my head, tossing it to the side before she pulled at the waistband of my pants as she took in the large erection straining against my zipper. "I want to see you."

"Not yet, Blue Jay." I dropped down beside her and turned her on her side to face me.

"Why?"

"Because I've had a wicked case of blue balls for weeks, and to say I'm hard as a rock right now would be a fucking understatement. And we're not having sex tonight. *Not yet.* I'm going to prove to you that I'm all in, so if that means a little more discomfort, so fucking be it. I want to do this right."

She smiled and my fucking chest squeezed. *What the hell was that about?* There was just enough moonlight coming in through the windows in my bedroom to illuminate her gorgeous face. Large indigo eyes, plump lips, and porcelain skin.

"Well, there are things I can do without us having sex, right?" she said, stroking me over the fabric of my jeans.

I reached down and wrapped my hand around her wrist. "No. If you unleash him, I won't be able to restrain myself. Trust me when I say, it's taking all the restraint I have."

I released her hand and she moved it to my face, running it along my jaw gently, and I loved the feel of her soft skin against mine. Her fingers moved up and tangled in my hair, running back and forth along my head. The sensation so great I almost forgot about my angry dick still throwing a temper tantrum beneath my zipper.

"You're full of surprises," she said.

"Yeah? Well, I'm just getting started."

Her cheek settled on my chest, and her fingers continued to move through my hair, soothing me in ways I couldn't explain. She was naked aside from her lace panties, and I wrapped my arm around her, running my hand up and down her back. Her perfect tits were pressed to my chest, and it took everything I had not to flip her on her back and take her the way I wanted to. The way she wanted me to. Monroe was different.

Special.

And I needed to remember that.

"Okay. Well, I guess this is a good time to ask you questions. I mean, we've already fake dated, broken up, you're my brother's best friend, and now I'm practically naked in your arms—seems like as good a time as any to find out more about you."

"Ask away," I said, kissing the top of her head because I couldn't stop myself. This was new. This need to take it slow and do things right. I was a fucking kick-ass lover—no doubt about it. Tender and sweet weren't really my thing. But everything about this girl had me reacting differently and I didn't mind it. Didn't mind waiting for her either. Somehow, I knew she was worth the wait.

She pushed up just a little, resting her elbow on my chest and looking at me. Her hair was a wild mess from writhing beneath me just minutes ago. Her face was relaxed and sated and fucking glowing. Her indigo blue eyes sparkled in the moonlight and she studied me. "It really wasn't hard for you to walk away from football? Everyone thought you would go pro, right?"

"That was the plan. But honestly, no. It wasn't even an option after my dad died. I've never been someone who struggled with making decisions. I know what I want, and I make it happen. It's that simple. I never waver. And I was done with football. My family needed me, and I didn't struggle with the decision like everyone thinks I did."

She nodded like she understood. "Yeah. It was big news when you walked away. I remember wondering if it was hard for you to hear them talk about it for months after you left."

"Not at all. Everyone wanted to dissect that shit, but it was much simpler for me than everyone thought. I wasn't under any sort of obligation to my family. Not one person pressured me. I struggled to return to USC after my father died because I knew my family needed me. But I also knew that my father would want me to finish school, and I wanted to have that degree under my belt too. I didn't need people acting like I just got a free ride at the family business, I'm not about that. Yes, I was born into an affluent family and I'm grateful for everything I have. But I've worked hard to get where I am and I'm proud of that. And attending school in Los Angeles made it easy to commute home to Napa often. But the minute I graduated, I knew it was time to come home and help my brothers."

"Good answer," she said with a smirk. Her hair falling all around her shoulders as she bit down on that juicy bottom lip of hers.

"What I want to know is how you know so much about this? Were you keeping tabs on me back then? I thought you hated me?"

Her cheeks pinked and she dropped down on her back. I rolled over, propping myself above her while I waited for her to respond.

"So, I may have had a little crush on you back then which is why I may have hated you for sleeping with my nemesis." She covered her face with her hands as she spoke, as if this were the most sinister secret.

Fucking adorable.

I tugged her hands away and waited for her to look up at me. "I would never have done that if I'd known."

"I know you wouldn't. It was kid stuff. But I'd told my friend Gwen about my ridiculous crush and I guess Tiffany overheard. She couldn't wait to flaunt your *sexcapades* in my face the next day." She shook her head and laughed.

"Sexcapades? Is that even a word?" I chuckled. "Well, that makes sense. She came on strong. And I was young and stupid. I never would have looked at you back then, being Buck's little sister. I always thought you were hot as hell, but you know, you were off-limits. But I wish I'd known Tiffany was playing games, because I wouldn't have let her do that to you. Did you beat her at every race from there on out?" I asked, pushing a loose piece of hair away from her pretty face as I ran my knuckles back and forth along her cheek.

"I certainly did. I stopped feeling bad about it after that too," she said through her laughter.

I rolled over to lie on my back and pulled her across my chest again, running my fingers through her silky hair. "Well, I'm glad we're here now and you forgave me for being a stupid, horny, young prick."

"Who said you're completely forgiven?" she teased, and her tongue swiped out to wet her bottom lip. "So, what's different now? You said you wouldn't have even looked at me that way back then because of Miles. But now you can?"

I sucked in a long breath. I was in a battle with myself. Loyalty meant something to me, and Buck was my best friend. "I don't have a choice. Now that I *see you*, I can't seem to look anywhere else."

It was the fucking truth. I don't know when it happened or how it happened. But she was all I could see now. She was everything I never knew I wanted.

She nodded. "When was your last relationship?"

I used the pad of my thumb to run it along her pouty lip. "Before my dad died. I had a girl I was seeing for a few months, nothing serious. After that, I just kept it casual, you know, that way no one gets hurt."

"Were you protecting them or you?" she asked, studying me like she needed to know the answers to her questions. Like the journalist she was deep in her core.

"Probably both, if I'm being honest."

She nodded. "Losing your dad was a big loss. I'm sure you still miss him every day."

"I do. Always will. It's been six years, but I swear I still feel like it was yesterday. Never want to hurt like that again. It's a deep to your soul kind of hurt. I already love my mom and my brothers, so I can't change that. But I definitely think I intentionally stayed detached from the women I saw over the last few years. Until you walked through the door."

I could feel her heartbeat racing against my chest. "Why?"

"No fucking idea. But I can't stop it and I've learned to trust my gut. And my gut says that this is something. Something worth fighting for."

"Fighting what?" she whispered, her gaze searching mine.

"Fighting every fucking fear I have about letting someone in. Fighting my best friend. Fighting the feeling that I could fail and fuck it all up."

"That's a lot of fighting, Montgomery," she said, laying her head back down on my chest and hugging me tight. "I don't know that I'm worth all that."

"You're worth it all, Little Bird."

"How are you always so sure of everything?" she asked, her breath tickling my chest.

"It's a gut feeling. Something I don't feel often. But I feel it with you. No doubt about it. I wouldn't risk all this if I didn't."

She nodded, her fingers running along my chest. This was definitely the most intimate moment I'd ever shared with a woman. Hell, usually I just had sex and tapped out. Left. We hadn't had sex and I was telling her things I never told anyone.

"I don't know that I'm worth that risk." She pushed up to look at me, and her eyes welled with emotion.

"Why would you say that?"

"I don't know," she said, biting down on her lip and shaking her head.

"Hey, I just told you my secrets. Tell me. Did that fucking asshole ex-boyfriend of yours make you feel small? Where is this coming from?" I asked, studying her.

She settled her head on my chest again, as if looking at me was too much. "No. He wasn't great, but he was fine. I guess I settled when I chose to date him. What you and I have—well, it feels too good to be true, you know?"

"In what way?" I continued to run my fingers through her hair. I wanted to know. Needed to know what I was up against.

"I guess I never thought I deserved to be completely happy."

I slipped my fingers beneath her chin and tipped her face up, forcing her to look at me. "Explain."

She sucked in a long breath, and anxiety rolled off her gorgeous body. "I don't know. I mean, when you enter the world the way I did, you sort of feel cursed. My mother died giving birth to me. Not exactly the best way to make your debut." She chuckled, but it was forced and laced with hurt. "My father lost the love of his life. My brother lost his mother. All for me. I've taken enough already, haven't I? So, I've always just sort of felt like I had something to prove."

A sharp pain settled in my chest. The brutality of the situation was hard to swallow. "None of that was your fault. You didn't take anything. It was a horrible tragedy. That's not on you. What do you have to prove?"

She shrugged as two tears streaked down her cheeks and my chest tightened. "Maybe that I was worth it. Worth my mom giving up her life in exchange for mine. So, I've worked hard at everything from as early as I can remember. I wanted to be the best runner I could be. The best student. The best journalist. But even when I achieve my goals, it still feels—like it's not enough. And sometimes I just feel so tired."

"It's enough, Blue Jay. It's more than enough. You're just finding your way. And your father and brother, yeah, they lost someone special but they both gained *you*. They could never blame you for what happened. And I can speak for Buck because the dude has been my best friend for years. He adores you. Worships you even." I used my thumb to swipe away the liquid beneath her eyes. "I think he and your dad see you as a miracle. The angel that arrived during a dark time. And what about what *you* lost? You grew up without a mother. That couldn't have been easy. No one blames you for what happened—well, aside from yourself maybe. And that's something you need to let go of. That's why it feels like it's never enough when you achieve all of these amazing things."

"Why?" she whispered, looking up at me with big trusting eyes. I swore in that moment that I would spend every day of my life proving to her that she was enough. More than enough.

"Because you're holding on to something that isn't your fault. You need to let that shit go. Accept that you are the light that came out of something dark. And your mom would do it again over and over for you. So, be the best at everything because you're a fucking rock star, not because you think you owe it to anyone." I'd learned a lot about this in therapy after my father died. Ford carried unnecessary guilt and I think we all tried to live up to unattainable expectations that first year. Ford, Harrison, and I dealt with our grief differently, but therapy had been helpful to all three of us. I was thankful my mom had insisted on it.

She nodded. "I can't believe I'm telling you all of this. I've never told anyone these things."

She settled back on my chest and I could feel her body relax against mine. "I like you telling me things."

"Yeah? What else do you want to know?"

"Why don't you want me to tell your brother about us?"

She pushed up to face me again. "Because it will complicate things. He has nothing to do with it. I love Miles, but he's almost too protective. I also don't want to risk hurting your friendship, and if this doesn't end well, he won't forgive you, trust me. And that's not fair to you." She settled back down against my chest, her fingers running softly up and down my arm. "I want this to just be our thing. Just you and me for now. See where it goes. The whole world was in our business when it wasn't real, but now that it's, er, something, I don't want to share it. I want to give it a chance."

"So, you finally agree there's something here, huh?" I teased her and pulled her up so I could taste her sweet mouth.

"I agree there's something, but I don't know what it is. It's foreign to me. It also terrifies me. I don't usually put myself in positions to be hurt," she said, her words breathless and raspy.

"I won't hurt you. I'm afraid you're the one in the position to do all the hurting."

She tilted her head to the side, lips swollen where I'd kissed her hard, and eyes narrowed and questioning. "How do you figure?"

"Because you're the one that keeps trying to fly away, Little Bird."

twenty

. . .

Monroe

I'D SPENT the past six nights at Jack's house. In his bed. He insisted I come to his place because he claimed Pussy liked me better than him—which was definitely true. The cat appeared to favor women over men and was slowly warming up to Jack. We'd publicly fake dated and now we were secretly seeing one another, but I was fairly certain Big Tony and Jack's brothers were aware of what was going on. I just wasn't ready to make it public. I feared once Miles found out, Jack would feel trapped with me, as dumping me would be the end of their friendship, and I didn't want to risk that. I needed to know if this was real without any outside factors adding pressure to either of us.

He still hadn't let me touch him, while he brought me to blissful orgasm night after night, and I was itching to return the favor. I didn't know what we were waiting for. He wanted to prove to me that this was something special, not just some sexual conquest. I knew he cared for me, there was no doubt about it. And I wasn't completely against being his sexual conquest at this point, because I'd never wanted anyone the way I wanted him. Did I think he would lose interest in me shortly after we did the deed? Probably. And I didn't want him sticking around out of obligation, which is why my brother didn't need to know what was going on. I didn't believe in fairy tales or happily ever after. Hell, I'd never seen one that actually worked out.

We'd spent the past few months together, and it was going to hurt like hell when this ended. He'd become a constant in my day—in my life. But nothing lasts forever, and I was the poster child for that slogan.

I stepped off the elevator and Pussy greeted me at the door. The name was horrifying, but the kitty was spectacular. He was an oversized cat, with the heart of a teddy bear. Sort of like his owner. Me and Pussy had a lot in common when it came to trusting others. But once he did, he was as sweet as they came. I scooped him up and craned my neck to see where Jack was.

"Hello?" I called out, looking down to see rose petals on the floor. What the heck. "Montgomery?"

"Follow the trail, Blue Jay," he shouted, and I didn't miss the humor in his voice.

Pink and white petals led a path to the dining room where the table was set, candles were lit, and a pizza box sat in the middle. My heart raced way too fast, and I set Pussy down to take it all in. Jack came around the corner wearing his navy suit pants and a white dress shirt with a few buttons undone sans his tie. His hair was a disheveled mess and he'd never looked sexier.

"What's all this?" I asked, noticing that the trail continued on in another path toward his bedroom.

"First we eat, and then we bathe." He pulled me onto his lap and rested his chin on my shoulder. Cedar and citrus had become my kryptonite, and I closed my eyes and breathed him in.

"Did you say bathe?" My voice rasped as he reached over and opened the pizza box.

"You heard me. Tonight, I thought we'd try taking our first bath together."

My head fell back in laughter. "What? Why in the world would we do that?"

He reached up, placing his thumb and forefinger on each side of my jaw and turned me to face him. "I want to do everything together. This is how I'm going to show you that I'm all in."

I could feel the heat rushing up my neck and across my cheeks. The thought of bathing with him was just—too much. I'd yet to even see the man naked. He'd seen me naked more times than I could count, but I hadn't been gifted the same in return.

"I've never bathed with anyone," I announced, before taking a bite of the best Margherita pizza I'd ever had. I groaned and savored the flavors as they exploded on my tongue.

"No groaning, please. The big guy, and I say that modestly because as you're going to see tonight, he's quite the sight. But he's sensitive these days and when you groan and you're sitting on him, well, it's just cruel, Blue Jay."

I laughed and turned to press my lips to his. I couldn't help myself. He was quite possibly the most lovable person I'd ever known. Jack Montgomery was the rainbow after a storm, the sunshine on a gray day, and the rain when you were in a life-threatening drought. He was an endless overflowing cup of sexy, beautiful man.

"Sorry about that." I turned to take another bite as I felt his impossible to miss erection poking me in my backside.

"I've never bathed with anyone either. So, these are all firsts that we will get out of the way, before you know…"

"What?"

"Before you trust me enough to let me rock your world completely."

"I've already given my full consent. I'm all in. You're the one who keeps saying no, which is slightly embarrassing since you have the reputation of a manwhore, and I'm rather inexperienced, yet I'm the one doing a hard-press to get you in the sack?"

His entire body shook with laughter now, which left me no option but to do the same. "Patience, Little Bird. I'm holding out because I want you to date me, not use me for my gorgeous fucking body, although I get it, I do. You aren't the first to want this, but I think you just might be the last one I give it to. So, I'm taking my time."

His words floated in the air around us, and my breath caught in my throat. Was he serious? Was this just part of his shtick? He didn't need any with me, as I'd already thrown myself at the man. Why would he say that? Did he mean it? Was he just being Jack the never-ending flirt and he knew those words would hit me hard? I tried to keep my face straight and not react.

He ate his pizza as if he hadn't just dropped a bomb on the room. The man just said what he thought. He didn't overanalyze or care how it sounded, and I loved that about him. But it also terrified me.

"Okay. Sounds fair."

"Good. Tell me about your day. You worked late."

"Well, I finished the article about how many dates there should be before you take your partner home for Thanksgiving," I said with a laugh. Thanksgiving was next week, and it was the only thing I could come up with to send to press this week.

"How many dates does it take?"

"I asked several people, and everyone seemed to think that somewhere between five and ten dates, depending on the connection with the other person, was acceptable." I chewed on the crust and glanced over my shoulder to see him watching me.

"Well, we've had at least a hundred dates if you count the fake dating time, not to mention I've known you for years." He reached for another slice.

"What are you talking about, Montgomery?"

"What are you doing for Thanksgiving?" he asked, and if I wasn't crazy, he appeared nervous.

"Um, well, my dad and Thelma are going to the Bahamas this year, and Miles is going to be in New York with that new girl, Sierra, that he met. They are going to spend the weekend in the city and see a few shows, do some holiday shopping, and eat at all his favorite restaurants." I laughed, because this is what he told me when he tried to sell me on joining them. "He invited me, but I'm not feeling the whole third wheel thing. I'll probably go to Becks' mom's house. I've done that the past few years."

"Not this year."

I finished chewing and narrowed my gaze to study him. "Why? I have fun there."

"You're coming to our home in Lake Tahoe. My mom really likes you and we do this big ole Thanksgiving, and the twins will be there. Come on. It'll be fun."

I admired how much time Jack spent with his nieces. He went over to their place every single day after work because he was convinced that they would forget him if they didn't see him daily. It was ridiculously sweet.

"We're keeping this a secret, and what if it's over by then?" I teased, but the words gave me a sick feeling in my stomach.

He rolled his eyes. "My family knows because *we* don't keep secrets. They're also protective and they understand why we are keeping it private for now, so they won't say a word. Hell, both my sisters-in-law are giving me tips on how to win you over, hence the goddamn rose petal map through my apartment, and the fat, mean cat that I now have to keep forever."

I smiled. He sure was putting in a lot of effort. "Okay," I said, biting down on my bottom lip as butterflies swarmed my belly. "I'll go with you. You do happen to have the coolest family I've ever met."

"The apple doesn't fall far." He wriggled his brows before reaching for his beer and taking a long pull. "What else were you working on so late? I highly doubt taking a date home for the holidays took you that long."

I thought about it. Jack was my boss who I was also secretly dating, and I knew him well enough to know that he wouldn't like what I was about to tell him. But it was inevitable and if I didn't tell him now, he'd find out tomorrow from Dan Arbor, which could potentially piss him off.

"I met with Dan about a story for my column."

"The Reynolds story is long over. What are you talking about?" He set down his beer and turned me to face him while I sat perfectly still on his lap.

"I got a lead on a story about Melissa Labrith and her shady husband. But I did what you recommended, and I shared the information with Dan."

His shoulders stiffened. "Governor Labrith? No. Let Dan dig into it."

I rolled my eyes. "No. I write an anonymous column, in case you forgot, and it's my lead. Her strait-laced husband is not who he seems to be, and I think there is trouble in paradise. His son hates him, and he throws these parties that are super sketchy. I'm talking drugs and sex, Montgomery. At least that's what we think. It's like a big ole orgy at the mansion. And our fair governor is not happy about it, but being an election year, she's sort of trapped."

"Who cares? It doesn't involve you." His voice was hard, and he showed no humor.

"What?" I pulled back, completely appalled by his words. "Well if that's true, then who cares how long one should date someone before bringing their significant other home for Thanksgiving? Who cares about the best hot spots in the city to meet eligible singles? *I don't*. But it's the news. I'm a journalist, and you own a damn newspaper. How can you even ask me that?"

"Do you know what Governor Labrith's maiden name is? Do you know who her largest donor was?"

"I do. So, what." Governor Labrith's father, Joseph Capetti, was a real estate mogul rumored to be involved in organized crime. He was a wealthy and powerful man, no doubt about it. Everyone who'd run against his daughter for governor mysteriously dropped out of the race and she ran unopposed. I knew why they bowed out and everyone else knew why as well. But the man covered his tracks like a pro. It appeared Governor Labrith's husband was fairly sly in his ways as well as I'd never heard one rumbling about the Labriths before now, but if something was there, I was damn well going to find out.

He pushed me to my feet as he stood, and his hands settled on his hips. "*So what?* Are you fucking crazy? She's off-limits, and you don't have permission to run with this story, do you hear me? Not happening. Conversation closed."

"You have got to be kidding me, you misogynistic, arrogant ass. You aren't the boss of me," I snarled as I shook my head.

"Technically I am. *I'm your boss*, whether you like it or not. And you aren't writing this story."

My mouth gaped open. Was he for real? "It's anonymous. No one will know it's me. And you can't tell me what to do."

"I can and I will. You aren't writing this story." His face was hard and there was no sign of wavering.

I stormed across the room and grabbed my purse making my way to the elevator. Two big arms wrapped around me, and his chin rested on top of my head. "Don't leave. Take a bath with me."

"Take a bath with you? I'm not some kept woman who you can tell what to do and then demand I bathe with you. That's not how this works."

He turned me in his arms and covered my mouth with his, lifting me off my feet as my legs wrapped around his waist and my body gave in to the desire I could no longer control. He pressed me up against a wall before pulling away. "We have to be able to separate work from our personal life."

"You can't tell me what to do," I said, my breaths coming hard and fast.

"What if we meet with Dan and Ford tomorrow and come up with a solution." His hands slipped beneath my blouse and his thumbs traced back and forth over my nipples that were now hard enough to cut glass.

My body was the ultimate traitor.

"What kind of plan?" I whispered against his mouth, wanting him to kiss me again even though I hated him at the moment.

"Maybe you can do the research and Dan will break the story. I don't want anyone to trace this back to you." He nipped at my bottom lip, and the ache between my thighs throbbed with need.

"You aren't playing fair."

"When it comes to keeping you safe, Little Bird, I'll never play fair," he said before covering my mouth with his and walking us toward his bedroom.

He set me down on the edge of the tub and leaned down to turn on the water. The bathroom was massive, with windows overlooking the city, white marble floors and gray cabinets. It was modern and sleek, very much like the man who lived here.

"We aren't done talking about this," I huffed, crossing my arms over my chest.

"We are for tonight." He unbuttoned the rest of his shirt and shrugged it off, tossing it on the floor.

"Says who?" I stood and made my way over to him. I'd be damned if he thought he could tell me what to do. I ran my fingers over the defined lines of his abs and cursed myself for being so weak when it came to this man.

"*Me.* Take your clothes off, Blue Jay." He reached for his waistband, and I studied his muscled chest, noticing the enormous erection tenting his pants. My mouth watered and I stood there gaping like a fool before I gathered myself.

"Why?"

He dropped his pants and his briefs slid down his legs at the same time and—oh my. I'd never seen a more beautiful man in my life. I'd personally never been a huge fan of the *penis.* Thyme's wasn't overly impressive, and I found it rather ugly. But this. This was something people painted and sculpted and dreamed about.

"Because I want to take a bath with you," he said, his voice gruff and sexy as his whiskey eyes bore into me.

I couldn't resist him. No matter how angry I was.

I tugged my shirt over my head and let my skirt fall to my ankles.

"Okay, let's take a bath."

He looked me up and down like he was trying to memorize every inch of me before he reached for my hand and led me to the tub. He stepped in first, pulling me in to settle between his legs. But there was a giant elephant in the room, which was currently poking me in the back, causing me to break out in laughter.

Yes, I was still mad at him for thinking he could tell me what to do.

Yes, we would continue this conversation tomorrow.

No, I couldn't walk away right now even if I wanted to.

Which I didn't.

"What's so funny, Little Bird?"

I rolled over on my stomach, resting my arms on his chest before allowing my hand to drift down below his waist and stroke him.

"Nothing's funny, Montgomery."

His jaw clenched, and I could tell that he was desperately trying to compose himself. "You like what you see?" He leaned back, both arms resting on the side of the tub as he closed his eyes and allowed me to touch him for the first time.

"I do. I like everything I see," I rasped. My hand moved up and down his length slowly, enjoying every moment.

"Tell me we can date, out in the open, and tell your brother—and this is all yours. I'm yours." He sucked in a long breath as I moved my hand faster.

"It's too soon."

His eyes opened, and he wrapped his hand over mine beneath the water and guided me to stroke him one last time before pulling my hand away.

"Then you'll have to wait, Blue Jay." And he covered my mouth with his, and it was the most erotic thing I'd ever experienced. Making out with this beautiful man in the bathtub. The closer I got to him the harder it would be when he walked away.

And he would.

Because nothing good lasts forever.

twenty-one

. . .

Jack

"EARMUFF THOSE BABIES, PLEASE," I said, as Harley held Everly and Laney Mae had Penelope propped on her lap. They both burst out in laughter.

"They don't know what you're saying, Jack-ass. They're babies." Laney Mae rolled her eyes, but when she could tell I wasn't kidding, she covered both of little P's ears with her hands. I stared at Harley before she did the same to Everly.

"Is there something a doctor can do for a wicked case of blue balls? I'm dying here, ladies," I said as we sat at a round table in the bakery.

They both continued to laugh hysterically before removing their hands from my nieces' ears.

"For god's sake, you're ridiculous. It's a couple of weeks. Man up," Harley said as she tried to compose herself.

"The best things in life never come easy. You like her, right? You really like her? So, stay the course." Laney Mae hoisted baby P over her shoulder and rubbed her back.

"If you count the fake dating part of our relationship, it's been months, not weeks. So, yeah, I've gone a long time. I'm a... sexual man. I don't even remember what I'm holding out for. She spends every night in my goddamned bed and you two have me brainwashed that I can't sleep with her." I pushed to my feet and paced around the dining space as I ran my hands through my hair.

"We didn't say you couldn't sleep with her, we said that you need to make sure she knows this is more than sex. She has her guard up with you, and it's fair. You're a well-known playboy," Harley said.

"You've slept with half the city, Jack-ass, and she knows that. She needs to believe this is real. That's why she won't tell her brother, because she probably thinks the minute you sleep with her that you'll dump her." Laney Mae chuckled when Penelope let out a loud burp.

"Well, then maybe I need to sleep with her and show her I'm not going anywhere. I mean, I've given her no reason to doubt me. And I hate lying to Buck. He calls me every fucking morning and I'm lying to the dude. He's like a brother to me, for fuck's sake. Oh Jesus. I'm sorry," I said, leaning forward and kissing the top of each baby's head.

"They don't understand it now, but they will soon, so you'll need to clean up your language. And try to get your brother to do the same while you're at it," Harley said, fighting back the smile on her pretty face.

"I will. I promise." I reached for Everly and pulled her to my chest. These little angels had a way of calming me and I fucking loved it. "And she agreed to come to Thanksgiving, so that's progress."

"That's a huge step. You're moving in the right direction. Let her take the lead. If she wants to take things to the next level, I think it's fine. She knows you're all in at this point. I mean, who invites someone to Thanksgiving that just wants sex?" Laney Mae said, winking at me. "Proud of you, Jack-ass."

"Yeah. It hasn't been easy. But she's worth it. All right, I need to get to work." I pushed to my feet and handed Harley the baby before kissing the tops of four beautiful heads. "I'd be lost without you."

"Love you," they both called out, as I pushed through the door.

Monroe had come to the office early to get some work done. I knew she was going to fight me on this Melissa Labrith bullshit. It was not surprising that there was a story there, but it wasn't one I wanted her to tell. Not by a fucking long shot. And she'd see how serious I was when we met this morning. I was pissed at Dan for even considering this knowing that it would be dangerous.

I made my way upstairs, popping the last of my donut in my mouth. Harley came in on the weekends and early mornings to bake and Laney Mae would come watch the girls for her so she could get things accomplished. She never left them with anyone who wasn't family and I fucking loved that Everly and Penelope were growing up surrounded by all this Montgomery love.

"Ford, Monroe, and Dan just headed over to the conference room. They asked me to have you meet them there," my assistant Sam said.

"Thanks. Here you go." I dropped a bag with a few treats on her desk.

"Have I told you that you're my favorite boss yet?" she said.

"Yeah, I overheard you saying that to Ford yesterday, you traitor." I smirked as I made my way down the hallway.

I pushed the conference room door open as a frown formed on my face, the minute I set my sights on Dan. But then my gaze locked with Monroe's and my lips turned up in the corner. Couldn't help it. My girl had a way of doing that to me. Blue Jay was the sunshine in a shit-storm. Hell, I missed her, and I'd woken up in bed with her only a few hours ago. I loved waking up with her sprawled across my body. Lavender and honey had become my favorite scent.

My weakness.

Hell, *she* was my weakness.

"Hey, we just wanted to have a quick meeting to discuss how to handle the Governor Labrith story," Ford said as I dropped in the seat beside my brother and across from Dan and Monroe.

"I'll tell you how we're going to handle it. We're going to kill the story. Who gives a fuck if her husband is into kinky shit or if their marriage is in the shitter? Not worth the heat on this one." I folded my arms over my chest and glared at Dan.

Dan Arbor had worked for us long before I came on board. He'd worked here when my father ran the newsroom. He was a good guy, a brilliant journalist, and I'd call him a friend. But allowing Monroe to step in the lion's den did not sit well with me, and I was sure as hell going to make sure he knew it.

"Who gives a shit? Um, the people of our great city, that's who," Monroe said, straightening her shoulders as her mouth morphed into a solid line and she stared at me hard. Those indigo blues could turn icy on a moment's notice. She was gearing up for a fight.

Buckle up, girl. I'm not going to back down on this one.

"I don't care. *You* are not running with this story. Don't we pay you the big bucks to cover the heavy shit, Dan? You're going to allow a newbie to run with a story like this? Really?" I hissed, and Dan's face startled.

"I, well, er, I didn't think it was a problem." Dan turned to look between Ford and me with surprise. He tugged at the collar of his light blue dress shirt—a habit I'd noticed over the years whenever he was uncomfortable. "She writes an anonymous column and I figured this would be a story we'd want to keep anonymous. It's more of a personal story, as it's regarding the governor's husband and not her. But most importantly, Monroe actually found the lead on this one and I thought it would be a good one to cut her teeth on."

Ford glanced over at me with a questioning gaze. He leaned forward in the black leather chair and folded his hands to form a teepee on the table. "That makes perfect sense. What is the problem with Monroe digging into this a little bit?"

"What's the problem? I'll tell you what the fucking problem is. Let's start with Joseph Capetti being Melissa Labrith's father. Come on, you both know better. She shouldn't be involved in this shit." My hand came down hard on the table and everyone jumped. The walls in the conference room were surrounded by floor-to-ceiling glass, and a few people out in the hallway turned and stared from the other side of the glass.

"Excuse me, but *she* is sitting right here. Don't act like I'm not part of this conversation. And why the hell should I not be involved in this? I'm a reporter, for god's sake." Monroe pushed to her feet with her hands braced on the table as she spewed her angry words at me. She wore a cream dress that hugged her curves in all the right places, and I couldn't help but stare at her perky tits as they pressed against the fabric.

Focus.

"Listen, I'm not sure what's going on here and I apologize if I made a bad call. She came to me with the story and I was impressed. She's, I mean, Monroe, you're hungry and I respect that. I didn't think Joseph Capetti would be part of the story as this is about Professor Labrith, but you're right, Jack, it's something to consider. He's going to protect his daughter at all costs." Dan glanced over at Monroe and she dropped back down in her seat.

"Melissa Labrith is estranged from her father. That's public knowledge. This has nothing to do with him. We aren't digging into organized crime here. It's a personal piece about a politician's husband. You're being dramatic." She raised a brow with pursed lips.

Ford chuckled to my right and I turned and stared hard at him before he pulled his shit together and straightened his face.

"Estranged my ass. Every fucking candidate who ran against her backed out. He was her largest donor. You don't find that interesting being the reporter that you are?" I clenched my jaw as I tried to calm myself.

"Sure, he keeps an eye on her. It doesn't mean he can protect her from a story breaking. He can't. It's news. That's the way this works," she said, her tongue dipping out to wet her bottom lip and it took all the restraint I had not to pull her on my lap and taste her sweet mouth. Hell, I was pissed at her, but I still wanted her. What the fuck was this girl doing to me?

"You couldn't be more wrong, Blue Jay. He *can* protect her from whatever the hell he chooses. *And he will.* And you're foolish if you don't believe that." I sat back in my seat and closed my eyes for a minute to tamper down the anger brewing. What the hell were they thinking even considering letting her do this?

"Oh, I'm foolish now because I don't agree with you?" she hissed.

"You're foolish for thinking one of the most powerful men in the city, who happens to be linked to organized crime, can't shut you the hell up. And shame on both of you for allowing it to get this far." I pointed my finger at Ford and Dan.

"Oh my god. So, we just kill the story because her dad is powerful?" Monroe shouted, begging me with those indigo blues to see her point.

"Yes." I shrugged. It wasn't fucking worth it.

There was a light knock on the glass and our assistant Sam stood on the other side. I waved for her to come in and she let us know that our next meeting was running late. She smiled at me because Sam knew me. She knew when I was losing my cool, and I was definitely losing my cool. I nodded, and she stepped out of the room.

"Okay, listen. I hear what you're saying, brother, but we do report the news, and Monroe was brought on as a reporter. She found this lead on her own. Her column is anonymous. No one will know who writes it, so anyone that doesn't like it will come after us, not her."

"You think it's that difficult to figure it out? Come on, you're smarter than that, Ford."

"I think we look into it. We don't make any decisions yet if we'll run with anything. For all we know, it's just bullshit. This is very secondhand information, from the girlfriend of her son, and it could all lead nowhere. Monroe wants to find a way into the party undercover and just see what she can find out. The next event we know of isn't until New Year's Eve. A lot can happen between now and then, and the whole thing may blow up. If we get that far and we can get her in, we'll have people in place to protect her. We'd be parked outside nearby, and she'll just be an observer," my older brother said, looking between me and Monroe.

Asshole.

I nodded. "All right, then I'll go too. Hell, Victoria will score an invite to this ridiculous shindig. I'll have her take me as her date."

Monroe's hands came down hard on the table. She pushed to her feet again and glared at me. "I do not need a babysitter. This is just an excuse for you to take some ho-bag to a party."

Ah… she sure as shit wanted to keep our relationship a secret, but she didn't like the idea of me being seen with another woman.

Good. Maybe jealousy would knock some fucking sense into her.

Ford and Dan chuckled before righting themselves. These two assholes thought this was funny, but this was not a fucking joke to me.

"So, I have a source on the inside. We may be able to get her in through the catering company that the Labriths use. Apparently, these types of events have you sign a nondisclosure statement, so we'd have to maneuver around a lot of different factors, but I'm working on it. It's still a ways away so we can't do much as of now. But you can't attend,

Laura Pavlov

Jack. It's a private after-party that is handpicked for obvious reasons. You'll never get an invite to that event, as you own the largest newspaper in the city. They won't do anything with you there, and you know it," Dan said, giving me an apologetic shrug.

He was fucking right, but that wouldn't stop me from being there.

"They don't know *me*. I can go in undercover and just see if there's anything there. Unfortunately, your face is too known, *playboy*." Monroe refused to meet my gaze now.

"Let's all remain calm. Come on, how often do these things blow up before we even get there? It might not even happen. For all we know, this is a rumor," Ford said.

I pushed to my feet. I wasn't happy. But it was three against one, and I wasn't getting anywhere with them. I'd sure as shit find a way to be at that party, and they'd all have to deal with it.

I stalked out the door without saying a word and made my way to my office, slamming the door behind me and pacing the room. The door swung open and Sabrina waltzed in and shut the door behind her. Could this day get any fucking worse?

"Hey, boss," she purred as she walked over to me and rubbed her body against mine. "It sounds like you're having a tough day and I thought maybe I could help."

I gripped her shoulders and pushed her back. This wasn't the first time I'd turned down her advances, and it was grating my nerves. "Are you kidding me with this shit? You need to leave."

My door swung open again, and Monroe stood there slack-jawed. "Oh. This looks cozy," she spat. "We need to discuss what just happened in the conference room. If you can spare a minute for a work meeting." Her arms crossed over her chest and she narrowed her gaze at me.

"She was just leaving." I rubbed my temples as Sabrina made her way out of my office and I slammed the door behind her.

"What the hell was that?" Monroe huffed, placing her hands on her hips.

"That was fucking nothing."

"It didn't look like nothing. This is why I can't trust you," she hissed.

"No. You don't get to play that card." I stepped into her space, pressing her back up against the wall. "She thinks I'm fucking single. Whose fault is that? I've made it clear I'm not interested in her multiple times."

"Fine. If you say so," she snarled. "What the hell was that back in the conference room?"

"That was me trying to talk some fucking sense into you." I placed a hand on each side of her face. The girl was driving me crazy.

"By taking some skank to a party. This is your idea of proving to me that you want something with me? Then I walk in the office and find Sabrina grinding up against you."

Ah… she was more pissed about Victoria and Sabrina than me interfering with the story.

"I assure you there was no grinding. She took her shot and she missed. I asked her to leave. And I'm not letting you go in alone to that fucking party, and I sure as shit can't take you as my date if you're undercover. So, I'll be there. One way or another. And you know that I'm not interested in anyone but you." My nose rubbed against hers. Our breaths were labored as desire lingered whenever we were together.

"Who's Victoria?"

"Some chick I used to see. No one important. But she's a socialite and she's on every guest list in town. I'm sure she can get me in the door."

"So, you're going on a date with someone else?" She pushed my chest back and glared.

"I'm trying to keep you fucking safe. You're playing with fire, and I won't have it. I don't give a shit about Victoria and I'll make sure she knows it. But I'll be at that party keeping an eye on you."

"I don't need you to be there." Her gaze softened, and she tugged me close.

"I don't care. I'll be there."

"Why?" The word came out breathy, and her gaze searched mine.

"Because I'm fucking crazy about you. And I don't give a shit who knows it. Hell, I want it out there. And I want your fucking brother to know the truth. I want everyone at the office to know the truth. I'm tired of hiding. It's not my style and you're making this more difficult than it has to be." I ran a hand through her silky hair, settling my fingers at the nape of her neck. Her chest rising and falling in response.

"I think Dan is a little confused by that show you just put on in there. I mean, he thinks we broke up."

"I don't give a shit. I'm pissed at him," I said, waiting for her to respond to the rest of what I'd said.

"You know why I don't want to involve Miles right now. Nor do we need all the people in the office in our business. Why can't this be something that's just for us?"

I rested my forehead against hers. "What do you want from me, Little Bird? What's it going to take for you to believe I'm all in?"

Her fingers traced the scruff on my jaw, and she looked up at me. "I only want you. That's it."

I covered her mouth with mine. Hungry and needy. I was done holding back. Done following rules that made no sense. If she wanted this just between us, so be it. I just wanted her.

Only her.

"Let's go," I said, pulling away abruptly and tracing her swollen lip with the pad of my thumb.

"What? Where are we going?" Her words were raspy.

"You want me. I want you. What the fuck are we waiting for?" I said, picking up my office phone to let Sam know to cancel my morning meetings.

"We're leaving?" she whispered.

"I asked you what you wanted and I'm giving it to you. I'm done torturing myself, and you."

Her eyes were big as saucers as she wrung her hands and shifted on her feet. "What changed?"

"Nothing. Just done waiting. You either trust me or you don't, Blue Jay. So, I'm going to show you." I pulled her flush against my body.

"Show me what?"

"That I'm all in when it comes to you," I said, grazing my lips against her ear as I spoke.

"What are you waiting for?" she whispered.

She insisted on leaving the office first so it wouldn't look obvious.

But after the way I'd lost my shit this morning in the conference room, I highly doubted Dan wasn't aware something was going on. Sam winked as I walked by, so I figured she was on to us as well. Obviously, my brother knew. So, Monroe could keep this little game going as long as she wanted, but I was done holding back.

Hell, I was just getting started.

twenty-two

. . .

Monroe

BIG TONY WAS WAITING at the curb when we stepped outside, and he drove us to Jack's place. Panic flooded through me. This man had touched me more times than I could count, but he'd never let me touch him aside from the teaser last night. He'd never let us take things further *together*. And now it was happening. In the middle of a workday. *This was so not me.* But I couldn't get past the thrill coursing through my veins. The anticipation had me buzzing.

I pushed away my concern about finding Sabrina in his office. She certainly was persistent, I'd give her that. And Victoria—who the hell knew what was going on there. I needed to tread with caution. Jack wanted to go all in, but how could I?

He reached for my hand and tugged me closer. "Don't overthink it, Blue Jay."

I raised my brows and tilted my head toward the driver's seat, reminding him that Big Tony sat just a few feet away. I wasn't about to discuss this with him in the car.

"I'm fairly certain Big T thinks we've been sleeping together this whole time." He grazed his lips against my ear, and I squeezed my thighs together to control myself.

Jesus. This was not okay.

I looked up to meet his gaze and chuckled, before holding my finger to my lips, desperate for him to stop talking about it in the car.

He leaned forward and nipped at my finger, pulling it between his lips and sucking on it before letting it go. "So sweet. Every inch of you."

"Oh my god," I whispered before we stepped out of the car and made our way to the private elevator.

Once the doors closed, he was on me. He pressed my back against the wall and kissed me hard. My breaths came hard and fast, and I melted against him. I'd wanted him for so long I couldn't think straight now that it was actually happening.

The doors opened and we stumbled into his apartment. "Sarah," he called out and she hurried out to greet us.

He wrapped his arms around my middle, his chest to my back, and I patted my hair in place and said hello to the sweet woman who probably thought we looked insane. We were both panting, and I was fairly certain my blouse was unbuttoned, but too nervous to look down at the moment.

"Well, hello," she said, using her hand to cover her smile. "What can I do for you?"

"Take the rest of the day off, paid, of course. Go see a movie, grab some lunch, treat yourself." He handed her what looked like a wad of cash.

She chuckled. "You got it. I'll see you tomorrow."

As soon as the door shut, he turned me in his arms, lifting me off my feet. My legs came around his waist and I tangled my fingers in his hair. "I can't believe we left work. What if we get in trouble?"

"I'm your boss. You won't get in trouble. We both work too damn hard anyway," he said before his mouth came over mine and he carried me to his bedroom. I'd slept in this bed a dozen times, but now I was nervous. I didn't know why.

He set me down on the bed like I was a precious piece of china. "I've waited a long time for you."

"Right back at you, Montgomery." My words were so breathy and needy, that my cheeks heated in response.

"Tell me what you want." He stood at the foot of the bed, hovering over me.

"I want you. All of you. No more holding back."

Well, so much for being cautious. I'd lost control of myself. Something about this man pushed me past boundaries I'd never crossed. Jack Montgomery was a bulldozer, knocking down walls and barriers since the day I'd met him.

"No more holding back." He licked his lips, and I could no longer wait. I sat forward and reached for his belt, tugging at his dress pants, and yanking them down. He didn't stop me this time.

"Someone's anxious." He laughed as he stood there, letting me take the lead.

I reached for his dress shirt, unbuttoning each button, and he tugged it off, tossing it to the floor. He stood there, completely naked, and I couldn't look away. He was so beautiful. Sculpted muscles, tan skin, tall and lean. Sure, I'd seen him before. We'd bathed together. I'd slept naked in his arms. Yet, it was like the earth was shifting beneath us. We were taking this to the next level. And I was so ready. Ready for everything that came with it. If it bit me in the ass, so be it. It would still be worth it. I couldn't stop this freight train if I wanted to.

He leaned down and unzipped my dress before pulling me to my feet. "Too many clothes. I want you naked. Now."

I giggled as my dress puddled at my feet. He had my bra and panties off in seconds. I stepped back until the backs of my knees hit the bed, and I fell onto the mattress. He propped himself above me.

"You sure you're ready for this?" he asked, his voice gruff.

"I'm positive. Condom?"

He chuckled. His lips pressed to my neck. "Slow down there, baby. I've never waited so long for someone. I'm going to take my time."

I laughed. "You've been touching me for weeks."

"But I didn't know it was going to end with me buried inside you. That changes everything." Oh my god. This was happening. His lips moved down my neck, tasting and torturing every inch of me.

He buried his face between my thighs, and I was lost in this man. I writhed beneath him. Needing more. Needing everything. The orgasm so powerful, I screamed out his name as tears streaked down my face.

He moved up and propped himself above me, swiping at the liquid running down my cheek.

"You okay, Little Bird?"

"Yes," I said, surprised as my voice cracked and my words broke on a sob. "This is just—intense."

"What is?"

"These feelings that I have for you. I haven't had them before. It's foreign to me," I admitted before he pulled me on his chest and wrapped his arms around me.

"It's new for me too, baby."

I swiped at my face and wiped away the last of the tears. "Well, this is sexy, huh? I'm blubbering about my feelings before we even have sex."

"It's the sexiest thing I've ever seen." His voice was raw. Honest. "Telling me you feel the same way I do. It was worth the wait."

He kissed me hard, and I reached down between us, gripping his throbbing erection. "No more waiting."

He flipped me on my back and reached over to his nightstand and grabbed a condom. He pushed up to sit on his heels while he covered himself. I watched in absolute amazement. This big, beautiful man wanted me as much as I wanted him. I'd never wanted anyone like this. Never felt anything close to what I felt for Jack.

I tried to push those thoughts away. My instinct was to run—to protect my heart because feeling this way was terrifying. But I wasn't going anywhere. I was going to enjoy every moment, for as long as he stuck around.

He chuckled as he leaned forward, settling between my legs. He moved slowly, as if he were savoring every moment, as he filled me, inch by glorious inch.

"Fucking perfect, Blue Jay." His eyes were closed, and he groaned his words.

I gripped the sheets in my fists as I savored the most erotic feeling of my life. It was both pleasure and pain. Too much and not enough. And I wanted more. I wanted everything.

He moved slowly, allowing my body to adjust to his size. The pain dissipated as we started to move in sync, and oh my god—nothing had ever felt so good.

"Jesus, baby. You were made for me," he said, rolling us over so that he was on his back and I was on top.

His hands gripped my hips as he guided me at first, before I took control. The feeling so overwhelming, my body moved of its own volition. Faster and faster. His hands found mine and our fingers intertwined as I rode him into oblivion.

I yelled out my release, and he went right over the edge along with me, calling out my name as my body fell limp on top of him.

"Holy shit," he grumbled against my neck.

I couldn't speak as I lay on top of him gasping for air. He wrapped his arms around me and held me tight.

Once I came down to Earth, he tipped me on my back and pulled out slowly, tugging the condom off and walking to the bathroom to dispose of it. He came back to bed and pulled me on his chest once again.

"You okay?"

"I'm great." I pushed up to meet his whiskey-colored gaze. "You?"

"Never fucking better."

My head fell back in laughter. A part of me had worried that maybe I wouldn't be enough for him. He was more experienced than me, no doubt about it, but we just fit. In and out of the bedroom. And maybe that was the most surprising thing about it.

"What are you thinking?" I asked as he studied me intently.

"That I want to do that again."

I chuckled, reaching for the clasp on my locket and setting it on his nightstand. "Well, you are the boss. So, if you think we've got time, who am I to argue?"

With those words, he tipped me on my back and buried his face in my neck. I arched into him, needing him in a way I couldn't put into words.

I should be terrified. But the only thing I felt was—happy.

———

"Hey, Dad," I said as he stood and pulled out a chair for me. My father and I met every other Friday for lunch. Just the two of us. Even when I was in college, he'd meet me near campus. It was the only time I got to see him without Thelma because she had a standing nail appointment every Friday.

Praise the Lord for small miracles.

Miles was meeting us today as he was in town for a meeting.

"Hi, sweetheart. You look good, kiddo." He kissed my cheek before pushing my chair in. "Miles is running late, so he sent me his order because I know you need to get back to work."

The popular restaurant buzzed with chatter and laughter. Servers hurried from table to table, but we were seated in the back corner per my father's request, so it was a bit quieter here. A few people gaped at him when we first walked in. I was used to it. He handled it with such grace, taking his time to greet people and sign autographs when they requested it. But sitting in the back definitely meant that we could have a conversation without being disrupted.

"Thanks," I said, shaking off the thought of the kiss Jack had sent me off with. It had been a few days since the first time we'd had sex, and to say we'd been making up for lost time was an understatement. I was floating on a cloud twenty-four hours a day. I'd never felt like this.

"What's going on with you? You look different," my father said before we paused to place our order.

"Just happy, I guess. Work's going great."

"Good, honey. You know your mom would be so proud of you if she could see you now."

His words took my breath away. We didn't speak about my mother often. It just seemed to make everyone sad, so it was always the elephant in the room. The topic we avoided.

"Thank you. That means a lot to me."

"She was driven, just like you. So damn focused. You get your work ethic from her. You know me and Miles prefer to enjoy life a bit more." He laughed and I sipped my iced tea as I watched him. His face lit up when he spoke about my mom.

"Tell me about how you met her. We've never talked about it. I mean, I know you met her in college, but I don't know the details."

He nodded. "Have I never told you this?" I shook my head no and he continued. "Well okay, your mom was something. The most beautiful girl I'd ever seen. Still is today, aside from you." He winked. "You're the spitting image of her. Catches me by surprise sometimes. And she wanted nothing to do with me. I had a bit of a reputation on campus, you know, I thought I was hot shit back then."

My parents had both attended UCLA and my father was the star quarterback. My brother attended the rival school and played for USC and they loved to razz one another about it.

"Go on." I giggled. I loved hearing this.

"I wore her down, because I swear to God, from the moment I laid eyes on her, I didn't want anyone else. It was always her. She was apprehensive, but over time she came to trust me. I had to show her I was serious, but it eventually happened. And that was it for me. *She was it for me.*"

I nodded. It was sweet to hear him talk about her. He dated such different women since she passed that it confused me. "You haven't felt that way about your other, er, wives?"

His head tipped back, and he chuckled. "No, sweetheart. I think there are different types of love. She was my one great love. My soulmate. I never believed in that shit before your mom. She gave me you and Miles, which kept me going after I lost her. And sure, I'm not a man who likes to be alone, so I've found partners that are with me for the same reasons I'm with them."

I tilted my head to look at him. "Which is?"

"Companionship. That's all I'm really looking for these days. Until I'm reunited with your mother."

My jaw fell open. He'd never been so open. How had we never discussed this?

"Wow. I had no idea. I always wondered why you dated the women that you did, to be honest." I shrugged. "I mean, the way you described Mom made her sound so—different."

"There's no replacing the other half of your heart, honey. That's why I didn't care much for that herb kid you dated all those years. There was nothing there. I want you to have what I shared with your mother. You'll know it when you find it."

My stomach dipped at his words.

"How did you know she was the one?"

"Because I missed her when we were apart for just minutes. She made me a better man. Loved me more than I loved myself. I couldn't get enough of her, even after all the years we'd been together. I'm guessing you didn't feel any of that with what's-his-face." He laughed and I rolled my eyes.

"No. I think I settled with Thyme. He was safe because our feelings didn't run all that deep. I figured he couldn't hurt me, although I learned that even if it wasn't an amazing relationship it still hurt to be cheated on. But I'm not much of a dater, so I think I just liked having someone to call my significant other, even if it wasn't magical. It was easy."

"Well, of course it hurt, sweetheart. Betrayal by anyone is painful. But it didn't gut you—it hurt your ego. That's different. You'll know when it's special because you'll be questioning the way you feel every single step of the way. It'll be foreign and scary but wonderful at the same time. Trust me. You'll find it." He just summed up my feelings for Jack in a nutshell. My heart raced at the thought. I didn't want to go there, allow myself to think I could have those things with him, and end up disappointed. As if he could read my thoughts, he continued. "Whatever happened with Jack Montgomery? I've always liked him. Thelma told me you two broke up?"

I didn't want to lie to my father. I'd already allowed him to think the relationship was real when it was fake, and now I didn't know what it was. And it terrified me.

"Sorry I'm late. Did you order?" Miles interrupted and I was grateful.

"Hey," Dad and I said in unison.

Miles patted Dad on the shoulder and kissed the top of my head before taking his seat.

"What did I miss? Catch me up." Miles reached for a roll from the bread-basket, and chugged half of his beer while he waited for a response.

Dad chuckled. "Guess someone's hungry. Well, we were actually just chatting about your mom."

Miles narrowed his gaze. "Good. We don't talk about her enough."

"And I was telling Monroe that her ridiculous ex wasn't good enough for her," Dad said, with a wink as the waiter set our plates down.

"Herb boy? Couldn't stand the dude. You can do so much better. He was boring as hell." My brother shrugged before picking up his burger and taking an enormous bite.

"Yeah, agreed. I was just asking her about Montgomery. I was surprised that you were on board with them dating, but I think he's a great guy."

Miles choked on his food and I patted his back and laughed. He took a long pull from his beer. "Jesus. Did we never clear that up with you? We made that shit up, Dad. Sorry, but your overzealous wife was being a bit relentless to Monroe about coming to her birthday dinner alone. So, they both agreed to go along with it. But then she posted that shit all over social media and Mon and Jack had to play along for a few weeks. *It was fake.* That's why I was okay with it. I'd kick his ass if he touched her otherwise."

Now it was my turn to cough. First off, he'd just outed us to my father who I'd never lied to before. Second, I actually was sleeping with his best friend, and seeing how angry he got at just the thought made me cringe.

"Sorry, Dad," I winced. "It was Miles' fault. Please don't tell Thelma, it's a bit humiliating that I had to make up having a boyfriend."

"I won't say a word, sweetheart. But you should never feel like you have to pretend to have a boyfriend to come home. But I actually thought you and Jack seemed happy together. Your fake relationship was a hell of a lot better than your real relationship."

Wasn't that the truth.

Miles chuckled. "Jack's my best friend. But if he ever hurt Mon, he'd be dead to me. Be thankful it was fake. The dude is a heartbreaker."

I sucked in a long breath at his words. My phone vibrated on the table and I glanced down to see a text.

Jack ~ Longest lunch ever. Miss you, Blue Jay.

I sucked in a long breath and dropped my phone in my purse. It had been forty minutes since I'd seen him, and I missed him too. What was I doing letting myself fall for him?

I was playing with fire.

And if you played with fire you were going to get burned.

twenty-three

. . .

Jack

WE ARRIVED in Lake Tahoe a few days before Thanksgiving, and I was happy that Monroe had agreed to come. The slopes were covered in fresh snow, the sun was out, and the air was crisp. It was a perfect day to ski.

"Jesus, Blue Jay, slow your ass down," I shouted from behind her.

The girl gave me a run for my money on the slopes, and it shocked the shit out of me. Her hot little ass swooshed from side to side in her white ski outfit as she moved at mach speed down the hill.

She made a sharp turn at the bottom, spraying snow up behind her as she came to an abrupt stop. She raised her goggles and burst out in laughter. "Are you winded, old man?"

I unclipped my skis and yanked her against me. "Not at all. Just worried about you getting hurt."

She tipped her head back and kissed me before she fell back in the snow and I braced our fall with my hands. I wanted to take her right there. Now that I'd had her, I wanted more. I couldn't get enough of this girl.

"Get a room," Ford barked as he made a hard turn and stopped inches from us, shooting snow all over the back of my head.

Asshole.

"Don't need one." I pushed to my feet and helped Monroe to hers. Her skis had come loose, and she reached over to grab them.

"Where's Harley?" she asked. Monroe, Harley, and Laney Mae had been spending a lot of time together since we arrived earlier in the week, and I was glad to see how well the three of them got along. Like they'd known one another for years.

Monroe Buckley just fit well everywhere. My sisters-in-law loved her, my brothers adored her, and my mother and her had formed a friendship over the past few days as I found them sipping coffee alone every morning out by the fire. They were the first ones up, and Monroe said she looked forward to that time with my mom. I had to remind myself several times when I'd pouted because she was gone from our bed in the morning, that she'd grown up without a mother, and she craved that maternal connection. And my mom was the rock star of all mothers, so who better to share her with.

"She's coming. No one can keep up with you two. It's ridiculous," Ford said, looking up at the hill for his wife.

"Oh my," Monroe said as she spotted Harley making her way down, snowplowing the entire way. Harley was new to the sport, still nursing two babies, and she did not appear to be enjoying this at all. We all chuckled as she came to a rolling stop. She didn't have enough speed to need to put in much effort to halt her forward movement.

"I hate this. I'm cold. I'm hungry. And my breasts are engorged because those two humans you put in me won't stop eating," she hissed when she yanked off her goggles and we all burst out in laughter.

"Baby, you'll get the hang of it. Let's try one more time," Ford said.

"*Baby*, if you ever want to have sex with me again, you need to cut me loose. I love you, but I hate this. And Monroe, what the actual hell? How did you learn to ski like that?"

"My father and brother tortured me most of my life dragging me out on the slopes on vacation and forcing me to keep up with them. I've been skiing since I was a little girl, so I've had years of practice."

Always so humble.

Ford stepped out of his skis and moved toward Harley, wrapping his arms around her middle. "How about lunch, guys?"

"Yeah, Harrison just texted me to meet them in the lodge," I said.

"Lunch I can handle. And then I'll get back to the house and relieve your mom from baby duty," Harley said, moving beside Monroe and leading us to the restaurant.

Laney Mae and Harrison waved us over and we joined them. Monroe was dressed for the arctic and she pulled off her white beanie with the pompom and her ski coat. I wrapped an arm around her, rubbing my hand against her sweater-covered shoulder to warm her up.

"How was it? Laney and I are going to make a few runs this afternoon. Doubt we'll get out tomorrow at all." Harrison set his menu down and we all paused to place our order.

A roaring fire blazed beside us in the restaurant. The place was buzzing because Lake Tahoe was a popular place over holiday weekends. We sat at an oversized booth and piled our coats on an extra chair that the server brought over.

"I'm done for the rest of the week," Harley said, raising a brow at Ford as she sipped her hot toddy. "And I promised your mom I would make a few pies today."

"Monroe, you and I are going to kill the side dishes this year," Laney Mae said.

"Yeah, I'm excited. I've never made Thanksgiving dinner. We'd always go out to eat, so this is nice." She leaned back in her chair, and I squeezed her hand beneath the table. Her cheeks were pink and she leaned in to rest her head on my shoulder.

"I get that. Gramps and I ate out after Gram passed away all those years ago. But a homecooked turkey is just so much better for some reason." Harley leaned over and adjusted the neck on Ford's sweater and he wrapped an arm around her.

"I'm looking forward to it."

"Have you two talked any more about the New Year's event at the Labriths'?" Ford asked, and Harrison shot him a look.

Monroe's body stiffened beside me. It was a sore subject. She'd be attending as an undercover caterer and I wasn't happy about it. I was still determined to be there, but Monroe begged me to let her do this on her own, as she insisted I would blow her cover. It was the first time in my life I cursed my handsome, recognizable face.

"Dan has a lead at the catering company, so I'm going to be able to get in that way." She turned to look at me.

"Not happy about it. I'll be there somehow, even if it means sitting in the back of a van," I hissed.

Laney Mae laughed. "Never seen you this worried about anyone, Jack-ass. It's nice."

"I shouldn't be the only one worried." I glared at my brothers and then did the same to Monroe and everyone chuckled.

It wasn't fucking funny.

"So, when will you guys tell Miles you're dating? I mean, clearly, you're together," Harley asked, and I didn't mind the question one bit. It was the topic we avoided every time we were together. Lying to my best friend every day did not feel right.

"I'd like to tell him now." I crossed my arms over my chest.

"It's none of his business. I love him to death. But he's ridiculously protective. He doesn't get over things. And this is new, and it's wonderful, but if it doesn't end well, it will change their friendship forever." She let out a long sigh and leaned even closer to me as she fiddled with her napkin. "We're two consenting adults. Why would we add pressure to something so new? Jack hasn't had a relationship in years, and my last relationship ended horribly. Our track records aren't great. My brother will hold it against him regardless of what happens."

"That makes sense," both of my sisters-in-law said in unison.

It didn't add up completely. Miles was like a brother to me. He'd get over it. Because the truth was... I doubted I'd be the one walking away. It was Monroe who had the walls up. She was the one holding back. And not telling her brother was just another way of protecting herself. Sure, he'd be pissed at first, but once he saw how much I cared for her, he'd have no choice but to get over it. But lying to him would only make everything more complicated.

"So, I just lie to him every day? It's bullshit."

"I'm not asking you to lie to him. Tell him that you're seeing someone. Tell him all about it. Just don't say it's me." She shrugged and everyone chuckled.

I didn't laugh. Because it wasn't fucking funny. She was scared. I wasn't buying her bullshit excuse.

Ford's gaze locked with mine and he studied me. He could tell I wasn't happy. "So, has he always been protective?"

"He's always acted more like a parent to me, even though we're so close in age, I think it's because of the way we lost our mom. But we've always looked out for one another. And I appreciate it, but at the same time, I don't feel like I owe him an explanation if I want to date his best friend."

Ford nodded and glanced over at me. "I get that. I think we became more protective of one another after we lost Dad."

He was fucking right. I wasn't questioning my best friend's motives to protect his little sister. Hell, I wanted to protect her too. But I also thought he deserved to know what was going on. I wasn't fucking around with her—I had actual feelings for her. Real feelings. And I wanted him to know. Hell, I wanted everyone to know.

"I think that's normal. But at some point, you have to make decisions for yourself, and Miles still sees me as a little girl. So, I want to just enjoy this, and I am." Monroe looked up at me, clasping my hand under the table and smiling. "I want this to be about us, not anyone else."

Yeah, she kept saying that. But if she felt confident in what we had, she would tell her brother and force him to deal with it. I wasn't big on secrets, because I didn't have shit to hide. I was who I was, and I made no excuses. She was asking me to go against that, and I'd do it for a little bit longer before I took matters into my own hands.

"Well, you two sure seemed to be enjoying yourselves when you were making out on the slopes," Ford said with a smirk. "I don't know how long you can keep that shit hidden."

Everyone burst out in laughter and I flipped my brother the bird.

But he was fucking right. We sure were enjoying ourselves.

———

"This feels so good," Monroe said, leaning her back against my chest as we settled in the hot bathtub.

"You feel so good," I said, burying my face in her neck and rubbing my scruff against her soft skin as she giggled.

"I've never had sex this much. I mean, I never really cared to."

I wrapped my arms tighter around her. I hated thinking about her with anyone else. "Really?"

"Nope. I've only had two partners before you and neither were anything spectacular. In fact, I sort of hated sex before. My high school boyfriend and I were just inexperienced. I can count on one hand how many times we actually *did it*. None were anything memorable. Just quick and awkward," she said, pausing to chuckle. "And Thyme and I had no passion. In hindsight, I hate him a little bit less these days."

"Why's that?"

"Because we were just a couple out of convenience, I think. We were too lazy to end it and start over. There was nothing there. And if he and Sage share anything close to what I have with you, I get why he jumped ship. I mean, I would have preferred him to end it before hopping in the coat closet with her, but I get it."

"Yeah? What do you have with me?" I wanted her to open up. I needed her to trust me enough to do that. That's when she'd be comfortable telling her brother about us. She still didn't trust me.

She rolled onto her stomach to look up at me. Her chest settling on mine, her hair was tied up in a knot on her head. "I'm obviously attracted to you—but it's so much more than that. I don't know how to put it into words."

I nodded, brushing the hair that had broken free from her bun away from her gorgeous face. "Do you trust me?"

"Sure." Her gaze avoided mine.

"Listen, Blue Jay, I get it. You don't trust easily, and your asshole of an ex didn't help matters. But I'm not playing here. I'm all in. I like you. Hell, I like you more than I know what to do with. I want to be with you all the time. *I'm not going anywhere.*"

Her lips turned up in the corners and her ocean eyes were wet with emotion. "I'm not going anywhere either. I'm happy when I'm with you, and I'm not used to that."

"Yeah? I'm happy when I'm with you too." I leaned down and kissed her sweet mouth.

"Have you ever been in love before?" she asked abruptly, and I studied her.

"No. Have you?"

"I said it to Thyme. I think I wanted to be in love, because we'd dated for so long, but I never felt it. It's scary feeling that strong about another person, right?"

"Not really. Not for me. I don't run from shit like that."

I knew I loved Monroe Buckley right then and there, but I also knew she wasn't ready to hear it. She needed to feel it. Believe it. Because I knew she felt the same fucking way about me. But loving someone meant there were risks. There was something to lose. And for the first time in a very long time, I had something to lose. But I didn't give a shit, because when I wanted something, I fought hard for it. And Monroe was worth the fight.

———

Thanksgiving morning, I woke up to an empty bed once again. Four mornings in a row, she'd slipped away. I pulled on some pajama bottoms and a T-shirt and made my way down the long hallway. The house was quiet, even as I passed Ford and Harley's room. The twins were up late, and Monroe and I had taken a shift walking them up and down the hallway a little after midnight to give their parents a break. So hopefully they'd all gotten some sleep.

I came to a halt just outside the kitchen when I heard Monroe whimper as my mom spoke.

"I understand being afraid, sweetheart. That's only fair. It sounds like you've been protecting your heart your whole life. But sometimes you need to take risks to find what you really want," my mother said, her tone soft and soothing.

Monroe gasped a few times as if she were trying to catch her breath and my instinct was to go to her, but I wanted to give her and my mom this time. Hell, she never fell apart with me. She was always so strong and stoic. I envied my mother for being able to see this side of her.

"I think I've spent my whole life avoiding this feeling, you know?

And it terrifies me because the loss would be really great if he walked away at this point."

What the fuck? Was she talking about me?

"Listen, I lost the love of my life, so I understand this more than you know. You lost your mom before you entered the world, so in a way, I think you've had a shield around your heart from the time you took your very first breath. I've had a shield around mine since the day Ford Senior died. Maybe it's time we both set them aside and start living, huh?"

A lump formed in my throat. The two most important women in my life were hurting, and I couldn't fix it. They were more similar in that moment than I'd realized. Both extremely strong and confident, yet tender and vulnerable beneath all that armor. My mother never broke down in front of us, but I'd heard the sobs coming from her bedroom many times since my father's passing. And Monroe had been born with her armor in place, and her brother and father had worked as a shield most of her life. Setting all of that down and taking a chance on someone was a risk. One I finally understood. That's why she didn't want to tell Miles, because she was guarding what we had.

"I'm trying so hard. But I'm terrified. And letting Miles in, or allowing the outside world to chime in, will only add to that, you know? Everyone will try to tell us why *we shouldn't be together,* and right now, I just want to be with him. But I know it hurts his feelings that I want to keep it between us for now. But it's only because I want to protect what we have," Monroe said through muffled sobs.

"Honey, let me tell you something that I know for certain. My youngest son has a much more tender heart than he lets on, and he is one of the most understanding men I know. What you're feeling is fair. And you'll tell your brother when you're ready." I glanced around the corner and my chest squeezed. Mom sat on the built-in dining bench with Monroe in her arms as she rubbed her head and patted little circles on her back.

"Thank you for being so understanding." Monroe pushed to sit up, and I took a step back to give them another moment. I made a promise to myself not to pressure her anymore about telling her brother. She needed time, and I'd give it to her.

Laura Pavlov

"You helped me as much as I helped you. I think we all tend to try to protect ourselves from getting hurt. But the key is, knowing when you can trust someone enough to let your guard down. Maybe we both need to work on that."

"I will if you will," Monroe said, swiping at her face and pulling herself together.

"Count on it, sweetheart."

I came around the corner, just as Monroe stood.

"Good morning, ladies. What did I miss?" I asked.

"Just a little girl talk," my mother said as her phone chirped and she let us know it was my aunt, before excusing herself to take the call.

Monroe reached for my hand and tugged me down the hall to our room. I pushed the door closed and dropped on the bed beside her. Her eyes were red and puffy, lips chapped, and she looked fucking beautiful.

"You okay?" I asked.

"Yeah. I just had a nice chat with your mom."

"She's the best, isn't she?"

"She is. I just realized what I've been missing all these years," she said with a chuckle, and I wrapped my arms around her and held her close. "I hope I'm just like her with my kids someday."

My chest squeezed tight. Because I suddenly had a dying need to put as many babies in this woman as she'd allow me to.

Monroe Buckley wasn't just the first woman that I loved.

She was the only woman I'd ever love.

She was my future.

twenty-four

. . .

Monroe

"PUSSY, if you don't get away from my woman, we're going to have a problem," Jack said, and I fell back laughing.

His cat had warmed up to him, but when I was over, which was pretty much every day, his kitty favored me. Jack had impressed me the way he'd stepped up as a pet owner. There were toys, litter boxes in two spots in his massive penthouse, and even a holiday-themed collar for Pussy.

I loved this time of year, but this year was even better because I spent my evenings with Jack. Something had shifted in Lake Tahoe, and our relationship was solid. He hadn't pressured me to speak to my brother again, but I knew it was coming because we'd be seeing Miles over the holidays. It was time. I don't know why I was afraid to tell him. Maybe saying it aloud made it real? I'd never shared a connection like this with anyone in my life, and I just wanted to protect it. It thrilled me and terrified me all at the same time. I loved Jack in a way I'd never loved anyone, and a part of me feared that the minute I told him those words, the minute I admitted them to my brother—everything would go away.

It was a bit of a pattern in my life.

When you enter the world in darkness, it's hard to hope for a happily ever after. But for the first time in my life, I felt like I could reach out and touch it. I wanted it. I needed it.

Pussy purred and vibrated as he rubbed the side of his face against my neck before jumping down. Jack flipped me on my back on his couch and settled above me.

"I hate when you work late. Are you hungry?"

"Starving," I said, running my fingers through his hair.

"What were you working on?" He kissed my neck and my head fell back with a moan.

"Just getting some of the details together for the Labrith party. We have everything lined up with the caterers."

He tensed, pulling back to look at me. "That fucking party is the bane of my existence."

"Don't be so dramatic, Montgomery. I'm going as a caterer. What could go wrong?" I chuckled, but his face remained hard.

"So, many things, Blue Jay. And that scares the shit out of me."

I turned in his arms and moved to his lap, placing one leg on each side of him. I kissed him hard because I understood his fears. Because I felt it too. I felt it to the very core of my soul. Just like one needed food and water to survive. I needed Jack Montgomery.

"I understand that. That's why we'll be extra safe, okay?" I said when I pulled back and watched as his gaze softened. The moon shined in through his floor-to-ceiling windows and soft classical music played in the background.

"Okay. Have you talked to your dad about Christmas yet? My mom asked if we preferred to have Christmas Eve or Christmas Day at her house."

My stomach fluttered and flipped at his words. I wanted to share everything with Jack. But I needed to talk to Miles on my own first.

"Well, I think Christmas Day being your birthday is a must. What if I do Christmas Eve with my family and then share Christmas Day with you?" I stroked his wild dark hair away from his face. I didn't miss the hurt that filled his gaze and a heavy weight settled in my chest.

"You don't want to be together on Christmas Eve?"

"Of course, I do. But Miles will be in town, and I figured I would talk to him on my own that night."

"I don't know why we can't do it together."

I fiddled with the buttons on his dress shirt before looking up to meet his gaze. His handsome face nearly took my breath away as he ran his fingers up and down my back.

"I think it's best I explain the reason we kept him in the dark. That's on me, and if he's angry about it, I want to take responsibility for it." My stomach wrenched as the thought of making this public terrified me. I didn't want things to change.

He nodded. "How do you think he'll take it?"

"I think as long as we're both happy, he'll be fine with it. I just don't want him to put our relationship under a microscope, you know?"

What I wasn't saying was that I didn't want Miles, my dad, the whole damn world to put expectations on what Jack and I had. It was human nature to ask what was coming next, and I wanted to stay right here. I didn't want Jack to feel trapped once Miles knew we were together.

"I can see that head of yours doing it again," he said, pulling me against him and wrapping his arms around me.

"Doing what?

"Overthinking. You worry too much," he said, burying his face in my neck.

"It's a curse."

"I wouldn't change a hair on your beautiful head," he said before pushing me to sit up. "Come on, let's get some food in you so I can take you to bed and have my way with you."

This had become our new normal. Him taking care of me. Me taking care of him. And I didn't want anything to change.

———

"I'm so glad you finally agreed to cocktails. I thought you were pulling a Gwen," Becks said, as the two of us sat at a high-top table at our favorite bar in the city and ordered martinis.

Jazz music pumped through the speakers, and the bar area was illuminated with light from the crystal chandeliers overhead, causing small diamond shapes to glisten on the surrounding walls.

I laughed. "I've been busy with work."

"You've been busy with your secret boyfriend." She rolled her eyes. "I don't mind it. You dated that douchebag for years and you never seemed into him at all. Now you're secretly dating your brother's best friend and you seem ridiculously happy. I can't complain. And he's hot as fuck, so there's that."

I leaned forward, holding my finger to my lips to remind her to keep her voice down. The place was buzzing with conversation and laughter. Servers moved around the space like a fine-tuned machine.

"You're so crude sometimes. But yes, he's hot. No argument there."

"And the sex?"

I felt my cheeks heat, and a wide grin spread across my face no matter how hard I tried to hide it. There were no words to explain how good it was. How amazing and life-changing being with Jack really was. The way he made me feel. The way he touched me. Butterflies swarmed my belly and I bit down hard on my bottom lip to contain myself.

"It's really good. That's all I'm saying."

"That's all you need to say." She raised a brow. "Your face gives you away. Like I said, *hot as fuck*."

I smiled and took a much-needed sip of my cocktail, pulling the olive off the toothpick and popping it in my mouth. "My face gives nothing away. I'm a journalist. I'm trained to hide my feelings."

She chuckled. "Sure, you are. All I know is that when I used to ask you about sex with Thyme, you would wince. Like it was painful. I knew he was a shit lover even if you never admitted it."

My head fell back in laughter. "He's texted me a few times, actually. Apparently, he misses me now that he has a knocked-up girlfriend. Go figure."

She gasped and reached for my phone, scrolling to find his texts. "Um, he texted you twelve times. What the fuck, Mon? And you've never responded. He's a complete stalker." She continued to scroll through the texts and say aloud everything she was reading. "He broke up with Sage? She's pregnant, for god's sake. What's his deal? Please let me respond for you."

I yanked my phone out of her hands, just as our waiter stopped by the table and Becks ordered another round of drinks. She flirted with him, per usual, and he didn't seem to mind one bit. Once he walked away, she turned her attention toward me, and raised a brow as if she were waiting for an answer.

"We're not engaging."

"What does Jack say?" she asked.

"I haven't told him. He'll just get pissed, and it's his birthday in three days. I don't want to ruin it with silly drama."

She studied me before pausing to take a sip of her martini. "That's part of being in a relationship, girl. Silly drama comes with the territory. How would you feel if he had an ex texting him and didn't tell you?"

I growled and shook my head before I could stop myself. "This annoying girl at the office, Sabrina, keeps hitting on him. Today she came in to drop something off to him while I was sitting in his office, you know, for an actual meeting. She leans over, pushing her big old breasts in his face, and looks over at me and winks. Later, she tells me that my loss is her gain because she thinks we're broken up. I freaking hate her."

Her head fell back in laughter. "What did Jack do?"

"He keeps telling me we could end all of this if I'd just let it be known that we are together."

There was a large ruckus in the bar area and we both turned to see a woman had slipped off her barstool. She jumped to her feet and waved her hands in the air to let everyone know she was okay. We both chuckled before turning to face one another again.

"Girl. This guy is too much. I love him for you. Just what you needed. A confident dude who tells you how he feels. No games. No bullshit. He's crazy about you. So why not just tell your brother and let the world know?" She shrugged.

My stomach tightened as I thought about it. "Do you ever feel like, I don't know, like maybe you don't deserve to be happy? Is that weird?"

"Yes. It's weird. I feel like I totally deserve to be happy. And I'm not settling for anything less. What the hell do you even mean? You're the best person I know, Mon. Why wouldn't you deserve this?"

"I don't know. I'm not sure that's even the right word. It's like I'm waiting for the other shoe to drop. I'm so afraid once we admit we're together, that it will come to an end. And I don't know if I could handle it if he got tired of me or moved on from this. Don't even get me started on how often he gets hit on or propositioned. And that scares the shit out of me."

There. I said it. I was afraid Jack would leave me. And why not? It was par for the course for me. I always held back just a little bit from allowing myself to be completely happy. Because the fear of actually being happy and then losing it, was apparently less scary than not allowing yourself to be happy at all.

She reached across the table and squeezed my hand. It was an uncharacteristically thoughtful move for Becks. Affection was not her superpower. "Girl, you're the bravest person I know. You're writing shit that blows up powerful people. *That is scary.* Allowing yourself to be happy, shouldn't be scary. Maybe you've just gotten so used to protecting yourself, that actually having real feelings for someone terrifies you."

"I don't know why I'm this way. I want to charge the tundra. Seize the day. But when it comes to letting myself enjoy this… I freeze. It's almost a paralyzing fear. It makes no sense," I said before pulling my hands away and reaching for my drink.

"Well, I'm no Freud, but I'm guessing entering the world where my mother died giving birth to me, having my father emotionally check out of all future relationships and date social-climbing heathens with no souls, and a brother who protected me so fiercely that I don't ever put my guard down… that'll leave a mark." She paused and reached for her fresh cocktail that our server had just set down and plucked the olive from the toothpick and popped it in her mouth. "It's time to separate all of those things, Mon. Your mom died giving birth to you. It sucks. But it happened, and out of it came this strong, fierce, beautiful woman who is making a difference in this world. Do you think she'd want to go through all of that for you to be emotionally unavailable? Doubt it, girl. So, tell your brother to back the fuck off. Tell your father to start living his life again and allow yourself to do the same. And tell that man of yours that you're crazy in love with him because you are."

She stared at me hard before reaching over and patting her own back. "Fucking brilliant, if I do say so myself."

"Didn't you get your degree in marketing? I'm feeling a career shift to therapist. That was not a bad assessment, my friend." I laughed as I continued to process her words.

"It's time to stop protecting yourself, girl. Live. Love. And all that hoopla. I think you found the guy that's worth taking the risk for. And please remember that I never told you to let your guard down with the douchebag herb."

I chuckled. "Thanks, Becks. Let me sit on this for a bit."

"No. Stop sitting on things. Time to ride your boy into the sunset, girl."

I choked on my drink and coughed before we both broke out in a fit of laughter.

"Love you. Thank you," I said before pulling my card out to pay the bill. "I've got this."

"You bet your ass you've got it. I just saved you thousands in therapy."

I hugged her goodbye before catching an Uber and heading to Jack's. I couldn't wait to see him. A few hours away from him had become torture.

When I stepped off the elevator, there was a massive floral arrangement sitting on the entry table. My heart fluttered, and I reached for the card.

Mon,

Please call me back. I messed up. I love you.

Thyme

My heart raced, because the only way these would be at Jack's place was if they'd been sent to the office and he'd seen them.

"Montgomery," I called out, my voice shaky.

He walked around the corner. His face hard, hair a rumpled mess. His dress shirt was completely unbuttoned, exposing his tanned, chiseled abs. His tie was long gone, and he leaned against the wall, arms crossed over his chest as he studied me.

"Something you want to tell me, Blue Jay?" His voice lacked emotion, but I could see the anger in his gaze.

"Listen. I didn't want to upset you," I said. "I haven't responded to him."

"Your fucking ex-boyfriend is sending you flowers to tell you he loves you, and you don't think I deserve to know that? Why would you though? No one in the office knows we're dating. Your fucking family doesn't know we're together. Why the fuck would I think you'd tell your ex-boyfriend you were with me?" The disdain in his voice startled me. Jack had never been upset with me. Not really. Sure, he didn't want me to attend that party at the Labriths, but he was able to speak to me without—disdain.

Disappointment.

I reached for my phone in my purse and handed it to him. "Read the texts. I just didn't want to upset you right before your birthday."

"Of course, you didn't, Little Bird. You've been holding me at bay this whole time. Did you ever stop to think that maybe I'd like to send you flowers to the office? Or take you out to a restaurant and hold your hand?" He held my phone in his hand, but he never looked at it. His eyes never left mine. "Or tell my fucking best friend that I finally found someone that makes me want to be a better man and it's his baby sister?"

His words were like a sharp knife to my heart. I put my hand to my chest as the tears started to fall.

What had I done?

How selfish had I been?

He handed my phone back to me. "I don't need to read this. I needed to hear it from you. My girlfriend. If that's what you even are."

His phone vibrated on the counter beside him a few times, and he finally picked it up and ran a hand through his hair. He held his phone up for me to read the screen.

"It's your brother. He's on his way over here. He wants to hang out and catch up. What do you want to do about that?"

I'd never seen Jack so angry. His demeanor was stiff and hard. His jaw clenched. But his whiskey-colored eyes nearly broke me. They were wounded. And for the first time since we'd been together, they appeared distant and guarded.

He didn't trust *me*.

And I'd done this to him.

Tears ran down my face as I fought back the lump in my throat.

Fight or flight.

"I'm going to tell him. But not like this." I grabbed my purse and ran to the door.

"Take your flowers, Blue Jay. We wouldn't want Miles to think something was going on between us," he hissed.

I took my flowers and sobbed when the elevator doors closed. I dropped the card in the trash before setting the arrangement on the lobby table and making my way outside.

I ran away.

Because for the first time in my life, I had everything I wanted.

And so much to lose.

twenty-five

. . .

Jack

I'D HUNG out with Miles the night before and we'd drunk ourselves into one of the worst hangovers I'd ever had in my life. He'd asked numerous times why I was in a mood, and I'd written it off to stress at work.

The truth—I was pissed at his sister. She'd received fucking flowers from her asshole ex, not mentioned the fact that he'd been texting her, refused to tell her brother about us, which in turn forced me to lie to him for months, and insisted on keeping our relationship a secret. I'd been patient for as long as I could. I was done playing games and she could get on board and come clean with him, or she was going to have to walk away. She couldn't have it both ways. Not anymore. I'd give her the ultimatum today and let her decide what she wanted.

My head pounded and I felt like shit as I stepped off the elevator at Montgomery Media, and Sam handed me a coffee and winced when she saw me.

"Rough night?" she said.

"Something like that."

"Monroe is in your office. She seemed upset and insisted on waiting for you there."

"I'll handle it," I hissed. She'd texted me several times last night

200

and I'd ignored her. She was probably just worried that I'd blown her cover with her brother. God for-fucking-bid he found out we were dating.

I pushed my office door open before kicking it shut with my foot. I walked right past her and dropped in the chair behind my desk. She hurried over and put her hand on each side of my face. Her indigo blues searching mine.

"I'm so sorry." Her words broke on a sob.

"What does that fucking mean? You're ready to tell the truth? Or you just need a little more time?" I asked, my anger spewing as the words left my mouth.

"I'm going to tell him tomorrow. We're spending Christmas Eve together."

"That's right. We can't spend it together because he still doesn't fucking know. What's your deal with this, Blue Jay?" I pushed to my feet, pacing the length of my office needing to put some space between us. "Are you embarrassed of me? Ashamed? What the fuck do I have to do to show you that I'm all in? What's it going to take? What the fuck do you want from me?" My words boomed around the space, and I stopped in front of her. Tears streamed down her face.

My office door flew open, and Miles stormed in with Sam on his tail. Could this day get any fucking worse? His sister stood before me sobbing, my head was ready to blow, and I held my hand up to my assistant to shut the door and leave us.

"Is this for fucking real?" Miles shouted, tossing Monroe's locket on my desk. "I went into your room to find some Tylenol and instead I find my sister's fucking locket. On your motherfucking nightstand beside your bed. You looked me in the fucking eyes and told me nothing was going on."

"It's not what you think," I said, running a hand over my face.

"It's not? You going to feed me a bunch of bullshit again? Because from where I'm standing... this is the second time I've walked in to find my sister crying. How long have you been keeping this from me? I asked you one fucking thing, Jack. One fucking thing. Not to fuck around with my sister."

"Miles," Monroe shouted. "You don't know what you're talking about. This is my fault."

"Don't fucking apologize for him, Mon. How could you fucking do this to her?"

I was completely done with this whole situation. I'd put my heart out there, and she'd stomped on it. For whatever reason, she'd insisted on hiding this, and now here we were in the midst of a shitstorm. I couldn't even be mad at him. It looked like—well, it looked like I'd lied to him, which I had.

"I can explain," Monroe shouted.

"Oh yeah? Tell me I'm wrong?" Miles glared at me. His hands fisted at his sides.

"You're so fucking wrong, brother." I pointed my finger at my best friend. "You think she's crying because I hurt her? You couldn't be more wrong. It's your sister doing the hurting. I'm the fucking one getting crushed here, man. Yeah, that's right. I'm fucking head over heels in love with her, and she won't even fucking admit we're dating. So, who's fucking who over?" I stormed past both of them, and Monroe reached for my arm, but I didn't stop.

I was over all of it. I'd lost my best friend and the girl I loved and all for what? Because she was too afraid to admit how she felt?

Fuck that.

Ford hurried toward me as I stormed out of my office. "What the fuck is going on? Who are you screaming at?"

"I'm done. I'm leaving. Cancel my appointments."

He followed me to the elevator and held the door open. "Jack. What the hell is going on?"

"I put myself out there and guess fucking what? I got crushed."

He stepped back and let the doors close.

I stepped off the elevator and walked right out the front door. I called Big Tony and he pulled up at the curb.

"You all right?" he asked, opening the back door for me.

"No. But I will be." My phone chimed with a reminder that I had an appointment in ten minutes. Fuck. I couldn't get a break today. "We need to make one quick stop and then you can drop me at the helicopter. I'm going to Napa early."

There was only one person I wanted to speak to. The one person who always made things better. My mom.

———

It turned out the best cure for a bitch of a hangover and a broken heart was some time with your mom followed by a five-hour nap. I'd turned off my phone and spent a quiet evening at the home I'd grown up in, which was exactly what I needed. Mom and I talked about everything, and she understood my frustration, but she empathized with Monroe.

It's not that I didn't understand Monroe's fears. I did. But things had gone too far, and I was done playing games. Either shit or get off the fucking pot. And obviously, Monroe wasn't ready to do either. She could find me when she was ready to own how she felt to both me and her brother.

Harrison and Laney had offered to stop by, but I didn't want to discuss this with anyone else. My mom had my back, and she was the person I relied on most when I was unsure about what to do. We'd gone to bed early, and I'd slept off the remnants of my hangover, and woke up feeling a shit ton better the following day.

It was Christmas fucking Eve. Thankfully I didn't need to go to work. Mom was having everyone for dinner, and it was good to be home. I hadn't spoken to Monroe since storming out of my office yesterday, nor had I heard from Miles. When I'd last seen him, his mouth had gaped open and he'd looked completely shocked by what I'd shared. I'd said my piece and they could do with it what they wanted. I'd admitted that I loved her, and that hadn't been the way I'd wanted to tell her. I'd planned to tell her when I gave her a Christmas gift. But fuck it. It is what it is. I'd played along with this ridiculous game for too long, and now it was out there. Time to face the fucking music. I'd never lived my life running from things or hiding who I was, and I shouldn't have allowed it to get this far. But there are firsts for everything. And loving Monroe Buckley was a first for me. And it fucking pissed me off that this was how it had all gone down.

Christmas music played throughout the house, and I made my way out to the kitchen as the scents of pine and cinnamon flooded me.

Nobody did Christmas quite like my mother. Every corner, every nook, every tabletop was covered in holiday décor. Reds and greens and angels and elves sat atop every surface. Mom called it our own little holiday wonderland.

I dropped to sit. There was a gaping hole in my chest, which was foreign to me. Like someone had reached in and tore out my heart. An ache that wouldn't go away no matter how hard I tried to numb it, sleep it off—it was waiting for me the moment I opened my eyes this morning. My mother came to sit with me.

"How do you feel, Jackie boy?"

"Like shit."

"Language, sweetheart."

"Okay. Like poop. Better?"

She laughed. "Have you talked to her?"

"No. I laid it all out there, Mom. She needs to come to me. The ball's in her court," I said.

She nodded. "I hope she still joins us tomorrow. I told her that her family was welcome to come as well."

"I'm guessing she won't come. We haven't spoken, so it's unlikely she'll just show up to Christmas dinner." I shrugged. "Maybe I'll start the morning with some coffee, extra Baileys."

"No. That's not how we deal with things." My mother placed her small hand atop mine and patted it a few times. "Don't numb yourself because you're hurting, Jack. Feel it. Learn from it. Don't run from it, sweetheart. You told her how you felt. Trust me, she feels the same. Let her process this."

"How do you know she feels the same?" I asked, running my hands through my hair.

"Because anyone who sees you two together knows how you both feel. You can't miss it." She squeezed my hand and kissed my cheek. "It's Christmas Eve. Let's decorate some gingerbread cookies. That sounds much better than getting drunk before noon, doesn't it?"

Not really.

Not at all, actually.

The thought of getting drunk and sleeping it off sounded a hell of a lot better than drawing faces on cookies I was just going to eat. But I wouldn't tell her that. "Sure, Mom."

She brought over a plate of cookies, bags filled with different colored icing and containers of sprinkles. Not really what I felt like doing. But it was Christmas Eve and my mom was the last person I would complain to about my pain. She lived it every day. I could suck it up and do this for her.

————

We all sat around the dinner table, and my spirits had only worsened as the day went on. Even the babies couldn't turn my mood around. I was tempted to head back to the city. I wanted to be alone. But I couldn't do that to my mother. Thankfully, by five o'clock when everyone arrived, she wasn't micromanaging my beverage intake any longer, and I sucked down several glasses of wine.

"I hate sulky Jack," Harley said, and everyone remained silent, while my mom covered her smile with her hand.

"I'm not sulking," I hissed.

"She's right, Jack-ass. You're no fun when you're a sad sack," Laney Mae said, and my mother finally gave in and chuckled.

"I'm sorry I can't be your entertainment tonight, ladies. Can a guy not have one off night?"

"That fight yesterday was all the talk in the office. Monroe and Miles left shortly after you, and she looked pretty upset. What went down?"

"I'm sure you heard plenty," I said, raising a brow at Ford.

"So, Miles knows about the two of you. So what? It's out there. Now you can date the normal way like the rest of us," my older brother said.

"Jack told her that he loved her. Well, he told Miles that he loved her, and she heard it." My mother passed me the basket of bread while she spilled the dirt.

"Thanks for the discretion, Mom." I rolled my eyes.

"We're not a secret-keeping family, Jackie boy. You know that."

"Oh my gosh, you did it, Jack-ass. You told her?" Laney Mae asked, as she set her utensils down and studied me.

"I did. I said it for the first fu..." I paused and motioned for my brother and Harley to earmuff the girls and waited with little patience for them to do so before continuing. "I did it for the first fucking time and I said it to her brother. And guess what she said?"

Harrison and Ford studied me with concern and Laney Mae and Harley were wide-eyed and eager for more and they both spoke at the same time. "What?"

"*Nothing*. She said nothing. She just cried. So, there you have it. I waited twenty-five years to drop those three little words on the only girl I've ever loved, and I got... crickets. Motherfucking crickets. For god's sake, will you earmuff those babies," I said, pushing to my feet and pacing the room.

I was angry. I was fucking pissed. And I didn't want to talk about it at our family Christmas Eve dinner. Especially in front of my two little nieces. But I was about to lose my shit and I didn't know what to do about it. This is why I would have preferred to be alone.

"Hey," a voice said from behind me, and I turned around to see Monroe standing there nervously shifting on her feet. "I hope it's okay that I'm here."

"Of course, it is, sweetheart," my mother said as I stood there dumbfounded. She wasn't supposed to come until tomorrow. Tonight, she was going to be with her family, but seeing as we sort of moved up the conversation she planned to have with Miles, I guess things had changed. "We're so happy you're here."

"I, um, I just needed to do this in person." She remained on the other side of the large dining room table from where I stood.

"Why don't we give you two a moment alone," Harley said, moving to pick up Penelope.

"No. Please. Don't leave. This is something I need to say in front of all of you. It's something I should have done a long time ago. It was fear that kept me from being honest about how I felt," Monroe said, and a tear escaped down her cheek.

It took all I had not to move toward her, but I needed to hear what she had to say. Harley dropped back in her chair and everyone sat in silence.

"You asked me what I wanted from you yesterday before you left. There's only one thing I want." She shrugged.

"What's that, Blue Jay?" I asked.

"I want you to promise to live one minute longer than me so that I never have to exist in a world that you aren't in." She covered her mouth with her hand as tears streamed down her face before she continued. "Because I love you so much that it terrifies me and excites me, and I don't know what to do with that. But I know that I love you, and it only seemed fair to tell you so."

I made my way around the table, lifting her off the ground and pulling her into my arms. "Thank Christ, because according to everyone here, I'm a sad fucking sack and nobody likes a mopey Jack."

The table erupted in laughter before they all returned to eating, and I pulled Monroe to the table and insisted she sit on my lap. There was an empty chair beside me, but I wasn't letting her sit that far from me. Not after spending a night apart, not knowing what would happen. No. I needed her with me. She smiled as I handed her a set of utensils and piled more food on my plate.

"Is everything okay with Miles?" Harrison asked.

"Yes. He wasn't happy with the way *I* handled the situation. He feels bad for assuming the worst yesterday, and that's on me. He understands now. And if it's still all right, I'd love if my dad and Miles could join me here tomorrow. He'd like to speak to you in person."

"Of course, they can. We'd love to have them," my mother said.

"What about Thirsty Thelma?" I asked, as I buried my face in her neck, inhaling all her goodness. Lavender and honey and sweetness.

"It's been an interesting twenty-four hours." Monroe shifted on my lap and whispered so only I could hear. Penelope and Everly were putting on a show of shouting gibberish while everyone gaped and clapped, but I focused on my girl. "I'm not the only one who was keeping secrets. Apparently, Dad and Thelma have been sleeping in separate rooms for over six months and he filed for separation after Thanksgiving. That trip was a last-ditch effort to salvage things, and it didn't work. He said he's tired of being unhappy and he wants to start living."

"Can't say I'm totally shocked. They didn't go together at all. Good for him. That's a step in the right direction."

"Yeah. The three of us stayed up all night talking about things. Why Dad was in a miserable marriage and has been with women who don't make him happy since Mom passed. Why Miles feels this need to protect me and act like he's my parent, and why I'm terrified of loving someone the way I love you."

I studied her beautiful face. "Yeah? What did you conclude?"

She smiled. "Life is messy. The loss of my mother had a profound effect on all of our lives. But in the end, she would want us to live. She would want us to be happy and to love and to make each day count."

I nodded. There was a lot of that going on here too. "Yeah. It says a lot about someone when their passing affects so many lives, right? We all struggle with grieving my father's death to this day. But I know he's looking down on us and happy that we're moving forward. One day at a time."

Grief was a bitter pill to swallow. It didn't come with a manual and it didn't take vacations. Monroe and I had each faced our own profound losses in our lives. And what I'd learned was that though we'd both been affected by the deaths of our parents—in a way they'd led us to one another. Neither of us had allowed ourselves to let our guards down with anyone else before now; yet somehow we'd been able to do it for one another. The one that mattered. I'd like to think my father had a role in leading me here.

She settled back against me and I wrapped my arms around her. "You're exactly right."

"Glad you're here, Little Bird."

"Me too."

twenty-six

. . .

Monroe

CHRISTMAS with the Montgomerys was better than I could have ever imagined. Monica was the epitome of what a mother should be. She made everything magical, and I reveled in it. Their family had also survived the loss of a man who meant the world to all of them, but she was moving forward, and they all followed her lead.

I'd spent the night there after dinner, and we all stayed up late talking and laughing. Christmas morning was everything it should be. Family and food and celebration. The twins were still too young to know what was going on, but we all sat around passing out gifts.

There was thought in every present I received, and it warmed my heart the way they'd all embraced me. Monica had given me a framed photograph of Jack and me that she'd taken in Lake Tahoe. It was a candid shot, and it captured us brilliantly. I cherished it. He had me on his lap and my head was tipped back in laughter as he looked down at me like I set the sun. I fought back tears as I stared at the photograph in a gorgeous silver frame.

"I love this. Thank you so much." I hugged her tight.

She'd given Harley, Laney Mae, and me all matching charm bracelets as well, and it meant the world to me that she treated me like I was part of the family.

It was also Jack's birthday, and everyone doubled up on his gifts. He received sweaters and boots and photographs of himself and the twins. I'd given him a luxurious robe and matching slippers, as taking baths together had kind of become our thing. He gave me a beautiful pair of pearl earrings and a framed picture of me, him, and Pussy that he'd taken on his phone. It was placed in a frame that said: family. My heart raced when I opened it. I didn't feel the need to run this time—but I had the strongest desire to stay. Exactly where I was.

With him.

Laney Mae and Harrison went back to their house to shower while Ford, Harley, and the girls went out to the guesthouse to get ready. Jack and I went to his room to take a bath.

"So, you know last night we didn't get to have any time alone, so you haven't gotten to see me naked yet," he said, pinning my back to the wall in the large bathroom.

I laughed. "Yep. It was torture."

"Well, there was a reason for that. I was hiding a little something for you. I have one more present to give you. I did a little thing yesterday before I left the city." He tore his shirt over his head.

His chest was covered with a white piece of gauze over his heart and I reached for it. "Oh my gosh, what happened?"

"Relax. It's a gift for both of us." He peeled off the gauze, and a gorgeous tattoo of a blue jay was inked over his heart. Indigo blue and pops of gold and orange shaded the wings. It was stunning.

"Oh my gosh. I can't believe you did that."

"Yeah. Yesterday was rough. But I knew whether you came around or not it didn't really matter. My heart was yours. It was up to you what you did with it."

I covered my mouth with my hands as tears streamed down my face. How had I gotten so lucky to be loved by this man? It didn't matter. I was done questioning it. I was going to enjoy it. Revel in it.

"I'm sorry I put you in that position. Miles wasn't happy with me. He feels really bad for assuming the worst. You know he loves you like a brother, right?"

"I'm not upset with him. I was pissed at you," he said, raising a brow. "You're the first woman I've ever said those words to. And I fucking mean them. I love you so much, Blue Jay."

"I love you, too."

He dropped to sit on the bed and tugged me toward him. I moved to sit on his lap, one leg on each side as I straddled him.

"Fear can be all-consuming. I'm sorry I put you through that," I said.

"Well, seeing as you did put me through a bit of hell, maybe you'll consider not going to the Labrith party to make up for it." His voice was all tease, but I didn't miss the serious look in his gaze.

"Isn't announcing my love for you in front of your entire family enough to make up for it?" I chuckled as my lips grazed his.

"I just got you to finally admit you're mine. I don't want to lose you." He flipped me on my back and settled above me.

"I'm not going anywhere, I promise." I reached up to trace the edge of the little blue jay on his chest. No one had ever done such a grand gesture for me.

"And if your ex-boyfriend reaches out to you, I want to know about it."

"Deal. I did respond to him yesterday because he continued blowing up my phone asking if I'd received the flowers. I told him that I was not only dating you but that I was in love with you and that he was going to be blocked from contacting me any further."

His lips turned up in the corners. "Such a pesky little herb. You do realize you told your ex-boyfriend you loved me before you told me."

I laughed. "Well, you told my brother you loved me before you told me, so we're even."

My phone vibrated on the bed and I reached for it, pausing to read the text.

"Come on, lover boy. My dad and Miles are on their way in from the city. We need to get dressed." I stood and tugged him to his feet.

"Shower first?" he said, walking behind me and leading me to the bathroom.

"Well, we do have to look presentable." I giggled as he tugged the pajama shirt over my head and dropped his joggers to the floor, standing there naked and looking like a piece of art.

A girl could definitely get used to starting her day this way.

———

When my father and Miles arrived, I ran outside to greet them. They had a bag of gifts in tow.

Jack stood in the doorway and Miles beelined toward him. "I'm sorry for jumping to conclusions, brother. Didn't want to say it in a text. Wanted to tell you in person. I was a fucking idiot and I'm sorry. I know you better than that. Can't think of a better person to date my sister," Miles said, and Jack pulled him in for a hug.

"I get it, man. Sorry for lying to you for so long."

"Trust me, Monroe explained everything, and she's very persuasive when she wants something, so I get why you did it," Miles said.

Men were so different. They didn't hold on to things. These two were already over it and acting like nothing had happened. Jack shook my father's hand and Dad pulled him in for a hug. My father seemed lighter now. I think he was making positive changes and I couldn't be happier about it.

We all gathered around the large table for an amazing spread of ham and turkey and more sides than one could count. Monica winked at me as I took it in.

"There are a few extra sides for our vegetarian this year," she said, and I bit down on my bottom lip to keep from crying. It was ridiculous really, but the way she cared for me was something I'd always craved.

I realized in that moment, as everyone chatted and laughed around the table that the gaping hole I'd always felt in my chest was no longer there. Jack had somehow filled it. He'd completed me in a way I couldn't explain. He made me feel whole. And his family just added to it with all their warmth, acting as if I belonged there.

We sang "Happy Birthday" to Jack and ended the amazing holiday with his favorite cake made by his favorite baker, Harley, who stood to make a toast.

"Happy Birthday to an amazing uncle, brother, son, and friend. Enjoy your favorite cake. You've got your favorite girl here to watch you eat it," she said with a chuckle. "And her brother no longer wants to kill you, so we can all live happily ever after."

She raised her glass and we all cheered. I squeezed his hand beneath the table before turning to look at him and whispering. "Happy Birthday, Montgomery."

"It's the best one yet, Blue Jay."

———

It was a short week between Christmas and New Year's and most of the employees at Montgomery Media were off on holiday. But Dan and I had things to do to prepare for the upcoming party, and Ford and Jack were both putting in full days, along with a small skeleton crew who were busy at their desks. Unfortunately, Sabrina was one of them. Dan had his staff here working on a few projects, but we'd kept the Labrith story under wraps as we didn't even know if it would go anywhere at this point.

I stepped in the breakroom for coffee and Sabrina and Bailey had their backs to me, deep in conversation.

"Yeah, my boyfriend wants to tie me down, but until he makes it official, I'm still on the market, and you know who I have my eye on," Sabrina said as she flipped her hair. Her dark jeans were skintight, her black top fitted, and her oversized boobs were spilling out of it.

"Are you still on a Jack Montgomery kick? You don't think that ship has sailed?" Bailey asked, and my blood boiled.

She was still trying to make things happen with Jack? It was my fault for not announcing to the world that we were together. It was time to let her know he was most definitely not available.

"Girl. Men like him take time." She chuckled before turning around to see me standing there watching them. Her makeup was caked on so thick I couldn't help but gape. "Um, take a picture. It lasts longer."

This girl gave *mean girl* a whole new meaning. I knew girls like Sabrina, and I usually steered clear. But she wanted Jack, and I was here to tell her that wasn't happening. He was mine.

Mine.

Butterflies fluttered in my belly every time I thought about him.

About us. Last night he'd insisted we take a horse and buggy ride through the city. We'd bundled up with hot chocolates and talked and laughed as we made our way through the busy streets. He was so unpredictable, so romantic, and I loved it. He owned my heart. One I hadn't even known was still there.

"Yeah, I just wanted to let you know you're wasting your time. Jack and I are together, so, you can stop plotting and move on." My tone came out harsher than I meant it to, and I didn't mind at all.

She rolled her eyes. "On again. Off again. How can one keep up?"

Bailey shifted on her feet in discomfort and gave me an apologetic shrug like she didn't know what to do about her friend.

"You don't really need to keep up. Just be aware that we're *very much* together." I squared my shoulders as she stepped closer to me. What the hell was this girl's deal?

"We'll see about that, Monroe." She stalked out of the breakroom.

What would we see about? The girl was batshit crazy.

"I'm sorry," Bailey whispered as she peeked her head out the doorway to make sure Sabrina was gone. "She's slightly obsessed with Jack. He's never paid her any attention, so don't let her get to you. I'm happy for you."

Bailey had always been much kinder to me.

"Thank you. I'm not quite sure what her problem is?"

"Sabrina is just... *a lot*," she said on a long sigh. "I don't actually know her that well. She just tells me all sorts of stuff at lunch, most of which I don't even want to know, like her rocky relationship with her boyfriend, her obsession with Jack, and being quite the party girl. But I'm new here, and I just want to be friendly, you know?"

Her kind eyes told me more than she was saying. She was afraid to be disliked by Sabrina, which I could understand. Me, on the other hand, I didn't care. I wasn't looking for friends, especially ones that I didn't like. But Bailey was sweet, and she was definitely hanging around with the wrong girl.

I nodded. "I get it. Thanks for the heads-up."

"Thanks, Monroe."

I walked down to Jack's office, because I already missed him, even though we'd driven to work together this morning. His office door was open, and I stopped in the hallway when I heard voices.

"Yeah, you're going to need to cut the shit. I've made it clear I'm not interested. I'm in a relationship and I also own this company, and your persistence is starting to work my nerves. Don't force my hand. I don't want to make this an HR situation. I know Dan is happy with the job you're doing, and I'd hate to have to report this," Jack said, his voice remained even and silky smooth.

I knew before she spoke that it was Sabrina. "I'm just having fun. Please don't go to HR. I like my job and I don't want to lose it. I didn't realize you were in a relationship. I just thought we shared a mutual attraction and wanted you to know that I had a no-strings required policy." Her voice grated my nerves. I just told her that we were together, and she'd raced right over here.

My feet moved of their own volition as I turned to stand in the doorway. "I thought I made it perfectly clear that Jack and I are in a relationship just five minutes ago. If I didn't, *please hear me now*. We are very much together and if you can't respect that, we're going to have a problem."

A wide grin spread across Jack's handsome face as he sat behind his desk.

"I guess I misunderstood," Sabrina said with one brow raised and a smirk I wanted to wipe off her face. "It won't happen again."

"I hope not." I raised a brow in return and settled my hands on my hips, giving her my most threatening pose.

She chuckled on her way out the door. "It's really no big deal. I actually have a boyfriend."

I held on to the door handle and stared at her as she made her way out. "Great. Then stay the hell away from mine."

I slammed the door and turned to face Jack.

"Damn, Little Bird. I love seeing you all fiery and jealous." He laughed and patted his lap for me to come sit.

"I can't stand that girl."

He studied me, tipping my chin up to meet his gaze once I settled on his lap. "Did she do something to you?"

I rolled my eyes. "She just gets under my skin. I just told her we were together and she comes in here and makes a move?"

"I'll call HR. She's given me more than enough reasons to terminate her at this point." He reached for the office phone and I put my hand over his.

"I don't want her to lose her job over this. I can handle Sabrina. Dan likes her, and I think she got the message loud and clear just now."

He cocked his head to the side. "You sure? You say the word and she's gone."

Jack didn't make threats. He was a man of action. And there was no doubt in my mind that he had my back. And I had his.

"I'm sure."

I rested my head on his chest and inhaled all of his goodness. Cedar and citrus and beautiful man.

"I like seeing you claim what's yours. And I am," he said, wrapping his arms around me even tighter.

"You are what?"

"Yours."

I smiled and leaned against all his hardness, feeling every muscle in my body relax with his warmth.

"Damn straight."

He chuckled, and we just sat that way for the next twenty minutes.

Because he was mine.

And I was his.

twenty-seven

. . .

Jack

I WOKE up with Monroe sprawled across my chest, and a pit settled in my stomach. I reached for the remote and opened just one set of the floor-to-ceiling blackout curtains in my bedroom as we both had a busy day today and we needed to get up. It was gray and gloomy out. The sun stayed hidden behind dark heavy clouds, and the view matched my mood.

Tonight was the Labrith party, and I didn't have a good feeling about it. Maybe it was just the lack of control that I felt. There was a fine line between being protective and smothering the one you loved, at least that's what my girl told me multiple times last night.

It was New Year's fucking Eve, and I would be spending it in a van while my girlfriend played caterer at some sort of orgy. Victoria couldn't even get an invite to this event. She was the biggest socialite I knew. She told me she heard that Charles Labrith was, and I quote, "a kinky fucker, and he liked them young." Apparently, he had friends in high places in the drug world and was into more than just sex. How the hell had this stayed under wraps for so long? My guess was that it was exactly what had me on edge. No one wanted to piss off Joseph Capetti. And going after his daughter's husband was the same as going after her.

Ford, Dan, a few guys from our security team, and I would be in the van parked not too far from the house. Monroe was working with a small skeleton crew for the catering company. She, Dan, and Ford had all assured me repeatedly that she was just going to be a fly on the wall and see what went down. We weren't running with anything until we had all the facts. She just wanted to dig a little further, and she'd begged me not to ruin this for her. It took everything in me not to blow this shit up. But I loved her so damn much, I didn't want to crush her.

I was at a crossroads. Fighting every instinct that I had when it came to this girl. But she'd assured me it would be a few hours, and then we were going to get on a plane and fly to Cabo San Lucas, Mexico for a much-needed break. Just the two of us. I'd bide my time and go along with this ridiculous plan—for now. Ford was fairly convinced there would be nothing to see, and this would all be something we would laugh about later. He encouraged me not to force her hand, and to allow her to follow her gut and trust that we would keep her safe.

But Monroe was everything to me, and I couldn't risk losing her. I'd kill the story if I thought it would put her in danger, and I already made that clear. If I thought her investigation would bring the wrath from Joseph Capetti, she could hate me all she wanted, I'd make sure that story never saw the light of day.

"Hey, handsome," she purred, and looked up at me. Her hair was a wild mess and Pussy was sprawled on the other side of her. I didn't like him up on the bed, but the sneaky bastard always crept in after we were asleep.

"Hey," I said, pushing the hair out of her face, and smiling down at her.

"It's pretty dreary out, huh?"

"Yeah. Looks like we're going to get a storm. Are you sure you don't want to can this whole thing and get on the plane now? We could be on the beach with cocktails by this afternoon."

She pushed up to sit, wrapping the black silk sheet around her bare body. Her blue eyes looked more gray than ever this morning, matching the sky outside. "We're leaving in less than twenty-four hours. Come on. Don't make this a big deal. I'll play caterer and serve some cocktails and scope out the place. We'll be on our way to Mexico in no time. If you don't like what I find, I promise to hear you out and we can discuss whether or not to run the story."

I tugged her down and kissed her hard. "Okay. Don't take unnecessary risks tonight. Don't make me storm the castle. Because you know I will."

"Don't be a barbarian, Montgomery." She giggled and tangled her fingers in my hair.

"I'm not fucking around, baby. I don't have a good feeling about this."

Her gaze searched mine. "Don't worry. It'll be fine. You need to trust me."

I covered her mouth with mine, because we weren't going to agree on this one. So, I'd choose my battles. The more time I spent with Monroe, the more I needed her. I needed this girl like I needed to take my next breath. She was all-consuming in the best fucking way. So, the thought of something happening to her terrified the hell out of me.

She pushed me back, her indigo blues danced wildly as she looked up at me. "You're insatiable, Montgomery. We've got the next week in Mexico for long mornings in bed. I have a big day today. I need to go meet Dan at the office to go over the plan."

"Only insatiable for you, Little Bird."

"Me too," she said as a big grin spread across her gorgeous face. Her fingers traced the stubble on my jaw, and I leaned down and kissed her neck. I couldn't help myself.

"Love you," I said as I pushed up and helped pull her to her feet.

"Love you, more." She clasped her fingers with mine and pulled me to the bathroom. "Do you want to come with me to the office?"

"It's not even an option. Of course, I'm coming. I'm not about to let Dan allow you to go rogue tonight. And I will be in that fucking van."

"Rogue?" She laughed before she leaned in and turned on the shower. "How about we save time and shower together?"

She knew how to distract me, and she was damn good at it.

"Obviously."

"So cocky this morning," she said, stepping into the oversized shower and I followed her in.

"Don't say cock-y when you're naked. It does things to me."

Her head fell back in laughter as water sprayed across her neck and chest and I hardened at the sight.

"Sit down, playboy." She pressed her hands to my chest, and I dropped down on the bench in the shower as she filled her hands with shampoo.

She massaged my scalp, and I buried my face in her perky tits. Now this kind of shower, I could get behind. I wrapped my lips around one perfect peak, and she gasped, tugging at my hair and pushing my head back to look at her.

"Behave," she said, but her body arched into mine and she leaned down and kissed me.

That's all it took before I pushed to my feet and lifted her in my arms. Her legs came around my waist and I pressed her up against the wall.

"I can't behave when it comes to you," I said, nipping at her ear as I settled myself between her legs, teasing and torturing her in the best way. "Do you really want me to?"

"No." Her voice was raspy and laced with need.

I pulled back, acting as if I would even consider stopping what we'd started. "But you're in a hurry, right?"

"Meh. I'm sleeping with my boss. I'm sure he'll understand if I'm late." She tangled her fingers in my hair as the water poured down my back.

"I think he'll be fine with it. But only if you're sure," I teased her entrance but didn't give her what I knew she wanted yet. Not until she said the words.

"Please," she whispered. "I need you."

I loved when she lost control with me.

"That's all I needed."

I buried myself inside her and moved her hips up and down until she moaned into my mouth. I moved faster, wrapping my arms around her to hold her close. Like I couldn't survive without her.

Because I couldn't.

———

"This is all standard, Jack. We just haven't done an undercover operation in a while. But she's just going to go in and find out if there is any truth to this story, though I am doubtful anything will go down in front of one of the members of the catering team." Dan sat back in the chair in the conference room and crossed his arms.

"Then why the fuck are we having her go in there at all?" I snarled.

Monroe shot me a look of disapproval. If looks could kill, I'd be a dead man. Lucky for me, they couldn't. And I was going to fight this every step of the way.

"Calm the fuck down. I think this is too close to home for you. Dan and I will go along with Edward and Calvin, and I can call you to let you know how it's going." Ford paced the length of the room and stared at me hard. Edward and Calvin ran security for our family. We trusted them immensely.

"Fuck, no. I'm going."

My brother nodded at me, because he knew when I had my mind made up, there was no changing it. I was already pissed that I wasn't going to be in there with her. No way was I going to not be in the damn van parked a few houses down. I needed to be close. If I had to storm the goddamn castle, no one was going to get in my way.

"Then you need to relax, brother. She is going to be a food server, look around, and report back to let us know if we need to dig deeper. Nothing is going down tonight," Ford said, and Dan nodded.

"Exactly. This is called due diligence. We're doing our fieldwork, putting in the time, and then we will see if there's a need to look further." Dan sat back in his chair with a brow raised.

Was this supposed to appease me?

"*We're* not doing shit. *She's* doing everything."

"Baby." Monroe came up behind me and wrapped her arms around my middle, settling her cheek against my back, and damn if it didn't work like fucking magic. The stress melted off my body. "Please don't ruin this."

I turned to face her, and her gaze nearly brought me to my knees.

Pleading.

Begging.

I nodded. "Okay. I got you. You're doing this. I'll stop."

"Thank you," she whispered before pushing up on her tiptoes and giving me a chaste kiss.

Ford's phone vibrated and he looked down to read the screen. "Game time. Edward is downstairs. We're dropping Monroe at the catering company. She'll enter the party with the caterers. Edward is going to find a way onto the property just as a precaution, so he will be close, pending he can blend in looking like security."

I clasped my hand with hers and led her down to the car. She wore a white button-up and black pants, per the caterer's request. A sick feeling settled in my stomach.

Maybe this was what happened when you truly loved someone? You feared anything and everything taking them from you. You didn't trust the outside world, because you had something to lose.

And I had everything to lose.

I remained quiet on the drive over, which was a definite first. I couldn't decide if I was worried or pissed, but every time Ford or Dan spoke, my anger grew. We were in an old, beat-up van and Monroe sat on my lap in one of the bucket seats. She turned to look up at me.

"We're going to laugh about this later, you know that, right?"

"Sure, Little Bird. I hope you're right." Then why the fuck did I have such a bad feeling?

"Do you remember when you would step on the field for your football games? Your mom probably worried the entire time. But you were totally in control and doing your thing. This is sort of like that." She held my hand and lifted it to her cheek, pressing it there and smiling.

"I think she just compared you to Mom," Ford said with a chuckle.

"Shut up. You were a pansy-ass when Harley gave birth. We all saw it." I rolled my eyes.

"She had two humans trying to break themselves out of her body. Monroe is going to be a food server at a political party, with lots of people around. What could possibly go wrong? Maybe she catches Professor Douchebag in the pantry with one of his guests. Not dangerous, brother. You're overreacting."

I chuckled for the first time today. Maybe he was right. Maybe I'd blown this up in my head. Part of what I loved about Monroe was her determination. I loved that she knew what she wanted, and she wasn't afraid to go after it. How could I fault her that?

I let out a long breath. "We'll laugh about this all the way to Mexico."

"There he is. See, it's all going to be fine. Love you." She kissed me quick before Dan opened the back door and walked her to the side of a building. Apparently, he had a good friend who owned a catering company, and also owed him a favor. It sounded sketchy but he told me not to ask. Dan had been a journalist for thirty years. He had "friends" everywhere.

Ford turned to face me as he sat in the seat beside me. "Not used to seeing you care about anyone this much. It's nice."

"Well, if anything happens to her, I'm going to punch you and Dan in the fucking faces."

His head tipped back in laughter. "Stop worrying. She'll be fine."

She would be.

There was no other option.

twenty-eight

· · ·

Monroe

THIS GIG WAS TURNING out to be a bust, but I didn't mind it, because at least I'd tried. That was part of paying my dues as a journalist. I would exhaust every resource. My current hunch—Lyle Labrith was probably an entitled brat with daddy issues. I'd seen nothing from Professor Labrith nor his lovely wife to give me reason to think anything was going on. They'd held hands at the party, chatted and laughed with guests.

My phone vibrated in my back pocket and I couldn't help but laugh. The highlight of my evening thus far had to be the endless slew of texts from my boyfriend. I think he'd finally relaxed as I'd been texting him constantly to keep him updated.

Jack ~ Still boring, Little Bird?

Me ~ Aside from working my ass off serving cocktails and appetizers... still uneventful. Don't gloat.

Jack ~ Not gloating, baby. Just wishing you were here. Actually, I wish we were at home. Naked in my bed.

My cheeks heated. He never held back, but he still managed to catch me off guard.

"Melody, things are winding down out there. Would you mind going around and collecting empty glasses? Check the bathrooms as well. When people get drunk, they tend to set their drinks down and forget about them," Elaine, the lady who owned the catering company and was a friend of Dan's, said. I'd used my go-to undercover name, though things had been completely uneventful.

"Of course. No problem." I grabbed an empty tray and made my way out of the kitchen.

The Labriths' home was large and a bit cold for my taste, but still gorgeous. Large crystal chandeliers hung from the ceiling, causing diamond-like shapes to cover the walls. Chatter and laughter filtered down the hallway as I made my way to one of three guest bathrooms. The crowd had definitely dwindled, and I was ready for this shindig to end. I didn't see any signs of a second party on the horizon, as people continued to say their goodbyes.

Music trickled through the speaker system throughout the estate and I collected more glasses than my tray could hold, as I tried to stack a few without dropping them. I turned down the final hallway, making my way to the last powder room that I doubted anyone used as it was fairly out of the way, and I heard whimpering. I set the tray down on the console table and peeked my head in the bathroom, but no one was there. I stood still as I tried to figure out where the sound was coming from. Muffled sobs had me turning down another hallway, abandoning my tray for the time being. A light was coming from beneath a door and I heard hushed voices. I stood beside the door.

"Listen, Melissa, how long can you keep this up? He's an asshole. He doesn't deserve you."

"I just don't know anymore. But how will that look?" Her voice broke on a sob, and I recognized it immediately. It was Governor Labrith. "How do I run for reelection when I can't even make my own marriage work?"

"We'll figure it out. Whatever it is. But you can't keep living like this," the other woman said.

"I know. But I got into politics because I truly wanted to make a difference. I wanted to do good and make Lyle proud. I wanted to give back." She sobbed. "But I can't seem to escape bad men. It's my cross to bear, I suppose."

A heavy weight sat on my chest as I listened to this beautiful, brilliant, powerful woman who sounded—broken.

"Lyle is proud of you every day. You are an amazing mother. But even he can't stand the sight of his father. You don't need to live in misery," the other woman said.

"I just can't believe he's throwing another one of his sick, twisted parties. He promised that he was done with this. How am I supposed to turn a blind eye anymore? He's blatantly cheating on me, and God knows who he's bringing here tonight? This is my home. This is where we raised our son."

"Enough is enough. You need to walk away," the other voice said.

My phone buzzed in my pocket and I quickly turned off the sound. The voices quieted behind the door before it cracked open and I met Governor Labrith's gaze.

"I'm sorry. Can I bring you something?" I squeaked.

"No. We're just leaving. Does anyone else know I'm in here?" she asked, swiping at her mascara-smeared eyes.

I leaned forward and handed her a napkin. "I don't believe so. The party is clearing out."

"Thank you." She cocked her head to the side and studied me. "What's your name?"

"Monroe," I said, and I don't know why I didn't give her my fake name. I was a bit awestruck to be speaking to her. I admired this woman immensely and the fact that she was living with a monster only made me want to support her all the more.

"I'm Melissa Labrith. And this is my assistant, Jenna." They each reached out to shake my hand before turning to walk in the opposite direction.

"Governor Labrith," I called after her.

"Yes?" She turned around to wait for my response.

"You're doing a great job. We need people like you out there fighting for us." I couldn't believe the words left my mouth, but she nodded and smiled before turning to leave.

I hurried back to my tray just as Elaine rounded the corner.

"There you are. I was afraid you got lost," she said, tucking her hair behind her ear.

"Oh sorry. I noticed the closet door was open and I found a bunch of these glasses in there," I lied and it seemed to appease her.

"Good job. Thank you. Do you mind lugging the bags of trash out to the side of the house? My feet are killing me. I'm getting too old for this." She chuckled. The other girl hired to help tonight was a complete airhead. Elaine had to keep pulling her from chatting with the guests and remind her that she was actually working the event.

"Of course. I've got it," I said as I set the tray down on the counter and made my way out the back door with two of the bags from the pile of garbage stacked against the wall.

The night was quiet. The Labriths' home was a grand red-brick estate, with pine trees forming a line along the side of the house. I set the bags down and sent a quick text to Jack.

Me ~ Looks like there's trouble in paradise. I think things are about to heat up. Will keep you posted.

Jack ~ Fuck that. Your job is done. Dan spoke to Elaine and she said you guys will be finished up in fifteen minutes. Whatever is happening next is not something you will stick around for. But now you know there's something to look into.

Me ~ Okay. Be out soon.

I tucked my phone back in my pocket and walked down the cement walkway where Elaine told me to set the bags. It was dark and quiet, and I thought about my conversation with Governor Labrith. I wondered how such a confident, strong woman ended up in a marriage like this? I understood that she probably felt trapped because they were portrayed as the perfect family, and she would be judged for leaving her husband. But should she be forced to suffer in a loveless marriage just to keep her job? No way.

"I'm sick of being patient," someone whisper-hissed in the distance and I stepped behind the tall evergreen to listen.

"Baby, it's almost over. I'll plant the drugs in her room tonight, it's enough to put her away for quite a while. You'll make the anonymous call first thing in the morning, and I'll be sleeping peacefully in my room. It's all finally happening," the deep voice said, and I had no doubt that it was Professor Labrith.

I held my breath, afraid to make a sound as I tried to make out the other voice. "How do you know she won't talk her way out of it? I'm sick of waiting."

The voice sounded familiar, but I couldn't place it. Was she a politician?

"Because of who her father is. People already have their doubts about her and seeing proof will be the final nail in the coffin. This place, all of this, it will be ours. We can finally be together."

"How will we afford all this on a professor's salary?" The voice caused the hair on my arms to stand on edge. Who the hell was she?

"Stop your pouting. How do you think I have enough cocaine to put my wife away for years? I've got my own side business going, and we won't need to worry about money. I can promise you that."

My heart hammered against my chest and I carefully placed the garbage bags down beside me once I realized I was still holding them.

"People will be suspicious if we're suddenly together and living the good life."

"We'll keep it a secret at first. Melissa and I have many investments, she comes from a lot of family money and everything is in both of our names. She'll go away and it will all be mine. No one will suspect a thing."

What the hell was happening? He was going to set up his own wife? The mother of his child? This man was a million times worse than I'd suspected. And who was his mistress? I'd heard her speak before. Maybe on the news? In an interview?

"If you say so. Just make it happen. I'm tired of waiting. There's plenty of men—" the woman hissed.

"Don't threaten me, darling. We've waited a long time to get here, let's not ruin it now. Go to the door for the after-party. I'll step back inside. We can have some fun right under that bitch's nose. She's already angry and I'm sure she'll retire to her room shortly."

"Okay. I'll meet you at the front door in a few minutes. Let me have a little bump before we step inside."

The sound of excessive sniffing came from where they stood, and I froze. They were obviously doing drugs. The crunching of leaves startled me and the light from above shined down just a few feet away from where

I crouched behind a bush, illuminating the face of the woman as she walked right past me, not noticing me in the shadows. My heart nearly pounded out of my chest. My mouth went dry. This was not happening.

I knew I recognized her voice.

Sabrina.

Her boyfriend was Professor Labrith?

No, no, no, no, no. This couldn't be. Clearly, she didn't know Dan and I were working on this story, or she wouldn't be here. How could we have missed this? This was the rich boyfriend she was talking about all this time?

I heard the back door close, so Professor Labrith must have gone inside. I reached for my phone and dialed Jack.

"Are you done?" His voice was deep and sexy.

"No. Something happened. It's not good—"

A hand wrapped around my mouth and my phone was removed from my hand. I tried to kick, attempted to scream, but the person holding me knew what they were doing. He held me tight, and the air left my lungs.

———

Panic coursed through my veins as I was placed on a seat in the back of what looked like a limousine and a strap came across my chest. A man slipped in beside me, and the car door shut before speeding off into the darkness. I looked at the other man sitting across from me in the dimly lit space. The moon illuminated his gray gaze as chills spread down my spine.

Joseph Capetti.

Oh my god.

What had I gotten myself into?

I sucked in a long breath and squared my shoulders.

Don't show fear.

"W-what do you want with me?" I asked, trying desperately to hide the quake in my voice.

"Miss Buckley, I'm sorry to drag you out here, but I find myself in an interesting predicament, and I believe you hold all the answers to my questions."

"What are your questions?" My words wobbled and I glanced down to see my hands trembling in my lap. I squeezed them together in hopes of appearing calm.

I'd been kidnapped and was in a car with a suspected crime lord. Joseph Capetti was one of the most powerful and feared men in the city. Why would he ever let me go now? How many times had I read articles that said you never get in the car with your abductor? But here I sat across from the man, as he spoke to me like this was totally normal. Maybe in his world, it was. And I didn't have much of a choice as I'd been taken against my will.

Jack.

He flooded my thoughts. He'd be worried sick. He'd predicted this would happen and I hadn't listened. Tears streamed down my face and I swiped at them before looking back up at Joseph Capetti.

"There is reason to believe that my worthless son-in-law is mistreating my daughter. My men have been trailing him, and we found you doing the same thing. I know you don't work for the caterer. I'm aware of your accolades in the world of journalism, and I have to say, for being so young, I'm quite impressed. I know who your father is. I know who your boyfriend is. I'm not looking to start a war. This is your opportunity to make this a peaceful meeting, Miss Buck-ley." He leaned forward and brought his face closer to mine.

There were crossroads in life, and I was at one. This story—it wasn't what I had expected it would be, nor was it one I was dying to tell. Governor Labrith was an innocent bystander, and the only thing I wanted at this point was to make sure she didn't get set up. If I weren't here, I'd be at the police station reporting what I'd heard. This was no longer about a story.

But I was here.

And I could only assume Joseph Capetti and I wanted the same thing. To help his daughter.

"I went there to see if there was a story. Word on the street is that Lyle hates his father, and that Professor Labrith throws questionable parties. I honestly didn't expect to find what I did," I said, my voice sounding a bit more stable.

"Go on." He studied me intently as I spoke, sending chills down my spine.

"Professor Labrith is going to set up your daughter tonight with what sounds like an absurd amount of drugs. His girlfriend, who happens to work for my newspaper," I paused to shake my head and sigh, "is going to place an anonymous call early in the morning to the police, and your daughter will be caught with bags of cocaine, I believe. He's going to plant them in her room, and his plan is for her to go to jail and he and his girlfriend will be together."

I sat quietly as he stared at me. "Did you hear me, sir?"

He chuckled, and my shoulders relaxed a bit. "I did. I've never been a fan of the man, but I have to say, this goes far beyond what I thought him capable of. My daughter isn't happy, but she's so damn fearful of losing her position, one she actually uses for good, that she can't bring herself to walk away."

I nodded. "Yes. She appeared upset tonight."

His gaze narrowed. "I'm surprised she allowed you to see that. She must recognize something familiar in you. I see it as well."

"What's that?" I shifted on my seat as we pulled over in an abandoned parking lot after driving for a while. It was dark and quiet, and I glanced at the large man beside me, certain that I couldn't physically fight my way out of here. There wasn't a building or a car in sight. There was nowhere for me to run. No one to call for help.

"*Good.* It's easy to see you and my daughter are similar in that way. This world needs more of that." He sat back in his seat.

"Are you going to kill me?" I asked, because I needed to know. I couldn't be pleasant with him if he was about to slit my throat.

He bellowed out in laughter and the man beside me chuckled. "Oh, my dear. You've watched too many movies, haven't you? I'm not in the business of killing people."

"Just kidnapping them for information?" I raised a brow.

He cocked his head to the side. "You weren't kidnapped. You were taken for your own safety. You were hiding behind a bush, and my men spotted you. You obviously knew you were on to something dangerous. I wanted to get you out of there."

"And get information from me," I pressed, squaring my shoulders. I suddenly felt a bit more confident.

"Looks like we were both looking for information tonight, no? She's my daughter. There isn't much I wouldn't do for her."

"And what happens to me now?" I asked.

"A message was sent to the Montgomerys that we would be delivering you shortly," he said, lowering the glass partition to speak to the driver. "Head to the address I gave you."

"You got it, sir," the driver responded before the glass was raised once again. Joseph Capetti wore a white dress shirt and black dress pants. His suit jacket lay on the leather seat beside him.

"Where are we going?" I asked, panic surging as I spoke.

"Relax. You'll be taken to Jack Montgomery's apartment. You'll receive your phone once you arrive. I suggest you don't reach out to the police or print anything about what you heard at this time. We'll be in touch."

I nodded. Not knowing what that meant. Or if I was really being taken to where he said. But for some reason, I thought he was telling the truth. And it made no sense. The man had taken me against my will, trusting him was probably a bad idea. But what option did I have?

Tall trees and greenery flew by as I gazed out the window like watercolors on a canvas. Everything blurring together as the car moved. We merged onto the freeway, headed in the direction of Jack's apartment.

At least I hoped that's where they were taking me.

twenty-nine

. . .

Jack

MY KNUCKLES WERE bloody from punching the wall. I paced the length of my apartment and reached for the vase on the entry table and smashed it against the door. I needed to break something. Punch someone. Tear down the fucking walls.

"Come on, brother. You need to calm down. They said they'd bring her here," Harrison said, his voice tentative, as he placed a hand on my shoulder. He wasn't certain she'd be brought here either, but he was sure as hell going to try to make me believe it. We were supposed to trust Joseph fucking Capetti? The man had a reputation.

"Fuck that. We don't even know who has her. Or why the fuck they took her." My words vibrated off the walls of my apartment, and everyone startled.

"Jack," Ford said, his cool voice cutting through the tension in the air. "I understand your anger. But breaking shit and losing your cool will not bring her back. Think logically. Why would they reach out to us via text if they were going to hurt her? That's not common practice."

"When did it become *common practice* to kidnap someone?" I shouted.

Our security team had been dispersed on the Labrith grounds, while we sat in a stupid van a few houses away. Edward had phoned to say that he saw a man toss Blue Jay into a black limousine but they sped away before he could get their plates.

I'd wanted to fuck up everyone inside that house. Elaine had phoned Dan to say that Monroe took the trash out and never returned.

And then this fucked up text came to Ford's phone.

Unknown Number ~ Do not do anything. She won't be harmed. We need information. She will be returned to your brother's apartment in an hour. You have my word. Do not inform anyone at the party that she's been taken or reach out to the police at this time. It is in your best interest and hers. JC

The phone could not be traced, as Edward and Calvin had used all their resources only to learn it was a burner phone. So, she was gone. And I was supposed to do what? Sit by and do nothing.

Fuck no.

"For now, yes," Ford said, his eyes searching mine as if he understood my pain.

He didn't. None of them did.

"I fucking told you this would happen." I pointed a finger at Ford and turned to find Dan sitting on my couch and pointed at him next. "Both of you insisted on letting her do this. I fucking knew this was going to happen. I need to call Buck. He and Ryan deserve to know what's happening."

"I don't recommend that, Jack," Edward said, moving to stand beside Ford. He'd run security for my family for years. My father trusted him. My brothers trusted him. Hell, I trusted him. He was a retired Navy SEAL. He knew his shit. He and Calvin had been on the phone and calling in favors from every resource that they had since she'd been taken. "Ford's correct. You don't normally get a text when someone is taken unless they're asking for something. They aren't requesting money. She has something they want, and they have agreed to return her. The last thing we want to do is get in the way of that happening."

"He's right," Harrison said, wrapping both of his arms around me and forcing me into a hug. "If you call her brother or father right now, they are going to call the police. What if that pisses Joseph off and he doesn't bring her here?"

A sob escaped my throat. The desperation indescribable. Panic attached itself to me like a second skin. I wasn't a crier. I cried when my father died, and I cried at his funeral. Those are the only two memories I have of breaking down. But now—it felt like someone reached inside me and cut my heart from my body. Gutting me and leaving me raw. My chest ached where a gaping hole grew with each passing minute.

What if she was hurt?

I knew she was fucking terrified and I couldn't do shit about it.

Jesus Christ, I didn't know what to do.

I wailed like a little bitch into Harrison's shoulder. Ford's arms came around both of us, and they just held me there. They'd always been there for me. They wouldn't allow me to spiral right now. But I was losing it. Time was standing still.

"Jack," Edward said as the elevator dinged letting us know the doors were opening into my apartment.

I pushed my brothers aside and charged the elevator as the doors opened and Monroe stood there. Eyes swollen. Lips trembling.

A broken little bird.

I rushed her, taking her into my arms before pulling back and running my hands all over her. "Are you all right? Are you hurt?"

"No. I'm okay," she said before she broke out in tears and I wrapped her in my arms. Her legs gave out and I scooped her up and walked to the couch, settling her on my lap.

Everyone gathered around us but kept their distance while I spoke to her. "Where were you?"

"I was in a car with Joseph Capetti and one of his guys." Her voice trembled, and a sharp pain settled in my chest.

"Did he hurt you?" I asked, tucking the hair that broke free from her ponytail behind her ear and stroked her face.

"No," she whispered. She was definitely in shock over what had happened, as she wasn't saying much.

"What did he want with you?" Harrison asked, bending down to face her.

Laura Pavlov

Ford ran his hands through his hair and paced the room. Dan's gaze locked with mine and I saw the guilt there.

She let out a long breath. "I went to take the trash out for Elaine. I overheard a conversation between Professor Labrith and his girlfriend."

"What were they saying?" Ford asked as he stopped to face Monroe.

Her body stiffened and I wrapped my arms around her tighter.

"His girlfriend is someone we know. It's Sabrina." She turned to look at Dan, whose face completely paled.

"My admin? Sabrina Callahan?"

She nodded. "Yeah. I knew she was seeing someone, but I never imagined it was Professor Labrith. They were talking about this plan to take down the governor."

Monroe went on to explain exactly what she heard. How they planned to place enough drugs in her room to put her away for a long time. How Sabrina was going to make the anonymous call to the police early in the morning and Professor Labrith would be sleeping down the hall. This was a plan that had been premeditated and well thought out. The man was working with drug dealers and going to set his own wife up for a crime she didn't commit.

"Jesus," Ford hissed. "Who the hell does that?"

"Sick motherfuckers," I said, dropping my head back against the couch. "And you filled in Joseph on what you heard?"

"Yes. He said not to call the police, nor to print anything in the paper at this time. He said he'd be in touch." She shrugged.

"I recommend doing exactly what he says. He's not going to allow his daughter to be set up on drug charges. If for any reason he doesn't step in, and she gets arrested, we'll go to the police at that time." Harrison squeezed Monroe's hand. "And he's been upfront with us at this point, so I think we let this play out."

She nodded. "I agree."

"So now we fucking wait," Ford said, as he pulled Edward aside and spoke to him quietly. I didn't even try to make out what he was saying, because I didn't give a fuck at this point. She was back with me, and that's all that mattered.

236

"I'm really sorry, Monroe," Dan said, running the palm of his hand over his face as he moved to stand in front of her.

"This is not your fault. We had no way of knowing Sabrina was involved, or that Professor Labrith was a complete monster." She buried her face in my neck.

"Well, I don't believe in saying I told you so—*but I fucking told you so*," I said, and Monroe smiled and pushed up to look at me. I heard my brothers chuckle and Dan even forced a smile, but the man was riddled with guilt. I'd let him off the hook in a few days. I wasn't there yet.

"You were right. I'm sorry." She placed her hand on my cheek.

"I'm fucking sorry I couldn't stop it. Are you okay?"

"Yeah. It was terrifying. He never seemed threatening, and he did tell me he was going to bring me here—but my mind still raced with every horrible scenario. I'm just so tired."

"Out. Everyone out," I shouted, pushing to my feet with her in my arms.

Ford rolled his eyes. "All right. Edward is going to have two of his men stationed downstairs just as a precaution."

"Love you, brother," Harrison said, clapping me on the shoulder. "I'm sorry, Monroe. Love you, girl." He kissed the top of her head.

Her eyes welled with emotion. "Love you, too."

Dan apologized a dozen more times before I all but pushed him out the door. Ford paused in the doorway and Monroe pushed against me to drop her to her feet.

"I'm really sorry for putting you in this situation," my brother said, pulling her into his arms. "I'm glad you're okay, because you're family now. And this one wouldn't survive if you weren't okay." He thrust his thumb at me.

"Thanks, Ford," she whispered before stepping back into my arms.

He nodded before walking out the door.

"Bath or bed?" I asked, as I guided her toward the bedroom.

"Bath."

I turned on the hot water and stripped her of her clothing before doing the same with mine. I stepped in and guided her to settle between my legs.

"I was so scared," she said, her voice so low I barely made out the words.

I ran my fingers up and down her arms as I tried to comfort her. "Me too."

"You were all that I thought about." She flipped over on her stomach to face me.

"Yeah? What'd you think about?"

"How much I love you. And the thought of never seeing you again..." She paused and shook her head.

"Hey, you're here. You're safe. I love you so fucking much."

She rested her cheek on my chest and we sat in silence as we both processed all that had happened tonight.

I was so fucking thankful she was okay. And back in my arms.

Exactly where she belonged.

———

The following morning, we woke up to a slew of texts and phone messages.

"Oh my gosh. Charles Labrith and Sabrina Callahan were arrested this morning and charged with drug possession and intent to distribute," Monroe said, holding the black silk sheet up to her chest as she stared at her phone screen.

"What about the governor?" I asked, pulling her closer to me as we both sat with our backs against the headboard.

"It says there are no charges against Melissa Labrith as she'd checked into a hotel late in the evening. She's cooperating with the police to make sure justice is served." She turned to face me.

"He works fast. Karma's a bitch, huh?" I asked.

She chuckled. "Guess who broke the story?"

"Who?" I asked.

"Brett Waters from CBS. He has a pretty good contact at the police department."

"Are you upset that you didn't get to break it?" I pushed to my feet and reached for her hand, leading her to the bathroom.

"Not even a little bit. This isn't the kind of story that I'd want to tell. There is something about her, Governor Labrith, that I really like. I hope she recovers from this. And I think Professor Labrith really *is* dealing drugs. It sure sounded like it. I doubt he'll get out of this. And I still can't believe Sabrina is his accomplice," she said, reaching for her toothbrush as Pussy leaped onto the counter to get closer to my girl.

"Well, it sounds like they're getting what's coming to them. What did I tell you about jumping up on the counters, Pussy? I don't like it. Get off," I said, staring the fat bastard down.

"I think if he could, he'd flip you the bird right now," she said, breaking out in a fit of laughter when my cat didn't budge.

I wrapped my arms around her and tickled her sides. "Is that so? Well, he's about to be really pissed off when he realizes we're getting the hell out of here. Seven days on the beach and the only pussy I'll be thinking about is yours."

Her head fell back in laughter. "You are so crude. Well, I'll be thinking about you, Pussy. We'll miss you. I saw you stocked up on treats and toys for him. I think you're all talk, Montgomery. You're going to miss him."

"Sarah will take good care of him. Maybe she can train the bastard while we're gone. How are you feeling this morning?"

"Like I was hit by a truck yesterday," she said, shaking her head. "I still can't believe everything that happened. I've never been so ready to get out of here."

I wrapped my arms around her and kissed the top of her head as I held her close. "Good. I told the pilot we'd be ready in thirty minutes. Get dressed." I slapped her on the ass and turned to get dressed myself.

A few minutes later she had her bags at the door. "You ready, Montgomery?"

"I was born ready, Little Bird."

thirty

. . .

Monroe

AFTER SEVEN DAYS at the beach with Jack, I was struggling to get back into the routine at work. We had a private villa on the ocean, and we swam, we ate, and we laughed. Oh, not to mention the hot sex on the beach, in the villa, under a palm tree, and in the water. I couldn't get enough of this man, and it only intensified the connection even more.

The office was still buzzing with talk of Sabrina when we returned. She'd lawyered up and claimed to be a victim. Word on the street was that she'd hired a hefty priced attorney and her parents were footing the bill. Professor Labrith was pretty much dead to rights, as Sabrina gave him up immediately, and agreed to testify against him in exchange for a lighter sentence. Governor Labrith had been hounded by the press but had yet to speak out. My chest tightened every time I thought about her. Becks told me that Lyle had been beside his mother since the story broke, and Tabi had even met her a few times over the past few days. I hoped that meant she was going to be okay.

My office phone buzzed, and I picked up.

"Hey, Talia. What's up?"

"Um, Governor Labrith is on the line for you." She didn't hide the giddiness from her voice.

"Thank you."

I clicked over to the line currently blinking with the waiting call. "Governor Labrith?"

"Hi, Monroe. I understand we've met? At the party?"

Shame all but engulfed me. "Yes. I'm, um, I'm sorry about that."

"Don't be. You didn't report what you saw. You didn't go public about finding me and my aide in a closet crying," she said. "So, I was hoping you and I could sit down. I'd like to give you the exclusive. You know, my side of the story."

My hand landed on my chest and I tried to calm my racing heart. "Really? Yes. I would like that very much."

"Great. I'm ready to put this behind me. Can you meet me in an hour?"

"Absolutely." I pushed to my feet and tried to control my breathing.

"You'll need to come to my house, as the press has set up permanent residence outside my gates. Security will let you in when you arrive. No cameras, please. Just you."

"No problem. Thank you. I'll see you soon."

I yanked my office door open and sprinted down the hall to Jack's office. He wasn't there. I made my way to the conference room, which was floor-to-ceiling glass walls. I could see him speaking to a group of people I didn't recognize. His gaze landed on mine and he smiled. Butterflies swarmed my belly, per usual, because apparently, I was a sap these days. I waved to let him know it was nothing important, and turned to head back to my office.

"Hey, get back here, beautiful."

I laughed before turning around to see my gorgeous boyfriend standing there, tall and strong, dark gorgeous hair and whiskey-colored eyes. But Jack Montgomery was so much more than just a good-looking guy. He was brilliant and kind. Thoughtful and generous. Sexy and commanding. Sometimes it felt like God had looked down on me and taken notes on everything I was missing in my life and delivered him in this perfect package.

"Go back to your meeting. It's not important," I said as he wrapped his arms around me and leaned down to kiss me.

"Anything you have to tell me is important to me. Speak."

I chuckled against his mouth. "Melissa Labrith just offered me an exclusive. Her side of the story. I'm heading over there now."

He lifted me off my feet and spun me around. "Everyone wants that story. But she knows you're special. Good always recognizes good, baby. And this doesn't have to be anonymous. It'll be the first serious political piece that you publish."

I squealed and he laughed. "Okay. Thank you. I need to go. I love you."

His lips grazed my ear. "What I wouldn't give to have you naked on the beach again."

I fanned my face when I pulled away. "Oh my gosh. I need to go." I turned back around and bit down on my bottom lip. "But you do paint a nice picture, Montgomery."

"Be careful, Blue Jay. I love you."

He said it all the time. I'd never been one for public affection, but I couldn't help myself when it came to Jack.

"Love you, too."

I grabbed my phone, stopped to let Ford and Dan know what was going on, and made my way to my car. My phone vibrated and I looked down to see a text.

Unknown Number ~ Do her justice. I'm counting on you.

I knew who it was. Joseph Capetti said he'd be in touch, but I'd never imagined it would be to get me an exclusive with his daughter.

I responded with a thumbs-up emoji, because what was the proper reply to a man suspected of organized crime who had also kind of kidnapped you? To my dismay, he sent back a winky face which made me laugh. I tucked my phone in my purse and drove to Governor Labrith's home. I hoped I'd never have to come face-to-face with Joseph Capetti again, and I wasn't happy about how he'd held me in his car to get the information he needed—but I understood it. He wanted to protect his daughter. My father would move heaven and earth to keep me safe.

When the gates opened and security led me in, I sucked in a long, slow breath. Just a week ago, my life had changed right on this very property.

But I was okay.

And I was getting the story of a lifetime.

———

Jack and I got a call to meet Ford in the conference room. We made our way there, and he pushed the paper across the table.

"This story is going to put you on the map, Monroe. I knew when I hired you that we were getting a talented reporter, but you have far surpassed all expectations with this. It's raw and real and people are going to eat it up."

"Thank you," I said, feeling my face heat.

Jack wrapped his arms around me. "Proud of you, Little Bird."

I chuckled, because he made everything a big deal, the big and the small. And I loved it.

"I'm glad you're both pleased. Governor Labrith had a story to tell and I'm just honored that she trusted me to help her tell it," I said.

"My phone has been blowing up all morning. Everyone is talking about it. You managed to turn this scandal in her favor. People weren't sure if she would recover, but you made sure that she did." Ford pushed to his feet and smiled. "Impressive shit, Buckley."

"That's because she is the shit," my boyfriend said, reaching for the box of pastries on the table and biting into a cupcake.

I thanked Ford as he walked out the door before using my finger to swipe at the icing on Jack's lip. I sucked it off my finger and smiled. "Thanks."

"Don't thank me for being proud of you. Governor Labrith opened up to you because she knew you wouldn't twist her words. You fought to help her get back on track, and Ford's right, that's impressive shit."

Melissa Labrith and I had spent four hours talking about her horrific marriage and her fear of losing the support of the fine people of San Francisco if she divorced him. Turns out, people love when politicians are real. And honest. And Melissa Labrith shared her story with the world and people appreciated it. Her words were heartfelt. She spoke about her father off the record, and it surprised me to learn that she truly loved him. They'd chosen different paths in life, but she didn't love him any less for it. And she never doubted his love for her. She'd asked me to keep that part of the interview out of the story, and I'd respected her wishes.

But her husband was a different story. He'd emotionally black-mailed her for years, and she regretted that she'd allowed fear to keep her in an unhappy place for so long. She spoke of the verbal abuse she'd been subjected to, and her efforts to keep her son shielded from his father's darkness. Her words were raw when she spoke of her love for her son, Lyle. She wanted to do good by our city, and she didn't want evil to prevail. We never spoke of the fact that her husband was planning to set her up, but I was fairly certain her father had filled her in when he moved her to a hotel.

Jack and I made our way to the elevator.

"Let's go home and check on Pussy. We just need to stop by my place to grab some clothes."

He interlaced his fingers with mine and led me down the hallway. "When are you going to decide if you'll move in with me? It's stupid to keep going to two places."

"How do you know you want to live with me?"

"I told you. I'm not an indecisive person. When I know, I know. I have zero doubts." He came to stand in front of me and tipped my chin up. "Zero doubts, Little Bird."

I nodded. "I have zero doubts too."

"Yeah? You'll make me and Pussy the happiest dudes around by moving in with us?"

"I'm all in, Montgomery."

"Fan-fucking-tastic. Come on, let's stop by the bakery. We need a box of cupcakes to celebrate with tonight." He wrapped my hand in his and I realized in that moment that I wasn't the same person I'd been when I first came to work here.

Jack Montgomery had healed all the broken parts of me. The gaping hole that had always been there, was no longer there. My fears and insecurities were replaced with confidence and hope.

Maybe that's what it meant to truly love someone. To give yourself to them and open up enough to let them fill in all the missing pieces. To trust them enough to love you the way you deserve to be loved. To see yourself through their eyes, and blossom into the person that's been hiding just beneath the shadows. To find your other half and finally become whole.

I'd found my other half.

And for the first time in my life—I was finally whole.

epilogue

. . .

Jack

THREE YEARS LATER

"Uncle Jack, pick me up," Everly said with her hands on her hips. The girl was wise beyond her three years and was a total girl-boss like her mother, and I fucking loved it.

I scooped the little brown-eyed munchkin up and turned to find Penelope watching me with a wide grin on her face. Her blue eyes sparkling as she blinked a couple times. She was the more reserved twin, and a bit standoffish with others, but she had a soft spot for me. Hey, what can I say? Most people had a soft spot for me. But seeing a smile spread across this little angel's face was hard to beat.

"Come here, Princess P," I said, scooping her up and propping her on my other hip.

Everly poked my cheek a couple dozen times with the tip of her finger, breaking out in a fit of giggles each time I gasped. Her dark brown ringlets bounced around wildly. Penelope rested her sweet cheek against my shoulder, her brown ponytail tickled my neck, and I kissed the top of her head. These two. They owned me.

"How did you get bigger in just three days?" Blue Jay asked as she sat on the couch at my mom's house in Napa, cooing to the little bundle in her arms. He was the newest addition to the Montgomery family, Ford Jackson Montgomery the fifth. I was honored Harrison and Laney Mae had named their son after Ford and me, and I intended to teach that little boy all my tricks when he got older. He was eight months old, and Monroe and I made it a priority to spend time with our nieces and nephew a couple times a week.

Seeing my wife hold a baby always did something to me. I couldn't wait to have a couple dozen of our own little birds. We'd married one year ago on Christmas Day. Making Monroe Montgomery my wife was the best birthday gift I'd ever received. We'd had a large ceremony at the winery in Napa, and Ford, Harrison, and Miles stood beside me as I pledged my love to the woman who owned my heart.

After Monroe released the story about Governor Labrith, her career took off. She was offered several gigs at other papers to be their lead political journalist, but of course she stayed loyal to Montgomery Media. She still wrote her column for the younger population in San Francisco, because she'd gained quite a following and she was grateful for the doors it had opened. She worked with Dan Arbor now, and they were quite the power team. We'd agreed that we didn't need to rush into starting a family until she was ready. But I was ready the day she came to interview at Montgomery Media, and she knew it.

"Baby, look at his eyes. They're the same honey-colored eyes as yours," Monroe said, stroking his blonde hair away from his face as his fat little fingers reached for a fist full of her blouse.

"I thought you said mine were whiskey brown?"

"He's a baby. We're calling them honey for now." She smiled and Laney Mae's head fell back in laughter.

"Of course, he got your eyes, Jack-ass. You couldn't help but make your mark on our baby," my sister-in-law said.

"Well, he's got Har-bear's dimples, your hair color, and Ford's first name. I'd say this kid is destined for success."

"I agree," my wife cooed, raising him above her head and blowing on his belly, causing him to break out in a fit of giggles.

"Uncle Jack, tickle me," Everly cheered, clapping her hands together.

"Oh, you want to get tickled, do you?"

"I do, I do," she shouted.

Laura Pavlov

Harley shook her head as she sat beside Monroe admiring baby Ford. "Girl, where do you get all that energy?"

"From my daddy." She fist-pumped the sky.

"You sure did, baby girl," Ford said as he dropped to sit beside his wife on the oversized sofa.

"How about you? Do you want to be tickled?" I asked Penelope and she shrugged, her little cherub cheeks turning pink.

I set her on the ground. "Stay put for just a minute, angel face."

I dropped Everly on the large chair and tickled her on each side and the squeal that escaped was a high enough pitch to shatter glass. And then I turned around and found Penelope gazing at me with her hands clasped together like she just couldn't wait to see what I would do. I reached for her and tossed her over my shoulder as I ran through the house.

"Is this better than tickling you?" I called out as her little body vibrated in laughter over my shoulder.

I settled her on the chair beside her sister. "You two are trouble."

"Daddy says that you're trouble." Everly giggled.

"I don't think you ah trouble, Uncle," Penelope said just above a whisper, unable to say the word *are* just yet. I tweaked her nose and winked.

"Don't go soft on me, P," Ford said.

"I tend to side with Everly on this one," Harrison called out.

I reached over and grabbed my nephew from Monroe and held the little stinker up to look me in the eyes. "And what do you think, Ford?"

He burped in response, which caused everyone to break out in a fit of laughter. "You're just like your namesake. A man of few words. I like it." I held him to my chest and walked into the kitchen to check on my mom.

"So, you ready to have everyone here tomorrow?" I asked, and she stopped chopping and turned to run her fingers through Ford Junior's hair, before patting me on the cheek.

"I am. It'll be nice to have everyone over."

We would all meet here for brunch on Christmas Day, just like we always did. Laney's parents, her brother and Gia and their little girl

would join us. Harley's grandfather was coming, and I looked forward
to my yearly chats with the wise older man.

"Monroe told me her father's coming this year," I said, watching as
a pink hue spread across my mom's neck and cheeks.

Ryan Buckley and my mom had been spending a lot of time
together since we married last year. She claimed they were good
friends, and she enjoyed his company. I had a feeling it was a bit
more, and I was happy for her. Hell, I was happy for both of them.
They'd both suffered tragic losses, and if they made one another
happy, I was all for it. My wife had sniffed it out first a few months
ago when she noticed them sitting close together at her birthday
dinner. She swore she saw her father clasp my mother's hand under
the table.

"Yes, of course he's coming. He wants to be with his daughter, and
Miles, Sierra, and the baby will be here as well. Why wouldn't he
come?" She smirked.

"You're suspect, Mother." I pointed two fingers at her and laughed.
"I think he wants to be here with you. Is that so hard for you to say?
We all want you to be happy."

She tilted her head to the side. "I am happy, Jackie boy. And yes,
maybe he wants to be here to see me as well."

"There you go. We all know there's something there, and we're all
happy for you. You deserve only the best."

She pushed up on her tiptoes and kissed my cheek. "Well, you
three boys and your beautiful wives and these adorable grandbabies of
mine are more than I could ever ask for. But yes, having a special
friend whose company I enjoy is an added bonus."

My head fell back in laughter. "A special friend? Damn, I love you,
woman."

"Uncle, I want you," Penelope said from behind me and my heart
exploded into a million pieces.

My mom's face lit up, and she reached for baby Ford. "This little
girl's got it bad for you, Jackie boy. And she sure is special."

"She sure is." I scooped her up and walked toward the dining room
as my mom called everyone for dinner. "I'm all yours, Princess P."

She settled on my lap and we all sat around the table laughing and chatting like we always did. Monroe reached for my hand beneath the table and squeezed it.

And damn if it wasn't the perfect way to spend Christmas Eve.

"Montgomery," my wife called from somewhere in the apartment and I startled from a sound sleep.

"Where are you, Little Bird?" I asked, sitting up in bed to find Pussy curled up on the pillow beside me.

"Be careful when you stand up… follow the trail," she said.

I stood up to see a line of cupcakes from my side of the bed to the door. "What the hell is this? Am I dreaming?"

Her laughter echoed from down the hall. I followed the colorful trail out of the room and out to the living room. Reds and greens and golds with glitter and sparkles on them were placed just a few inches apart, leading the way. When I got to the end of the trail, my wife sat beneath the tree in a white sheer nightie.

Sexy as hell.

"Is this a Christmas miracle?" I asked.

She smiled. "Come here."

I dropped to sit across from her. "You want to open presents, baby?"

Her eyes welled with emotion. "I couldn't wait any longer. I wanted to give you your gift."

I studied her. "You all right?"

She reached behind her for one more cupcake and handed it to me. It was a cupcake with pink frosting on one side, and blue frosting on the other. "What is this?"

"You're going to be a daddy," she said, biting down on her bottom lip and looking up at me like I set the sun.

"Are you fucking with me?" I pushed to my feet and leaned over to catch my breath. I couldn't fucking believe it. I reached for her hands, pulling her in my arms.

"We're having a baby," she whispered.

"You did it. I'm so fucking proud of you. Our own little bird. I want him or her to be just like you. Smart and beautiful and talented." I swiped at my eyes, and I'll be damned if I wasn't crying like a fool.

"I want him or her to be just like you," she said, tears streaming down her beautiful face.

"Thank you, baby. This is the best gift ever."

"I think you did most of the work." She blushed before pulling up on my shoulders and wrapping her legs around my waist like the little spider monkey she was.

"Loving you is never work." My mouth came over hers and I carried her back to the bedroom and dropped her on the bed.

"I love you, Jack Montgomery. Thanks for showing me what it means to be happy."

"I love you, Mrs. Montgomery. Every glorious inch of you," I said, dropping her on the bed and settling above her.

"We've got to get ready to go to your mom's. The kids will want to open presents." Her breaths came hard and fast, just like they always did when we were together. She tangled her fingers in my hair and urged me closer.

"They can wait. Right now, I need to show you how much I love you."

"You show me every day," she whispered.

"That's the plan." My mouth covered hers, and every time with this woman was like the first time.

Because she was all I needed.

All I'd ever need.

And I'd spend the rest of my life loving her.

The End

Do you want to find out if Jack and Monroe are having a boy or a girl and catch up with all of the Montgomery's? Read Monica Montgomery's second chance novella for FREE!!

https://dl.bookfunnel.com/1pfykb2az8

acknowledgments

Greg, Chase & Hannah, thank you for being my biggest supporters and always believing in me and encouraging me to chase my dreams! YOU are the reason that I work hard every day!! Even if you make fun of my endless social media posts…I love you to the moon and back!

Sissy, When I think of strong heroines, you are always the first person that comes to mind. Thanks for inspiring me to write characters that aren't afraid to take risks, dream big, and go after what they want! I love you!

Pathi, Abi, Natalie, Doo and Annette, thank you for being the BEST beta readers EVER! Your feedback means the world to me. I live for your comments and suggestions!! I would be lost without you!

Willow, I will never be able to thank you enough for all that you do for me. From encouraging me, snapchatting with me when we need a distraction, texts, voice messages, fuelings, juicing, home décor tips, editing, proofreading, plotting, fashion, holiday décor, recipes…we share it all and it is the absolute highlight of my day!! I am so thankful for you! Love you always!!

Thank you, Sarah Hansen (Okay Creations) for working your magic once again! I think this is my favorite cover yet!!

Sue Grimshaw (Edits by Sue), Thank you for your encouragement, your guidance and your support. Your feedback is always spot-on and I am so incredibly thankful for you! Thank you for believing in me and in this story!! I appreciate you more than you know!!

Tamara Cribley (The Deliberate Page), so thankful to get to work with you again. I love all of the little details that you add to the formatting and appreciate your patience and support so much!! Thank you, my friend!

Jo and Kylie (Give Me Books Promotions), you know how much I adore you, and cannot wait to finally meet you at the Four Brits Book Fest!! You keep me calm and handle every hurdle with absolute grace! So thankful for you!!

Ellie (My Brothers Editor), thank you for always making time for me and for being endlessly supportive! It means the world to me and I am so grateful for your friendship!

Sarah Ferguson (Social Butterfly PR), I have so enjoyed working with you over the last few weeks!! I am looking forward to many more releases together!! Thank you for all of your support and encouragement!!

Ashlee (Ashes & Vellichor), what would I do without you? Thank you for bringing my characters to life with your amazing teasers!! You amaze me each and every time you send me something!! So grateful for you!

Dad, you really are the reason that I keep chasing my dreams!! Thank you for teaching me to never give up. Love you!

Mom, thank you for your love and support. So excited for this release because I know Jack is your favorite!! Love you!

Sandy, thank you for reading and supporting me throughout this journey. Love you!

Pathi, I am so thankful for you! You are the reason I even started this journey. Thank you for believing in me!! Love you!

Natalie (Head in the Clouds, Nose in a Book), Thank you for supporting me through it all! I appreciate all that you do for me from beta reading to the newsletter to buddy reading so we can talk about all of the trauma!! Hahahaha Love you!

Catherine Cowles, thank you for encouraging me on the tough days and for helping navigate through SO MANY THINGS!! I appreciate you more than you know!! Love you sweet friend!!

Sammi Sylvis, Thanks for making me laugh and helping me stay sane through these releases! Glad we have one another to lean on!!

Kailie Phillips, Our lunch was an absolute highlight of 2020 for me! I can't thank you enough for making the most AMAZING book swag for my release! Love you so much, sweets!

To all the bloggers and bookstagrammers who have posted, shared and supported me—I can't begin to tell you how much it means to me. I love seeing the graphics that you make, and the gorgeous posts that you share. I am forever grateful for your support!

Lisa, Julie, Eric, Jen and Jim, I am very thankful to have such supportive and encouraging siblings in my life. Love you!

Steph, Nicole, Sue, Thompson, Pathi, Bell, Natalie, Annette, Carol, Margy, Mindy, Kristin, Laura, Anne, Abi, Kelly, Maggie, Leigh Anne, Julie, Nancy, Bev, Leslie, Florence, Tina, Renae, Cindy, Kelly & Kate, Darleen, Althea, Jess, Ariel, Heather, Shannon, Gabe, Brandon, Logan, Brock, Caroline, Hendershot, Liva, Kennedy, all the amazing ladies at d'annata boutique and Bloom boutique, and all of my friends who have supported me along this journey…thank you so much!!

keep up on new releases

Linktree Laurapavlovauthor

Newsletter laurapavlov.com

other books by laura pavlov

Cottonwood Cove Series
Into the Tide
Under the Stars
On the Shore
Before the Sunset
After the Storm

Honey Mountain Series
Always Mine
Ever Mine
Make You Mine
Simply Mine
Only Mine

The Willow Springs Series
Frayed
Tangled
Charmed
Sealed
Claimed

Montgomery Brothers Series
Legacy
Peacekeeper
Rebel

A Love You More Rock Star Romance
More Jade
More of You
More of Us

The Shine Design Series
Beautifully Damaged
Beautifully Flawed

The G.D. Taylors Series with Willow Aster
Wanted Wed or Alive
The Bold and the Bullheaded
Another Motherfaker
Don't Cry Spilled MILF
Friends with Benefactors